ANGEL OF MERCY

Angel of Mercy

Andrew Neiderman

G. P. PUTNAM'S SONS   NEW YORK

G. P. Putnam's Sons
Publishers Since 1838
200 Madison Avenue
New York, NY 10016

Library of Congress Cataloging-in-Publication Data

Neiderman, Andrew.
Angel of mercy / Andrew Neiderman.
p.   cm.
ISBN 0-399-13926-5
I. Title.
PS3564.E27A54   1994   93-31259 CIP
813'.54—dc20

Printed in the United States of America
1   2   3   4   5   6   7   8   9   10

For our grandson Dustin,
another generation of hope and promise,
a blessing

PROLOGUE

Faye Sullivan drove into the parking lot of the Murrays' apartment complex and hurried out of her car toward their unit. She was dressed in her nurse's uniform and looked as though she had just come from work. She pressed the buzzer, waited, then pressed the buzzer again. When no one came to the door, she dug under the welcome mat and came up with a key. She inserted it in the lock and opened the door.

"Susie?" she called. "Susie, are you still here?"

Faye raised her eyebrows quizzically in the ensuing silence. Her heartbeat quickened. Her sister had been cleaning and caring for Sam Murray since late in the afternoon, but when Faye called from the hospital just before the end of her private-duty shift, there was no answer. She knew what that usually meant.

Faye took a deep breath and made her way directly to Sam Murray's bedroom. She couldn't help but notice how neat and tidy the apartment was—clearly her sister's handiwork.

"Susie!" she screamed as she peered in through the bedroom door. She approached the bed. Sixty-six-year-old Sam Murray lay on his back, his left arm dangling over the side, his face locked in a look that suggested surprise more than anything else. Under his right hand, which was placed palm down on his chest, was a framed picture of him and his wife.

Faye lifted Sam's wrist and felt for his pulse. Then she

looked up and shook her head as if she were giving an anxious relative the bad news. She placed his arm beside his torso. After she closed his eyes, she turned to the night table where Susie had left the hypodermic needle and the bottle of insulin.

"A wad of cotton," she remarked out loud. She scooped it up and placed it in her pocket. Then she dug into her uniform pocket and pulled out a pair of her surgical gloves. She picked up the hypodermic needle and empty insulin bottle. She wiped them both clean before squeezing Sam's fingers around them and placing them back on the night table. Then she perused the room once more before turning to leave the apartment.

Twenty minutes later, she pulled up to her own apartment complex and parked in her carport space. She slammed her car door hard and hurried up the steps. Jabbing her key into the lock, she pushed the door open and stepped into the apartment. Her baby-blue eyes were cold with determination. Her normally soft, full lips were stretched thin with resolve.

"Susie!"

Her twin sister limped out of the kitchen and smiled. Except for the brace on her leg and the fact that her hair was shoulder length while Faye's was cut neatly just below her ears, they were identical. They even had the same dimple in their left cheek.

"Hi, Faye. Guess what? I did all our supermarket shopping already. I thought you should rest. You have a full schedule ahead of you, special nursing from twelve to eight every day for Mrs. Sylvia Livingston, right?"

"Forget about Mrs. Livingston. I just came from the Murray apartment."

"Oh. Did you see the smile on his lips?"

"Smile? What smile? I saw a dead man. That's what I saw," Faye snapped.

"He smiled like that when he set sight on Mrs. Murray, and realized they would be together again forever. I'm sure."

"You fool. You little fool. Do you know what I found on

the night table? A wad of cotton dabbed in alcohol." She held it up.

"What? Oh. I just try to do it right," Susie said.

"Even a half-assed policeman would wonder why a man about to commit suicide would care about disinfecting the area around the needle puncture."

"Oh. I didn't think of that. I don't think of the police."

"Well, you should."

Faye plopped into the easy chair.

"I'm sorry, Faye. I know I should, but I'm thinking too much about how happy they're going to be when they're together again. That's why I used insulin. It was her medicine."

"I know what her medicine was. I was her private nurse until she died, wasn't I?"

"Just like Daddy and Mommy, they'll be together again," Susie said, her face beaming.

"If Daddy and Mommy are truly together again, I assure you, they're not happy," Faye quipped.

"What? Of course they are, Faye. How can you say such a thing?"

Faye was silent.

"How can you?" Susie was almost in tears.

"Let's not talk about it, Susie. I'm not in the mood right now." She looked up sharply. "We're going to have to leave another place."

"No, we won't," Susie insisted. "You stopped in after me and made sure everything was all right, didn't you?" Susie smiled and relaxed. "Just like you always do."

Faye stared at her.

"I know you look after me. I know you always will. You're my sister."

Faye continued to stare at her. She always did look after her.

"What am I going to do with you, Susie?"

"I don't know. What?"

Faye just shook her head.

"Did you see how clean their apartment was?" Susie asked proudly.

"I saw."

"There was this terrible stain in the rug. I had to work like the devil to get it out. You would have been exhausted, but I kept imagining Mrs. Murray complaining."

"And she would have, too," Faye said. "All she ever talked about was that apartment. I can still hear her talking, stringing together one household experience after another, reminiscing about her home and her family chores as though she were telling old war stories, outstanding accomplishments."

"I know. Remember Mother? Remember how she would know if someone had moved the salt and pepper shakers two inches? Like the mother bear in 'Goldilocks and the Three Bears,' Mother would go raving through the house, crying, 'Who's been in my kitchen? Who's been sitting in my chair?' "

"Mother was a neurotic," Faye said. "Which was what drove Daddy away from her eventually."

"No, she wasn't."

"She became obsessed with cleanliness, with orderliness. Eventually, she even regarded sex as something dirty, no matter if it was sex between two married people."

"Stop it, Faye."

"You can't blame Daddy for the things he did."

"I don't blame him for anything. He didn't do anything. He loved Mommy and they love each other now and forever . . . in heaven."

"Right," Faye said sitting back. "In heaven."

Susie sat down and folded her hands in her lap, her face brightening like the face of a little girl about to be told a wonderful fairy tale.

"Tell me about your new patient, Mrs. Livingston. What's wrong with her?"

"She had a coronary and she's just been moved out of CCU because the doctor said she made enough improvement."

"Just like Mother," Susie said, "only her doctor was wrong."

"Mother didn't have a private-duty nurse, and by the time the floor nurse got to her, she'd already succumbed to the second heart seizure," Faye said.

But Susie's comparison made her think. Mrs. Livingston had been out of CCU almost the same length of time as their mother had. Tomorrow would be the exact number of days Mother had survived the first attack, and Mother, just like Mrs. Livingston, had had a strong, defiant heart, an organ that beat on almost out of anger. Sometimes it did seem to Faye as if parts of the bodies she nursed were at war with other parts. It wasn't a pleasant sight: people disappointed with their own kidneys, lungs, gall bladders, talking about their bodies as if they had been betrayed by trusted friends.

Nursing was a great deal more demanding than people thought, especially private-duty nursing. True, the patients were often comatose, and even if they were not, they were too sick to make many requests, but look how it affected her private life. Attractive and nearly thirty, she should at least have a meaningful relationship. Instead, she was living with and caring for her handicapped twin.

But most of the men Faye had met had resented her dedication to nursing anyway. She knew she should regret that, but she didn't. No matter how they complained about the time she gave to her work, she didn't regret a moment of it. Only now she had other problems.

Susie was getting out of hand. Soon, soon she would have to do something serious about her, something that would break her heart, but something that had to be done. She couldn't let her continue believing that she had been put on this earth to be an angel of mercy.

Could she?

1

"He's going into the wash!" Frankie Samuels screamed.

Rosina Flores turned the wheel sharply, sending their patrol car bouncing over the sidewalk and up to the top of the knoll. The hill descended into a cement gully constructed by the Army Corps of Engineers to prevent the sort of flash flooding that had nearly destroyed Palm Springs in the past. Still in the throes of a major drought, the area was bone dry, and there was no promise of rain in the white clouds that lay listlessly against the soft blue sky.

Their robbery suspect was attempting to escape by driving his motorcycle down the wash. They watched him maneuver over the rocks and earth. It looked like he might be successful, but at the bottom of the hill, he took a spin and flew headfirst over his handlebars.

Frankie got out of the car. He was five-feet-eleven, fifty-eight years of age, and his two hundred and ten pounds was a burden, most of it accumulated at the bar reviewing old war stories with retired cops. With soft brown eyes, thick brown hair, and a hairline that was barely receding, Frankie didn't show his age. Up until now, he had lived hard, too, rushing at life with a bulldozer mentality as if he would miss something if he didn't forge ahead at full tilt. His impulsiveness had gotten him into trouble on a number of occasions from kindergarten on, but especially since William Nolan had become chief of detectives in Palm Springs. An ex–military policeman, Nolan was a teetotaler and something of a physical fitness fanatic.

"Jesus fuckin' Christ," Frankie muttered under his breath. Nolan had deliberately made Rosina Flores Frankie's partner in order to rein in his temper and his barroom language. Frankie resented Nolan's aim, but he sincerely respected Rosina, who, in addition to being the best shot with a thirty-eight, was also the most intelligent member of the department. She was certainly heads above Nolan.

The suspect, a Caucasian who looked about twenty, rolled down to the wash but unexpectedly got to his feet and started to run.

"Shit," Frankie said as he began to run down the hill.

"Wait, Frankie," Rosina called. "We'll get back into the car and cut him off before Gene Autry Trail."

"You get back in the car. I'll pursue on foot," he insisted.

The trip down the rocky hill was difficult. Frankie slipped and slid and cursed when he scraped the palm of his right hand in an attempt to keep his footing. Finally, he hit the pavement and started after the younger man. Nolan's criticism of Frankie's weight and physical condition began to replay in his mind. With every added breath and stride, Frankie relived the most recent dressing down.

"You know, Samuels, I have nightmares about you. I see you pursuing a suspect, running down Palm Springs Boulevard on one of those summer days when the temperature hits a hundred and ten, and you bust a heart valve all over the sidewalk. The next day, the *Desert Sun* headlines: 'Overweight Palm Springs Detective Drops Dead in Pursuit of Shoplifter.' Have you lost any weight since we last spoke about it, Samuels?"

"Couple of pounds."

"It looks like they were off your brain."

Frankie hated to admit it, but as the blood pounded and his breath grew shorter, he realized Nolan wasn't wrong. He increased his stride, swinging his arms out and pounding the cement with every bit of energy he could muster. This son of a bitch wasn't going to get away from Frankie Samuels. No one had ever done it before. He just had to keep close on his ass and drive him toward Rosina.

But the bastard did something unexpected when he looked back, maybe because he saw how hard Frankie was huffing and puffing, his tongue hanging out like a hound dog's. He turned and started up the bank, digging his boots in with expertise and success.

Frankie felt his body go "Oh no" as he turned with the suspect and started to charge up that hill. His thigh and calf muscles felt as if they were being jabbed with needles and his heart was pounding so hard, he thought it would split his chest open. He started to reach for his pistol, deciding to fire a warning shot, when it hit him like a bullet from a gun inside him, shattering his chest as if it were made of thin crystal. He dropped his pistol and clutched his heart. The world around him spun. He gasped and tried to lean forward but was pushed back until the sky appeared. A moment later his back hit the ground and all went black.

He woke up in the ambulance and saw Jack Martin, the twenty-six-year-old paramedic who was on his bowling team, gazing down at him with a smirk on his face as the vehicle careened around a turn and sped down Sunrise Way toward the hospital.

"How are you doin', Grandpa?"

"Fuck you too," Frankie uttered in a hoarse voice.

Martin laughed and called to the driver.

"There's still some life in him."

"What the hell happened? Did the son of a bitch shoot me?" Frankie asked.

"Not unless you want to call yourself the son of a bitch," Jack said. He completed another check of Frankie's blood pressure, listened to his heart and shook his head.

"What?"

"Your ticker's really kicking up, Frankie. Just relax."

"Ticker?"

"When you have a physical last?"

"I dunno . . . a year, maybe . . ."

"Maybe two?"

"Jennie," he said thinking about his wife. She had been after him lately to get a checkup.

"She's meeting us at the hospital, but you better worry more about Nolan," Jack kidded.

"Shit. Where's Rosina?"

"Right behind us."

"And the perp?"

"Mexico by now."

"Fuck."

"Relax, Frankie. You've got other things to worry about at the moment," Jack said prophetically. Frankie closed his eyes. At least the pain had eased, but he imagined that was because Jack had given him some sort of shot. The wail of the ambulance continued, and the realization that he was its passenger drove him into a deep depression.

"I'm only fifty-eight," he muttered, "only fifty-eight."

Jennie was there the moment the doors were opened. He was groggy so her face looked cloudy, but nothing made him feel more secure than those light green eyes as she leaned over the gurney. The tears were flowing down on her cheeks. His arm felt like it had turned to lead, but he lifted it to touch her light brown hair. At fifty-two she had scarcely a gray strand. Beth, their twenty-six-year-old daughter, attractive in her own right, still felt intimidated beside her mother, one of those women who grew into a deeper, more elegantly beautiful woman with every passing day.

"Am I in heaven?" He closed his eyes and smiled.

"Frankie . . ."

"I'll be all right," he promised. She squeezed his hand as they wheeled him through the emergency room doors. He hadn't been in a hospital as a patient since he was a teenager and he had fallen off his bike and broken his arm, and despite his big, strong macho image, the realization put some panic in him. "Jennie," he called.

"Right here, babe. Right beside you."

He couldn't keep his eyes open and the voices around him drifted in and out. He was sure he heard Nolan's. He heard

Jennie's and he heard Rosina's. The doctors and nurses were all around him, hooking him up to all sorts of machinery. The beeps were everywhere and everywhere he turned it seemed there were white uniforms. Whatever they did, they did quickly, or at least that was the way it seemed to him, for after what he thought were only minutes but were really closer to hours, the doctor was peering down at him with Jennie at his side.

"Was it a heart attack?" Frankie demanded. He was breathing easier and, remarkably, only felt fatigue in his legs now.

"I want to do more testing and observe you, of course," the doctor replied, "but my preliminary diagnosis is hypertrophic cardiomyopathy."

Frankie pulled at his earlobe like Humphrey Bogart in *The Maltese Falcon.*

"My medical jargon is a bit rusty, Doc."

Jennie smiled.

The doctor, Pauling, a cardiologist at the Desert Hospital, pulled himself into a more formal stance and began as if he were lecturing to a classroom of med students.

"Hypertrophic cardiomyopathy denotes a condition in which there is a thickening of the heart muscle. This makes it more difficult for the heart to pump blood away from itself to the rest of the body. This can cause the blood to back up, creating such symptoms as shortness of breath. Have you been experiencing that, Mr. Samuels?"

Frankie shifted his eyes to Jennie, who was now smirking with irritation.

"Yes, he has," she answered for him. "But he's always telling me it's nothing."

"Well . . . I just thought it was because I needed to lose some weight."

"That will certainly help."

"How bad is this hyper . . . whatever?"

"Well, it won't stop you from performing your ordinary day-to-day activities. The condition becomes dangerous, however, when you engage in strenuous physical activity. As you've discovered," he added dryly.

"So I got a fat heart, huh?"

"Well, not fat as such. It's more analogous to the stretching of a thick rubber band compared to the stretching of a thin one. Your heart has a difficult time relaxing."

"My heart? Hell, my heart's always relaxed, isn't it, Jen?"

"This isn't funny, Frankie."

"I'm really not laughing. Okay, Doc, what do we do next?"

"After a few more tests, I anticipate recommending a permanent pacemaker," Dr. Pauling said.

"Pacemaker? Jesus." It was as if all of his years had hit him at once.

"The procedure requires only a local anesthetic. We will implant the device under your collarbone with a wire leading to the bottom of your heart. The pacemaker will reverse the contraction wave of your heart and as a result, ease the obstruction caused by the backup of blood."

Frankie just stared, wishing he were dreaming. Dr. Pauling turned to Jennie as if he saw that Frankie had fallen into a daze and was no longer listening.

"Usually, pacemakers are used to regulate the speed of the heart, but in this case it would simply alter the contraction pattern of the heart muscle."

Jennie nodded and Dr. Pauling turned back to Frankie.

"After I run you through a few more tests, you can go home for a while. We'll schedule the procedure in a week or so. In the meantime you will have to avoid any really strenuous physical activities."

"He will," Jennie promised. She glared at him. Frankie let his head drop to the pillow.

"I'll look in on him shortly," Dr. Pauling said as he left.

"Nolan's going to pressure me to retire now," Frankie moaned. "How can I be a cop with a pacemaker?"

"He doesn't have to pressure you, Frankie. You'll do it on your own," Jennie predicted. He widened his eyes and gazed up at her.

"Oh really?"

"Frankie, most people don't get second chances, especially at . . ."

"At my age? Go on, say it." He turned away. He hated feeling sorry for himself, but at the moment it seemed impossible to do otherwise. "Did you call the counselor?"

"What do you think?" Jennie replied. He turned back to her.

"Maybe he was in court."

"No, he was in the office. He should be arriving any minute."

Frankie pretended to be upset, but he was actually looking forward to seeing his son, Stevie. At twenty-eight, he was the youngest junior partner at Klein, Clapper, and Brogen, a prestigious corporate law firm in Los Angeles. Stevie's wife, Laurel, was a beautiful five-foot-ten-inch California blonde with a dark complexion and Wedgwood-blue eyes. She could have easily been in the movies, but instead was a production assistant for one of Hollywood's biggest producers.

"He said he's bringing Beth," Jennie added after a moment. Frankie turned his head and raised his eyebrows. He and his daughter seemed always at odds with each other these days. If she wasn't off marching and protesting with her chapter of NOW, she was carrying picket signs on Wilshire Boulevard in front of the federal buildings protesting the violation of animal rights or U.S. involvement in South America. Whatever cause it was, Frankie believed it was simply compensation for the early failures in her life, which included a fourteen-month aborted marriage and dropping out of college to work with a holistic doctor in Santa Monica.

Frankie felt himself sink deeper into the bed as if it were made of sponge. He sighed and shook his head.

"So what am I going to do, Jen, retire and take up golf?"

"You'll do what you have to do, Frankie. And you won't give me a hard time about it," she added firmly. "I never complained much all these years when you were on stakeouts that kept you away for days on end. I barely uttered a sound when you were shot at and when that teenager tried to carve you with a hatchet, or when that man on crack cocaine deliberately crashed his pickup truck into your car. I swallowed my fears, told myself this is what I took on when I married a policeman, and accepted. Now it's time for you to accept, Frankie."

"I don't know who's worse, you or that horse's ass we have for a chief of detectives. Since he was appointed, the whole atmosphere's changed at the department. He's got everyone growling at everyone."

"So maybe it's a good thing you get out now," Jennie said. She sighed, relaxing her shoulders. "I'm going to go get a cup of coffee. Rosina's still outside waiting to see you."

"Send her in," Frankie said.

Jennie leaned over to kiss him softly on the lips. For a moment she lingered, her hands gripping his shoulders.

"I thought I was going to lose you this time for sure," she whispered tearfully.

"You're not losing me, Jen. You might be sorry, but you're not."

She wiped her tears away and smiled. It rained sunshine down on him. How had he been lucky enough to have this beautiful, gentle woman fall in love with the likes of him? He never stopped being in awe of it.

A moment after Jennie left, Rosina Flores stepped into his room. She was a striking woman with olive-brown skin and hazel eyes. She kept her ebony hair cut just beneath her ears. Hardened by the difficulties she had endured struggling against prejudice and poverty, the twenty-five-year-old Mexican-born woman had excelled in public school and graduated as her class valedictorian. Like a star running back in football eluding tackles, she had held off the suitors who would confine her to a home and children, and went on to study law enforcement. Her initial goal had been to become a California highway patrolwoman, but her superior mental abilities found more challenge first in forensics and then in detective work.

"¿Cómo está, stupido?"

"Terrific."

"I told you to get back into the car and we'd cut him off at the pass. But no, not Palm Springs's Charlie Bronson."

"Not you, too, Flores. *Por favor.* What happened to the perp?"

"Cathedral City police picked him up walking along Highway One-eleven."

"Great."

"Nolan wants a full report by oh eight hundred."

"He just loves that military shit, doesn't he? Oh eight hundred. Did you salute?"

"He's on your case, Frankie."

"I expect so."

"He spoke to your doctor at length out in the corridor. How bad is it?"

Frankie described hypertrophic cardiomyopathy, using the rubber-band analogy.

"And just when you were supposed to teach me how to be a real detective, street smart." She smiled. "I'm just glad you'll be okay."

"Thanks."

"I'd better get to that report," she said as she started to leave.

"Hey, Flores."

"Yeah?"

"I still think you ought to marry that accountant and raise a flock of chicks."

She laughed and left the room. Frankie turned toward the wall. Alone for the moment, he permitted a small tear to emerge out of the corner of his eye, his way of saying goodbye to the young, determined, and dedicated policeman who had once inhabited his body. All the time he'd been in law enforcement, he'd worried about taking a bullet from the gun of some street punk, but now the bullet had come from within himself instead.

Where does our youth go when it evaporates, he wondered as he lay back, waiting for his doctor's return.

2

The heart monitor beeped weakly and then suddenly went into a flat line. Faye Sullivan ran to the door of the hospital room and screamed: "Stat." The unlucky intern on the floor, Dr. Brad Hoffman, looked up from the chart he was casually perusing and mouthed, "Oh, no." It was, after all, his first emergency, his first time all alone. He dropped the chart and turned from the elderly man who had been staring at him with liquid, dark eyes and hurried down the floor to the private room in which Sylvia Livingston had been recuperating. Faye was performing CPR, but stepped back respectfully as soon as Hoffman appeared.

The young intern looked at the monitor and at the patient and screamed for the defibrillator. Before he could request it, Faye Sullivan handed him a hypodermic of adrenaline. She smiled at him warmly and he gazed at her for a moment. Later, he would recall that smile. It was almost as if they were in the cafeteria and she had just handed him a cup for his coffee. There was also something very sexual about the way she focused on him and pursed her lips. It had made him hesitate a moment to gather his thoughts. Then he pulled back the sheet and injected the medicine directly into Sylvia Livingston's heart muscle.

The defibrillator was quickly wheeled in. He stared up at the heart monitor, hoping for a miracle before he began, but there was none visible. The line was deadly flat. He turned the defibrillator up to two hundred and placed one pad over Sylvia Livingston's right breast and one just under her left.

"Clear," he cried. The jolt lifted the fifty-five-year-old woman off the bed, but the line on the monitor remained flat. He glanced frantically at Faye. Again she wore a soft expression, her eyes gentle, but this time her smile calmed him. He knew she was an experienced nurse, and he thought she was attractive, even beautiful in an angelic way. At that moment she looked just like a competent special-duty nurse should look, he thought: no panic in her face, no flood of emotion in one direction or another, just a quiet efficiency. It filled him with renewed purpose and he attempted to revive his patient again, turning the defibrillator up to four hundred. Once again, nothing changed. He tried again, and again it was in vain.

When he looked at Faye this time, she shook her head softly. Just to go through the motions and convince himself and her he was doing all that he had to, he made one final attempt. The flat line didn't change a split second. Hoffman stepped back.

"We lost her," he announced.

"She looks peaceful," Faye said, gazing down at the dead woman. No matter how many times she confronted it, Death was still fascinating. Sylvia Livingston's eyes glimmered like stones under a cool mountain stream.

Hoffman stared at Faye for a moment and then looked at the expired patient. Faye was right. There wasn't any grimace; the patient's face was in repose, the eyes glassy and still. Death had already made its claim and turned her into a specimen, Hoffman thought. She was quickly beginning to resemble the cadavers upon which he had practiced and studied: anonymous bodies without names, without histories, without bereaved relatives.

Faye Sullivan closed Sylvia Livingston's eyes and stood beside her with her own eyes closed as though she were offering some last rites. Then she turned abruptly to Dr. Hoff-

man, her eyes so bright and excited that now she looked like
a little girl about to open her birthday presents.

"I'll call Mr. Livingston," she said. "He just went down to
the cafeteria to get a bite."

"Oh. I'm sorry," Hoffman said. He felt this need to apologize to someone and was glad it was the private-duty nurse
and not the patient's husband. "She's been out of CCU for
what, a little more than a day?" he asked. Faye nodded.

"Twenty-nine hours," she said. He shook his head.

"I'm sure her husband wasn't expecting this," he said sadly.

"No, but you did very well, Doctor. I'll be sure to tell
him," she added.

Brad Hoffman smiled gratefully. Yes, he had done everything he had been trained to do. It wasn't his fault. He barely
knew this patient, and despite the new emphasis on bedside
manner and personalizing medical treatment, he was grateful
for his ignorance about the woman and her family. It would
make it easier for him to forget, if he ever could forget that
cold, icy stare.

"Thank you. Er . . . if you need me when Mr. Livingston
comes up, I'll be finishing up my rounds," he said.

"I won't need you, Doctor," Faye said confidently. She
gazed at Sylvia Livingston's corpse one more time and when
she looked at Brad Hoffman again, he looked like he really
appreciated her. Couldn't she fall in love with such a man
and couldn't he fall in love with her? But then again, all the
unmarried nurses she knew fell in love with doctors and
wished doctors would fall in love with them.

She grimaced and took on her professional, stoic look.
"Unfortunately, I've had more than my share of these," she
added, and then left to call Sylvia's husband.

Tommy Livingston had just sat down with his tray in the
hospital cafeteria. He had taken only a cup of coffee and a
bran muffin, confident that he would not even eat much of
that. His stomach felt full, tight, and his chest had turned to
iron, making every breath an effort. He had this thing about
hospitals. The moment he stepped through the entrance, he
felt queasy. He tried to hide it from everyone, especially his

sons, but he had always had an anxiety about hospitals and rarely visited anyone there if he could help it, even members of his own family.

Of course, he couldn't avoid coming to see Sylvia. She had come so close. At one point her life had been down to a trickle; each beat on that monitor sounding like the drip, drip, drip from a melting icicle. He could literally feel the wintery air surrounding her in the CCU. Death was weaving its cocoon. He had been present at his own mother's final moments and still vividly recalled the way she had turned her eyes toward him and smiled just before she expired.

If I went to a psychiatrist, he'd probably tell me that was why I have this thing about going to hospitals, he thought.

But the boys don't have this problem. They should be here more often. Then he wouldn't feel so guilty about avoiding the place, he decided. Sylvia doted on the two of them anyway and had long since devoted more of herself to their sons than she did to him. She was a mother before she was a wife. He shook his head at the thought. Ridiculous, being jealous of my own children.

Anyway, it really was unfair to expect two men in their mid-thirties, both successful and busy, one an accountant in a major agency, the other owning and operating one of the biggest real estate firms in the Coachella Valley, to just sit around day and night in a hospital lounge or at their mother's bedside while she slept. For him time wasn't a concern; it didn't matter. As an architect, he had made plenty during the boom construction days in the desert communities. Now, he worked only when he felt like it. He could sit here for weeks, months. He just hated it.

Tommy sat forward and sipped some of his coffee. He started to cut a piece of muffin when one of those senior-citizen hospital volunteers tapped him on the shoulder. She was a short, gray-haired lady, someone's grandmother, with the pink uniform draped over her dress.

"Are you Mr. Livingston?" she asked. Her lips were curled in a friendly smile, but her eyes were a deep, dark gray, the eyes of someone who had been summoned to do a sad deed.

"Yes."

"I have a message for you to return to the step-down floor immediately," she said.

"Why? What's wrong?"

She shook her head and stepped back as if making any physical contact with him would infect her with his sadness and misery.

"They just asked me to find you. Maybe nothing's wrong," she said.

"But, they told you . . . immediately?" he said, flustered for a moment.

The old lady didn't reply. She pressed her lips together to seal in her true thoughts.

He rose to his full six feet, but his shoulders refused to straighten. For a moment he gazed stupidly down at his coffee and muffin.

"I'll take care of that for you," the elderly volunteer said.

"Thanks."

"I hope things turn out all right for you," she said. He nodded at her and started away, his legs carrying him as if they had a mind of their own and his torso had lost all control. He stabbed the button by the elevator with his right forefinger and waited impatiently, his heart pounding. The door opened and two nurses stepped out laughing. They didn't seem to notice him and for a moment, he did feel invisible. Alone in the elevator, he felt like he was being swept up in a dream and when the doors opened again, he would simply wake up.

But when they opened, he found Faye Sullivan standing there, waiting for him. He didn't have to ask. The sadness in her soft blue eyes, the way she tilted her head just a bit to the left and pressed her lips together told him. He didn't need to hear her say it.

"I'm so sorry, Mr. Livingston," she began. "Your wife was one of the most courageous patients I ever had."

"What happened?" he demanded. "What . . ."

"She must have had another seizure. The doctor on the floor did all he could."

"You mean, she's . . . gone?" He realized he had to hear it

spoken after all. A part of him refused to believe it any other way.

"She's expired, Mr. Livingston," Faye said. That was just the way the doctor had put it to her father when he had described what had happened to her mother. "Expired." As if her time had run out on the meter of life.

The words fell thunderously through Tommy Livingston's ears and sent his blood raging to his face. In fact, he felt as if all of his blood were spilling onto the hospital floor. He actually gazed down to see if he were standing in a pool of red.

"I'll take you to her," Faye said, and she marched ahead of him to his wife's room.

No matter how much Tommy had tried to prepare himself for such an event, he was still utterly devastated to stand at Sylvia's bedside. She already looked different to him. Without the spark of life, her face seemed more like a mask now, a replication. He hated looking at her, but even though his chest ached as sharply as it would have if someone had driven a knife into it, he didn't cry. He closed his eyes instead and felt himself sway until Faye Sullivan took hold of his arm.

"Here, sit down," she told him as she led him to the seat.

He started for it, then stopped.

"No, I've got to call my boys . . . Perry and Todd . . . and I've got arrangements to make . . ."

"There's sufficient time, Mr. Livingston. Catch your breath first. Believe me, I know of what I speak. Just sit down a moment. It's like you've been struck with a sledge hammer, I'm sure. No matter how big and strong you think you are," she added.

He didn't resist. Maybe she was right. She appeared to be very competent, a true professional. He let her lead him to the seat and sat down, gazing at Sylvia.

"The last thing she said to me was, 'Tommy, go home and get some rest.' She was always thinking about others more than she thought about herself."

Faye nodded.

"I'll leave you alone for a moment and get you a glass of cold water," she said.

After Faye had left him, Tommy went back to Sylvia. He held her cold hand, whispered his final words of devotion, and began to cry. He didn't hear Faye Sullivan return to his side a short while later, so he didn't hide his sobs. Suddenly, he felt her hand on his arm and he pulled himself back.

"Drink this," she said. He wiped his eyes with a quick sweep of his big right hand and then took the glass of water. He drank some and thanked her.

"I'd better call my boys now," he said.

"I've taken care of that for you, Mr. Livingston. They're both on their way."

"Really? But . . . how . . . I mean . . ."

"I took their phone numbers when I first met them. Just as a precaution," she added. "I hope you don't mind."

"Mind? No, I'm . . . just surprised," he said.

"I know how difficult a time this is for everyone concerned and especially for the husband," she said.

"Yes," he said.

"My father . . . survived my mother. We were with him when my mother died, my twin sister, Susie, and myself. All of his siblings were gone. My mother still had a living sister, but she was on the East Coast. Essentially, he had only us."

Tommy nodded, only half-listening and clearly not absorbing a word. Faye pulled her shoulders back. Why was she babbling like an idiot?

"Will you be all right?"

"Yeah, sure," he said. "I'll just sit here and wait for my boys."

"Fine," she said, and she left him.

After she had gone, he looked at Sylvia again and shut his eyes. He was filled with an urge to bolt out of this room, even out of the hospital, but he fought it back and waited for his sons.

While in the corridor outside, Faye paused to gaze out the window at the puffs of clouds that were making their way la-

zily across the horizon, moving like a caravan of marshmal-
lows through some child's panorama of sweet dreams. She
had sweet dreams, too, especially her dream of some day
finding someone who would love her and cherish her as
much as Tommy Livingston loved and cherished his wife.
Why were some people blessed with that and so many not?
What was the secret? What was she doing wrong? Surely
there was someone out there who would respect and admire
a woman dedicated to her work.

She was interrupted by what she first mistook for a reflection of herself in the window, but when she turned, she realized it was Susie.

"What are you doing here? If I've told you once, I've told
you a hundred times, I don't want you appearing unexpectedly. This is a hospital, not a social hall. The work I do is very
serious . . . life and death."

"I just came to visit Mrs. Livingston and you. I was bored
sitting at home," Susie whined.

Faye shook her head. Something in Susie's eyes told her
she hadn't just appeared in the corridor, however.

"You went into Mrs. Livingston's room, didn't you?"

"Yes," Susie admitted. "I didn't disturb him, even though
I saw how he's trying to hide the pain. You could see his terrible suffering, couldn't you?" she said excitedly.

"Yes," Faye replied in a tired voice. "I could see it, but I'm
a trained nurse. I can't cry with the close relatives of every
single patient I have, you know," she said sharply. Susie didn't
seem to hear or care.

"He's another one of those strong, manly types who thinks
any show of emotion is womanly," she said. "They're the
worst when it comes to facing tragedy. They boil up inside,
swell like an infection. Daddy tried to be like that. He didn't
want to cry in front of us when Mommy died."

"Daddy didn't cry in front of anyone when Mommy died.
Not even himself," Faye said.

"That's not so. I was there. I saw him cry. I saw him,"
Susie insisted.

Faye turned away to look out the window again.

"Mr. Livingston's going to need someone to stand by him, isn't he? Will you tell him about me? Faye, will you?"

Faye took a deep breath and then turned around and stared at her a moment.

"He has family, children," she said. She hoped Susie would leave it at that, but in her heart, she knew she couldn't.

"You've met them. You know they won't give him any real support. They're self-centered. Will you tell him I'm available? Will you? He needs me." She limped up to her sister. "Faye?"

Faye nodded softly, resigned.

"I'll tell him at the proper time, after the funeral," she whispered.

"Promise?"

"I said I would, didn't I?" she snapped.

Susie seemed to wither right before her eyes, growing smaller and smaller until she looked like a twelve-year-old girl again, always depending on her, even more than she depended on their mother and father.

"It's just that when I peeked in, he looked just like Daddy, sitting by the hospital bed."

Faye closed her eyes and opened them.

"You don't know what you're talking about. Daddy never sat at Mommy's hospital bed."

"Of course he did," Susie said smiling.

"All right, Susie."

"I don't know why you insist on saying these things that you know aren't so."

"All right."

"You just forget, that's all. You want to forget, so you just forget."

"Don't start!" Faye snapped. "Just go home," she ordered. Susie backed away, nearly stumbling over herself as if she expected Faye to reach out and slap her.

"You don't have to shout at me."

"Just ... go home, Susie. Please."

"You just forget," Susie insisted. She turned and started away. Faye watched her sister hobble down to the elevator. Then she started back to the room where she knew Tommy Livingston was still sitting, staring at his dearly departed wife.

3

"This is a helluva sight for a man who nearly had a heart attack," Frankie muttered when he and Jennie were forced to stop at a green light to let a funeral procession go through the intersection. Behind the metallic black hearse, Tommy Livingston, his two sons, and their wives and children rode in a gray stretch limousine with tinted windows. There were close to twenty-five cars of friends and relatives following. After the last car passed through, the light turned red again before Frankie could go forward. He had insisted on driving, reminding Jennie that the doctor had said he could resume normal activities until he returned for the pacemaker.

"His idea of normal and yours are quite different, Frankie," Jennie said, but she relented and permitted him to take the wheel. Now he twisted impatiently in the seat.

"I knew that light would change before we could pass."

"We're in no rush, Frankie," Jennie said. "You might as well get used to the slower tempo of life right away."

"Yeah, I suppose," he said, although he had no idea what a slower tempo of life really meant.

"Look at the mountains, Frankie," Jennie said. He gazed to his right. "Doesn't it look like a movie set, like someone just planted them there? I never get used to them."

He smiled. It was impressive—the city of Palm Springs built right at the foot of the mountain range, a true oasis in the desert. The light changed and they coasted down Palm Canyon Boulevard into the heart of the small city that had a native population of just over forty thousand. But it was still the season, still busy. Small clumps of people sauntered down the sidewalks and over the crosswalks.

Despite his constant stream of anger and self-pity, Frankie felt the tension drain out of his body. This lazy vacationer's mentality seemed to permeate the very air and infect every visitor with the same sense of relaxation. Here and there he spotted young lovers walking arm and arm, window shopping and giggling. People sat out on the sidewalks casually dipping plastic spoons into cups of frozen yogurt or ate salads and burgers under the protection of cool mists that emanated from the edges of the ceilings and awnings.

Frankie recalled how he and Jennie had first met in Palm Springs. They were both from larger cities, he from Los Angeles and she from San Diego. It had been something of a family foregone conclusion that he would work for his uncle in his uncle's import-export business, but Frankie was always fascinated with police work. He had started with the LAPD as a foot patrolman, graduated to a black-and-white, and then quickly moved into plainclothes before he met Jennie while vacationing in Palm Springs with a few of his policemen buddies. She had come to live with her aunt and worked as a receptionist in the hotel where he and his friends were staying.

It wasn't love at first sight for Jennie, but it was for him. He pursued her relentlessly until she agreed to the first date and then, as she revealed later, she saw a side of him that wasn't visible until she had spent some time with him. He was soft, gentle, and compassionate just under that crust of granite he dressed himself in every morning in order to function as a big-city policeman.

Once they became serious, it was her decision that they live in Palm Springs.

"I'll marry a policeman," she told him, "but not one who works in a big city."

At the time Palm Springs didn't suffer from the same sort

of criminal epidemic most of the bigger urban areas were experiencing. It was still small-time. Lately, however, with the growing population and the influx of poorer people, those old distinctions were fading quickly.

But despite its coming-of-age problems, Palm Springs still had a fresh new face, at least on the main drag. There was a jewellike glitter to the sunlight that reflected off window panes, sidewalks, and expensive automobiles. Absent were the urban buildings defaced with the graffiti of madness sprayed in a frenzy by children of the ghetto searching for a way to achieve notoriety and meaning. There was little or no litter on the walks and streets. Some of the policemen wore shorts and rode bikes. Music emanated from sidewalk coffee bars, and the Plaza Theater at the center of town announced a follies review featuring a number of old-time performers coaxed out of retirement.

The traffic picked up toward the south end of town and Frankie accelerated down Palm Canyon Boulevard South into what was called the Indian Canyons, where they had their three-bedroom hacienda-style home with its lemon, orange, and grapefruit trees. It was located on the west end in an area adjacent to a plush new eighteen-hole golf course. A condo development had been constructed right beside them. It was a gated development of blue-roof-tiled structures with two swimming pools, carpetlike lawns and colorful gardens, four tennis courts and quaint walkways that wove from one end to the other. Lately Jennie had been verbalizing a desire to give up the house and move into one of those units, but up to now Frankie resisted anything that smacked of retirement.

"I'm not old enough for golf yet," Frankie had quipped. Now he seriously wondered if golf would be considered too strenuous for a man with his condition.

They drove into their garage and entered the house through the kitchen.

"Why don't you just relax in the den, Frankie, and I'll make us some lunch," Jennie suggested the moment they had walked through the door. He scowled.

"Don't make me into a couch potato immediately, Jen," he said.

"I'm not. I just . . ."

"I'll be all right," he assured her. She nodded and bit down on her lower lip as if to keep herself from saying another word.

Frankie walked through the kitchen and did just what she suggested, however: he settled on the sofa. For a moment he just looked around. How wonderful it was simply to come home, he thought, and he looked around his home as if it were the first time he had entered it. It took a brush with the Grim Reaper to get him to appreciate what he had. While most of his contemporaries in urban areas like Los Angeles lived in small homes or apartments, he had a thirty-two-hundred-square-foot home with a marble-floored entryway. Unlike the inner-city apartments where some of his older acquaintances resided, he had an airy, bright, and cheerful house with new-looking beige Berber rugs, cream-painted walls, and large windows and skylights. The bathrooms had brass fittings and plenty of mirrors. There was a tear-drop chandelier in the dining room and the living room had a bay window that looked out toward the San Jacinto Mountains, giving them a rather breathtaking view. Just outside the kitchen, they had a small patio which they could use as a breakfast nook. Why was it he had never stopped to appreciate all this before? he wondered.

Jennie appeared in the doorway.

"I'll make some soup and a toasted-cheese sandwich, okay?"

"Sounds good." He smiled. "It's good to be home."

She returned the smile and went back to the kitchen. He waited a moment and then slowly, quietly, he reached over and lifted the telephone receiver out of its cradle. As gently as possible, he punched out the station's number.

"Billy," he said when the dispatcher responded. "It's Frankie. Give me Rosina."

"Frankie! How you doin'?"

"Good."

"What?"

"Good."

"Why are you speaking so softly?"

"Just give me Rosina, Billy."

"Right."

The extension was rung.

"Detective Flores," she responded.

"Who says you're a detective?"

"Frankie! You're home?"

"Just arrived."

"How are you?"

"Great. What's been happening?"

"Not a helluva lot," she began and then said, "well, actually a helluva lot."

Frankie smothered a laugh.

"What?"

"Seems this schoolteacher was porking the mother of one of his students . . . a divorcee, whose estranged husband remained possessive."

"Killed her?"

"Killed the teacher. It will be in tomorrow's *Sun*."

"At least it's open-and-shut. What else?"

"Had a suicide to investigate. Elderly gent who just lost his wife and seems to have offed himself by overdosing on her insulin."

"Whatever happened to gas ovens?"

"Theirs was electric. It's a sad one. He was very determined."

"What d'ya mean?"

"Autopsy revealed he took a fistful of Dilantin, too."

"Don't be a big shot, Flores. What's Dilantin?"

"Thought you former big-city detectives would know." She laughed. "It's used as an anticonvulsant and sleeping aid, but one of its possible side effects, especially in large doses, is insulin shock."

"I thought you said he overdosed on insulin?"

"I did."

"So he took these pills besides?"

"I told you he was determined."

Frankie was silent a moment.

"Where'd he get the pills? Were they his?"

"I'm not sure."

"Couldn't be his wife's if she had diabetes then and was taking insulin, right?"

Rosina was silent.

"You didn't go through the medicine cabinet, review their drug history, contact their doctor? . . ."

"I checked. There wasn't any Dilantin in their medicine cabinet."

"Not even an empty bottle?"

"No."

"So?"

"Nolan says it's open-and-shut and he doesn't want me spending any more time on it. I have to go stake out this pump station on Alejo that might be a drugstore instead. The owner of the Seven-Eleven across the way tipped us."

"You're satisfied closing this suicide investigation, Flores?"

"Hey, the guy was married for nearly forty years to the same woman. They live alone, one married daughter in Ohio. His wife kicks the bucket and he offs himself using her medication. We found him with their picture clutched to his chest. Nothing stolen that we can determine. Who'd want to hurt a bereaved old man? I know you don't like Nolan, especially these days, but . . ."

"Fistful of Dilantin, but no bottle? It's a loose end," Frankie insisted.

Rosina was silent for a moment.

"I'm going to miss you, Samuels. No one else has your urban cynicism here."

"What's the victim's name?"

"Murray, Sam Murray."

"Call the coroner and see if he can tell you how long the Dilantin was in Mr. Murray before the insulin kicked in, too."

"Why?"

"If he took so much sleeping powder and it would have knocked him out, he couldn't have injected himself with insulin, now, could he?"

"Frankie, Nolan's not going to . . ."

"Forget it. I'll look into it while you pump gas."

"Frankie."

"I'm bored."

"Already? You haven't been off the job a week."

"I haven't?" He laughed. "Seems like a month. I'll be in to see our beloved chief in a day or so. In the meantime . . ."

"In the meantime . . . Let there be a meantime, Frankie. I gotta go."

"Vaya con Dios."

"Great, you're bilingual." She laughed and hung up

Frankie pressed down the button on the cradle to redial and speak to forensics, but he felt Jennie's eyes. He looked up quickly and saw her standing in the doorway.

"I'm just . . ."

"Hang that phone up, Frankie Samuels," she ordered, her eyes full of fire. There was a crimson tint in her cheeks that told him she was about to erupt. Like a man under the gun, he obeyed. "You haven't been home five minutes."

"I just . . ."

"Don't start your lying, Frankie. I can't take it. Not along with everything else."

He started to raise his hand to swear, but her smirk aborted the gesture.

"Your lunch is ready, Frankie. You'll eat, go out on the patio and lie on the lounge. I'll bring you the papers. After that, you'll do what the doctor said and take it easy for the first day home. The children are coming down to have dinner with us tomorrow night. We're ordering in Chinese."

"Beth, too?" he asked.

"I don't know."

"Now who's lying."

"I don't know. She said she might go to Tucson to that demonstration, but . . ."

"That's where she is, Jen. I'm second when it comes to the cause."

"Please, Frankie, I can't take any more tension."

"All right," he said rising. "Let's eat."

Hours later, after he did fall asleep on the lounge on the patio, he came in and flopped into the leather La-Z-Boy chair in the den to flick on the television set and get some local news. The teacher-parent love triangle murder was the head-line story.

"I guess this ain't the paradise it used to be," Frankie com-mented when Jennie joined him. They talked quietly about the old days for a while until they were interrupted when Phil and Brenda Morton, their closest neighbors, arrived with a freshly baked coffee cake.

Phil had owned a hardware store in Akron, Ohio, and Brenda had been a school nurse. They were a pleasant, up-beat couple who had an almost monomaniacal drive to enjoy their autumn years. Their lives appeared to be built around their schedule of activities, from golf to bingo to senior-citizen day trips and show trips. The bulletin board on the right wall of their kitchen was inundated with messages and announcements concerning restaurants and department stores that awarded senior-citizen discounts and early-bird specials. Frankie used to joke about them, but for the first time, Frankie saw his and Jennie's future in the same terms.

Later, when he and Jennie finally had a quiet moment, sitting on their settee on the patio, he confessed he was tired.

"This retirement business can wear you down," he said.

"According to Phil and Brenda, there's never a lack of something to do."

"That's what I was afraid of. Let's not run ourselves down filling our lives with things to fill our lives, Jen," he warned.

"Don't worry about me, Frankie Samuels. You just make sure you watch your medications and diet and tell me imme-diately if you're too tired to do something."

"Don't start nagging. I can still go back to being a traffic cop giving out parking tickets," he threatened.

She laughed. He embraced her and they sat there while the night continued to fall and the stars continued to pop to the surface of the vast desert sky. Unencumbered by the bright lights of the city, they were far more visible.

They remained there until they were both tired enough to go in to sleep. Just after he closed his eyes and rested his head on the pillow, the memory of that funeral procession returned. It was just natural for cops to be superstitious, as superstitious as soldiers going into battle. Omens, talismans, charms, and curses made them take second looks, made them extra careful. Was it just fate that put him at that intersection exactly when a funeral procession was going by? If only he had checked out of the hospital a little earlier, or even a little later, they might have missed it and this dark, cold feeling that surrounded his heart would not be there the first night he spent at home.

He turned to look at Jennie. She was already in a deep sleep, only now, when he gazed at her before closing his eyes, he wondered if his would be a sleep from which he would never awaken. At least this way the last thing he would remember seeing would be Jennie's sweet face, he thought. He kept his eyes open a little longer, staring up at the dark ceiling and wondering how it would come. Would it come in his sloop or would it come when he was just sitting down to eat dinner?

He swallowed hard and pressed his eyes tightly closed for a moment. It was so quiet here. Usually, he was so exhausted by the time his head hit the pillow, he had no time to think about it. Well, now he would think about a lot of things he had somehow ignored.

Let this not be the beginning of the end, he prayed. He lay there listening to Jennie's breathing, concentrating on her rhythm. He would never forget the hollow sound of his own breathing when he was in the CCU unit at the hospital, that beat on the monitor, that breathy echo that seemed to embrace his very brain and bathe him in the realization that he was on the precipice looking down into the darkness of his own grave.

He got himself off these depressing thoughts by recalling his conversation with Rosina Flores. The man used Dilantin but it wasn't his wife's prescription and there was no empty pill bottle. Where did he get it, then? Was it his prescription? If so, where was the pill bottle? How did he know enough to use it along with the insulin? These questions should be answered before the investigation is closed, he thought.

Of course, on the surface Nolan was a hundred percent correct. There was no apparent motive for anything else and good reason to accept suicide.

But a man who just had a brush with the Grim Reaper and knew how dark and cold the face of Death was had a hard time accepting and understanding why someone would willingly embrace the grave.

I'm sure it's the only reason I'm harping on this, he thought, and he turned over to fall asleep to the sound of his own troubled heartbeat.

4

"He's surprised to see you here," Susie said.

Faye nodded. She, too, had seen the surprise in Tommy Livingston's face here at the cemetery when he had set eyes on her. He hadn't seen her in the crowd of mourners who had attended church, although she thought Todd, one of his sons, might have seen her.

"The poor man looks like he's had half his soul lopped off," Susie whispered. Faye glared at her so she would keep quiet. She didn't want to bring her to the funeral; Susie was always bad at funerals. The church was crowded, so she told Susie to remain in the car. She wasn't good attending church services anyway, especially funeral services. She would hobble down the aisle and stop where the immediate family was sitting and say the most outrageous things, especially to the children. In Susie's eyes, the children didn't suffer as much grief as did the surviving spouse.

That was all well and true if the surviving spouse had really been devoted to his or her lost loved one, but despite what Susie wanted to believe, Faye knew it hadn't been the case when it came to their father. Susie just didn't know it all; she just didn't know. There were things Faye didn't want her to know. Susie was too fragile. If she had endured one-tenth of what Faye had endured . . . but she was always asleep or in another room when Daddy paid his visits.

"Look at him," Susie continued, whispering into Faye's ear, "He looks like a man who's had half of everything he's lived for removed. He's like a one-legged, one-armed man tilting, ready to fall. Doesn't your heart go out to him? I feel like rushing forward to be there as his crutch."

"Don't you move," Faye warned. Susie was capable of simply doing what she said: stepping forward between the members of the family and taking Tommy Livingston's arm. "Get back in the car."

"What?"

"You heard me," Faye muttered under her breath. "Back in the car this instant."

"But . . ."

She turned and gave her one of her furious looks: her eyes wide, her lips drawn back so firmly there were patches of white in the corners of her mouth. As usual Susie cowered back and obeyed. Faye breathed with relief.

She thought Tommy Livingston smiled when he looked her way again. Most of the time, he had had his eyes down. He didn't really look around until the minister had completed the prayers and the mourners who had followed the hearse to the burial plot turned to go, some passing by him and shaking his hand, the women kissing him. She stood waiting as these people filed by. Finally, he said some things to his sons and started toward her.

"It's very nice of you to attend the funeral," he said. Instead of replying, she reached out and squeezed his hand. He appeared to appreciate that gesture more than any words anyway. "We have some refreshments at the house for close friends, relatives. Why don't you come?"

"I will," she said. He nodded and joined his family at the limousine. She saw from the expression on his son Perry's face that he didn't recall who she was, probably because she was out of uniform. The uniform did turn her into another person with an entirely different personality, as she thought it did for most people who wore uniforms. Everyone was a bit schizophrenic: cops, firemen, even doormen, because their voices changed, their posture, even the way they looked

at people changed once they put on their uniforms. She was
no different.

Faye hurried back to her car.

"Where are we going?" Susie asked.

"I'm going to the Livingston residence. You're going
home."

"Why?"

"I just know that's best."

"But . . ."

"Don't argue with me today, Susie. I'm not in the mood."

"But you promised . . ."

"I know and I will tell him about you."

"I should have introduced myself to him in the hospital instead of rushing off before he saw me," Susie complained.

"I said I would tell him and I will. Have I ever lied to you?
Well, have I?"

"You know you have," Susie said. She looked away quickly
so she wouldn't feel Faye's ire. In silence they drove back to
their apartment. Susie got out without a word and hurried toward the front door, and Faye drove on to Tommy Livingston's house.

He had a beautiful Sante Fe–style home on a small bluff
in southeast Rancho Mirage. From his rear patio, you could
look down on the Ritz Carlton Hotel and its grounds, and,
according to Tommy, if you came out in the early morning,
you could often see bighorn sheep grazing on the side of the
bluff.

The furniture was all Southwestern, with a lot of pinks and
blues in the carpets, wall hangings, and linens. Indian art and
replicas of Remingtons were exhibited in almost every one of
the seven rooms. There were skylights and large windows
that provided natural light during the long desert days and
great views of the valley and sky during the nights. Many of
the features, such as the remote-controlled ground lights and
the pool lights, filter, and jacuzzi blower, were state-of-the-art
and were features Tommy Livingston had put into all the
homes he had designed.

A crowd of about two dozen friends and relatives had returned to the house. The daughters-in-law were busy commanding the temporary servants and setting up the food and drink. The sons held court in the den, talking softly to their own friends. The children were relegated to the rear and told to stay out of everyone's way.

Faye wandered through, gazing at everything with interest, for the lives of her patients, more often than not, fascinated her, especially the patients who seemed to have had good marriages, people who really appeared to be in love. Despite what Susie thought, Faye believed love was a fairy tale.

Anyway, she often tried to imagine what their homes and their lives outside of the hospital were like, and Susie was always grilling her with questions when she returned from the hospital. Some patients did tell her things, even rather personal things about their families. More mothers than she cared to mention complained about their children or the women and men their children had married. Some wives complained about their husbands. On the whole, she found her female patients more open about their lives and families than the male patients.

Faye wandered into Tommy Livingston's office and gazed at the pictures of his family on his desk. Sylvia Livingston had been a very pretty woman, just like her own mother, Faye thought. She had the same sort of half smile, tantalizing, and didn't she have the same color hair about the same length? Hadn't her parents taken a similar picture on a stairway? Why was everything so foggy now, all her memories intermingling with the things she now saw? It made her dizzy for a moment and she leaned against the wall.

She was so far to the right, in fact, that Tommy Livingston didn't see her when he first came in and went to his desk. He took the wedding picture in his hands and stared down at it. Then his shoulders began to shake.

She wanted to slip away so she wouldn't embarrass him, but he turned around and saw her before she could leave.

"Oh," he said sucking in his breath. "I . . ."

"It's all right, Mr. Livingston. It's okay to have a good

cry. Keeping it pent up only makes it worse," she said. He nodded.

"Yes." He looked toward the doorway.

"You don't want to cry in front of your boys or your grandchildren, I know," Faye said dryly.

"No, I don't," he admitted.

As if she were back in the hospital and in control of things, she went to the den door and closed it. "I know you want to get away from people for a while," she said. "Come, sit down." She nodded toward the leather settee and he followed obediently. He sat with his hands in his lap and stared at the floor.

"Do you want something to drink . . . a glass of water?" He shook his head.

"It's nice of you to still be interested in us," Tommy said.

"My sister is always bawling me out for treating people like numbers. Most nurses I know do."

He started to smile skeptically.

"No, it's true. Why, I know some nurses who've walked past their former patients in department stores, not recognizing them anymore. I'm not that bad, but I do try to remain detached, especially when I know I have a critical case."

"I can understand that. I can't imagine going through this more than once," he said, nodding.

"We do what we must do," she replied. Then she looked toward the desk and the photographs. "But I'm glad I came here and saw what Mrs. Livingston looked like when she was younger."

"She was a very beautiful woman. I was very lucky."

"Yes, you were." She sat back and smiled as though she were reminiscing with him. Susie says husbands and wives grow closer in their senior years. Especially after their children are married and gone," she added.

"Sylvia never let go of her sons, marriages or no marriages," he said.

"A son must cleave to his wife and a daughter to her husband. It's only natural. It's harder for a mother to accept that than it is for a father, I suppose."

"You sound a lot older than you are," he replied, impressed.

"I am older in many ways than other people my age. I'm glad you see me that way, Mr. Livingston."

"Call me Tommy. You're not my employee any more."

She smiled. He was a very vulnerable, sad man. He needed Susie.

"So you have a sister?"

"Yes. I have a twin sister who lives with me here in Palm Springs."

"You don't say, a twin sister?"

"Yes, Susie."

"And what does she do?"

"Susie likes caring for people and keeping their homes clean and in order. She didn't go to college. She's had a number of different jobs, tried being a secretary and hated it. It took her a while, but she's really found herself now that she's gone into domestic service."

"Really? Is that what she's doing here?"

"Yes, but she doesn't work regularly. She likes to meet different people."

"She's not married then?"

"No. Susie is . . . rather shy. She was born with a leg problem, so she wears a brace. But it doesn't hold her back when it comes to work. She could be of great service to you, especially now. I don't expect you'll keep this house the way it used to be kept by your wife."

"Hardly," he said smiling.

"Susie could be of some help, at least until you adjust."

"Sure. Bring her around," Tommy said.

"I'll send her over tomorrow."

"Sure," Tommy said.

They sat there talking softly for a while and then she accompanied him when he returned to the den. All of the mourners gazed with curiosity.

"This is Faye Sullivan," Tommy announced. "She was Sylvia's private-duty nurse."

Perry and Todd nodded with recognition now. They

watched with interest as their father brought her to the food in the dining room. Faye was still sitting in the living room, perusing some family albums when Perry and Todd, their wives and children, were getting ready to leave.

"You can come to our house, Tom," Perry's wife said. Todd's wife immediately made a similar suggestion.

"No, I've got to get used to being alone. No sense in postponing it. You guys go on, get on with your lives, and don't worry about me," he said, pulling his shoulders up to resume his normal firm demeanor.

"I'll call, Dad," Todd said. "And if you need anything . . ."

"I'll stay with him awhile longer," Faye suddenly volunteered. Everyone gazed at her, the sons looking surprised at first and then a bit grateful; the daughters-in-law simply looked a bit amused.

"There, see. I'm still in the hands of an expert," Tommy said.

His daughters-in-law kissed him and his sons hugged him. Then they all moved out. Tommy followed them to the door. Shortly afterward the caterers left, too, even though there was cleaning left to do. Tommy voiced his annoyance.

"It's all right," Faye said, gathering the dirty paper plates. "I told them to go."

"You did? Why?"

"At a time like this, you don't need a bunch of strangers lingering around the house, banging pots and pans and vacuuming. You need peace and quiet, meditation time."

"But why should you . . ."

"I don't mind. I used to work as a maid, you know," she said. "While I was attending nursing school, I hired myself out and made what I needed for living expenses."

He stood there watching her sweep through the living room, adjusting furniture, fixing pillows, brushing crumbs off the coffee tables.

"Most of my father's extra money went toward medical bills in those days."

He closed his eyes and the moment he did, he swayed. Faye was at his side instantly.

"Easy," she said. "You're far more mentally and emotionally exhausted then you realize. Come on, get to bed. I want you to rest." She had looked around the house when she first arrived, so she knew where to lead him. He followed obediently, surprised and frightened by his weakness.

"All of a sudden," he explained, "my legs felt like they had turned into sticks of butter."

"Not unusual." She brought him to his bed. He sat down, dazed, and watched as she began to undo his tie and then unbutton his shirt.

"Got my own private duty nurse, huh?" he said, smiling.

"Oh," she said, pulling back suddenly, "I didn't mean to . . ."

"No, no, that's all right. I appreciate what you've done and what you're doing, Faye. Thank you. I'll undress myself and lie down awhile."

"Did the doctor give you any sedatives?"

"No, I don't think I'll need any."

"Yes, you will," she said authoritatively. "You're exhausted, but sleep isn't easy to come by when you're as emotionally wounded as you are now. Believe me, you'll drift off, but you'll keep waking up with a start, hoping this has all been a nightmare."

He stared at her. What she said made sense.

"Sylvia must have had some sedatives. I'll look in your medicine cabinet," she said. She already had and knew what was there. A few moments later, she returned with two red-tinted gelatin tablets and a glass of water.

"What's that?" Tommy asked. He had taken off his pants and was under the blanket.

"Chloral hydrate. It's a common sleeping pill," she added to relieve any anxieties he might have. She wouldn't tell him that this compound when given in larger doses was more famously known as a Mickey Finn. He nodded and smiled.

"Forgot I had a nurse." He took the pills and chased them down with some water.

"You just sleep," Faye said. "I'll stay as long as I can before leaving for the hospital."

"You shouldn't spend your time here, Faye. I'm sure you've got better things to do with your time off than care for a grieving husband," Tommy said. He closed his eyes when he felt her hand on his forehead. It made him feel secure and relaxed and he drifted off.

Faye stared at him and watched him sleep. He reminded her a little of her father after he had come into her room and crawled in bed beside her, moaning about how lonely he was. Mother hadn't let him sleep with her for some time. He always began by telling her he just wanted to feel someone he loved beside him. He just wanted to hold someone he loved, touch someone he loved. She kept her eyes closed but it happened anyway, and then afterward he fell asleep and looked just like Tommy Livingston, dead to the world.

When Susie thought Daddy was too lonely and should join their mother in heaven, Faye didn't stop her. He should be dead to the world, she thought angrily; and then afterward she thought, maybe Susie was right, if not about Daddy, at least about other people. Maybe people who were really in love and together so long really couldn't stand being apart. She never told Susie, but she wished there were something like eternal love between two people, because if it existed, maybe it would exist for her one day.

She looked at Tommy Livingston again and recalled how he had shuddered and cried when he came into that room and looked at his wife's picture, and then she was struck with an idea.

Wouldn't it be wonderful, she thought, if when he woke up, Susie was already here caring for him, easing his suffering. She knew how anxious Susie was. She rose quickly to call her, but at the phone, she hesitated.

I shouldn't do this, she thought. She knew what it would lead to, didn't she? But when she looked back toward Tommy Livingston's bedroom again, her resistance waned.

"I can't help it," she muttered. "Susie should be here. He does need her and she . . . needs to help him."

She closed her eyes and took a deep breath and then she made the call.

5

The thing of it was, she didn't feel like she was in a strange house. As the twilight came, Susie felt herself drifting back through time. This kitchen, this living room, these halls and these walls, even the vases on the tables and the painting above the fireplace had a certain familiarity. When she closed her eyes and inhaled, she thought she drew in the scents and the aromas of her own home. Not the home she was living in now with Faye, not the apartment on Palm Canyon Boulevard South, but her real home, her home when her mother and her father were alive and they lived in Pacific Palisades.

She noticed the Livingstons' family albums were still there on the glass-top center table, just as they had been in her own home. Someone always brought out the family albums at times like this, she thought. It was as if he or she were afraid Death would wipe the memories out of their minds, so they had better reinforce them quickly.

But when she sat down and opened the first one, instead of two little boys, she saw a pair of twins, and instead of Sylvia and Tommy Livingston thirty-some-odd years before, at the threshold of their marriage and their lives together, she saw her own parents. She sighed. How young and beautiful they were, how handsome and strong, how healthy and vibrant. Why couldn't they always be that way? Why did they have to grow old and sick, and why did one of them have to die before the other?

It made her angry. Couldn't God have figured out a different pattern, something more pleasant for people so in love? Why have something like love anyway, if this was going to happen? While He was at it, He could have prevented all this grief and sorrow with a swipe of His divine hand. Instead, she had to be called upon time after time after time.

She rose and moved slowly through the vaguely lit house, moving like an apparition that had just arrived and was unsure of its haunting grounds. She limped down the hallway and slipped into the bedroom.

Tommy Livingston slept so soundly. He resembled a corpse laid to rest in some funeral parlor. On his back, his nose up, his Adam's apple prominent but still, his breathing barely discernible, he metamorphosed before her eyes and became her daddy in his coffin. She could even hear the organ music off to the right and behind her.

She moved to him, her hands clutching her handkerchief. The tears were streaming down her cheeks. Vividly recalling, she reached out slowly and put her hand over his forehead. He felt stone cold.

"You're happier now, Daddy. I know you are. Good night, sweet Daddy."

She smiled through her tears and removed her hand. She was going to go to her knees and offer a prayer when suddenly the phone rang and shattered her memory like a window pane, the shards of precious images falling all around her.

Angry, she stabbed at the receiver and lifted it before the second ring disturbed Tommy Livingston.

"Hello," the voice on the other end said when she said nothing.

She reached around the phone and pulled the jack out of the base. The receiver went dead. Then she cradled it and went to her knees, only it was no good. The ringing continued when whoever it was called back. Frustrated, she rose and went out to the kitchen to answer.

"Mr. Livingston's residence," she said.

"Huh? Who is this?"

"Susie Sullivan."

"Susie Sullivan?" There was silence for a moment. "You're the nurse?" the man asked.

"No. I'm her sister. I was called here to stay with Mr. Livingston."

"What? Who called you?" the man demanded.

"Mr. Livingston asked my sister to call me. I keep the house clean and care for him during his troubled time," she explained. "Who is this, please?"

"This is Todd Livingston. Where's my father?"

"He's sleeping. My sister gave him something to help him sleep and he's sleeping soundly, finally," she said, emphasizing the 'finally' so he would make no request to have her wake Tommy.

"Well, if he should wake up before you leave, will you tell him I called?"

"Of course, but Faye said he would sleep through the night now."

"Oh. Well, do you think I should return?"

"No, that's not necessary. I'm staying."

"Oh. Well, call me if you need me. No matter what time. My number's . . ."

"I know your number, Todd. My sister put all the important numbers on the bulletin board here in the kitchen."

"Okay. Thanks."

"No need to thank me," she said. "Good night, Todd. Try to get some rest."

"Right. Good night," he said.

After she cradled the receiver, she returned to the bedroom to be sure Tommy hadn't been disturbed. Then she moved quietly through the room, gazing at everything: Sylvia's cosmetics, combs, and brushes on the vanity table, the pictures on the dressers, the clothing in the armoire and in the closets, and even the clothing in the drawers.

She did the same thing with the rest of the house: walking into every room, inspecting every closet, every drawer, studying every artifact, every picture. She knew where Tommy Livingston kept his rifles and his fishing poles. She knew where the supply of toilet paper was stored. By the time she retreated to the sofa in the den, she knew everything there was to know about this house and its contents, just as she had known everything about her parents' house.

Satisfied, she made a little bed for herself in the den. Then she got down on her knees, clutched her hands, closed her eyes, and recited her usual nighttime prayer.

"God bless Faye for all the wonderful work she does to help people who are sick, and God bless Mommy and Daddy in Heaven. Amen."

She took off her brace, snapped off the lamp and dropped herself into the comfortable warm darkness. Nighttime made her snuggle. She whimpered a little like a baby for a moment and then she closed her eyes and envisioned the photographs in the album, only this time the people in them could move and smile and laugh, especially the lovely couple: Tommy and Sylvia. Tommy was so happy, he positively glowed when he had Sylvia in his arms or beside him. And now, look at how unhappy he was.

But Tommy won't be unhappy long, she thought. No, not for long. Faye had brought her here to help him. And she would.

Tommy Livingston awoke with a start. It was almost as though Sylvia had nudged him. He half expected to hear her familiar "Wake up, Rip Van Winkle." He turned and gazed stupidly at the empty place beside him in the king-size brass-framed bed. Her place was untouched and cold, her pillow without a crease. None of this had been a bad dream. Sylvia was gone for good.

He sat up slowly, feeling years older than he was, and scrubbed his face with his dry palms. Funny, he thought, how he hadn't noticed how quiet the house had been with Sylvia in the hospital. Now that she was definitely gone, that silence was emphatic. In fact, if he concentrated, he could hear the whir of the refrigerator motor.

For the moment he couldn't remember how he had gotten into bed or when he had undressed. His mind was so cloudy. He recalled greeting people after the funeral and then ... when did he go to bed? He hated this confusion. Damn it, he thought, shaking his head as if he expected to shake his thoughts and memories loose. Instead he felt nauseous and dizzy and had to lie back again. After he got his breath, he sat up and gazed around the room.

Everything was neatly put away, no garments hanging over chairs, the closet doors and dresser drawers closed, the curtains drawn. When did he do all that?

His gaze went to the telephone and clock on his night table. It was nearly ten o'clock. He had slept that long? He never slept that long. He was a morning person. What surprised him even more was that no one had called to see how he was doing. Where were his sons, his relatives, his friends? Everyone else hadn't overslept, had they? But when his eyes trailed the telephone wire, he noted that the phone had been unplugged. He hadn't done that; he would never do that.

He started to swing his legs over the side of the bed when she appeared in the doorway.

"Good morning," Susie said, smiling. She limped quickly across the room to open the curtains and let in the sunlight. It was so abrupt and the rays were so bright, reflecting off the cream-colored walls and the mirror over Sylvia's vanity table, that he had to cover his eyes for a moment.

"What's happening?" Tommy asked. "Why are you here?"

"Oh, I hope you don't mind," she said quickly. "My sister called me last night and told me to come over. She had to go home to get some sleep because she's expecting to be scheduled for private duty shortly."

"Sister?" He thought, his eyes blinking rapidly. "Oh," he realized, putting together her limp and her longer hair. He realized also that this woman was dressed in a maid's uniform and not a nurse's. "You're ... the twin sister?"

"Yes. My name is Susie," she said. "I hope you don't mind my being here."

"No, I ... I'm just surprised to see you," he said. It began to fall into place . . . Faye helping him to bed, giving him the sedative. "When did you say you arrived?"

"Last night. I finished cleaning up while you were sleeping, and you were sleeping so soundly, I decided to keep people from bothering you. I hope you don't mind."

"You've been here all night?" He shook his head, still a bit confused. "I never heard a sound."

"I unplugged your phone so it wouldn't ring and wake you, but I took down the names of everyone who called this morning. I have the list in the kitchen."

"Where did you sleep?"

"On the sofa in the den. It was quite comfortable. I've slept on worse sofas and in pretty uncomfortable chairs, believe me."

Tommy nodded. He started to get up and stopped. She sensed his modesty and went to the closet to take out the robe. He was surprised she knew it was hanging inside the door. She brought the robe to him and he took it without comment, although dozens of questions were buzzing around in his head.

"I've got some oatmeal cooking, some juice and some coffee made. I also made some of those breakfast rolls your wife had in the freezer. Faye says you need something hot and substantial in your stomach. Grief wears you down, drains your body," Susie said.

He nodded.

"I'll just take a quick shower," he decided.

"I thought you would. I put a fresh towel in the bathroom for you."

"Thanks," he said and continued to gaze up at her. Susie and Faye Sullivan couldn't be much more than thirty, he thought. Either one could have been the daughter he and Sylvia had so wanted, but it was as if Sylvia's body had shut down after Todd's birth. She didn't get pregnant again for the longest time, and when she did, it was an ectopic pregnancy.

"I'll get your breakfast together while you take your shower," Susie said.

He rose and went into the bathroom. After he was freshly

shaved and dressed, he entered the kitchen to find his place all set, his orange juice waiting and his coffee steaming hot. She poured the oatmeal into a bowl and brought it to him with a hot roll.

"You want honey or molasses over it?"

"Honey's fine," he replied and she smiled, nodding.

"That was the way my father liked it," she said. She fetched the jar of honey and brought it to him, and then she poured herself a cup of coffee and joined him at the table.

"How is it? It's not overcooked, is it?" she asked the moment he brought a spoonful to his lips.

"It's great."

Susie nodded.

"I like to cook. Faye hates it," she said. "After our mother died, I did all the cooking for her and my father. Actually, I did a lot of the cooking before she died, too."

"What did she die of?"

"Heart disease, just like your wife."

"Everyone seems to think it's a man's problem," Tommy said. "I must say, I was surprised when Sylvia had a heart attack."

"Faye says that's a common misconception," Susie remarked. "Especially now that women smoke more than men and eat the same fat-filled diets." She blew on her coffee for a moment, her eyes fixed in a blank stare.

"You said there was a list?"

"Pardon?"

"Of people who had called?"

"Oh, yes." She rose and returned to the counter to tear a page off the notebook by the phone.

"Wow," Tommy said. "This many calls and I slept through all of it."

"Faye said she gave you a powerful sedative to be sure you got a good night's rest."

"Yeah, I remember now. Something of Sylvia's, she said. I don't take sleeping pills as a rule."

"I'm sure Faye thought you needed them. She wouldn't give anyone pills if she wasn't positive. She hates to overmedicate and she's very critical of doctors who prescribe pills like candy," Susie said.

Tommy smiled at the vehement way Susie defended her twin sister.

"I guess you two are pretty close, being twins and all."

"We've always been close, even when Faye was away at college. We look after each other."

Tommy smiled.

"With all that's going on in this rotten world, that's nice to see nowadays. Too many of the younger generation are into themselves," he remarked.

Susie picked up on it quickly.

"Faye says the generation gap just seems to be growing wider and wider. Different values, different priorities."

Tommy nodded. These were almost Sylvia's exact words.

"Both you and your sister seem very wise for women so young," he said.

"Faye and I side with the older generation more often than not, which is why we both work so much and spend most of our time alone."

"Neither of you has been close to being married, then?"

"Faye was once . . . with a young doctor," she replied.

"What happened?"

"He had a tragic accident . . . he took too many uppers to keep working and crashed in his car."

"Oh. That is sad. But how about you? You're just as pretty," Tommy remarked. She was. She had the same beautiful eyes, the same rich-looking hair and complexion and just about the same figure. Big deal, so she limped, he thought.

"Every time I measure a prospective boyfriend against the man my father was, a man like you, he comes up short. I just won't settle for anyone less," Susie added firmly.

Tommy smiled.

"Well, you're a very pretty and a very nice person, so the man who finally wins your heart is going to be a very lucky man," Tommy said.

Susie didn't smile. Her eyes suddenly turned cold and her lips firm.

"I'm not optimistic," she said. "And besides, when I see how much it hurts to lose the one you love, I'm afraid I hesitate to get too involved. It's a horrible paradox. The more you love someone and he or she loves you, the harder it is to face life without him or without her."

Tommy just stared up at her. He didn't know whether to feel sorry for her or admire her. Was she better off with this attitude? He certainly couldn't disagree with her description of the pain accompanying the loss of a dearly beloved.

"I know how much you're going to miss Sylvia," she said, "even though you're the strong, silent type. Just like my father was," Susie said wagging her head. "Men think if they keep their sorrow inside and let their tears fall behind their eyes, they're more manly and it hurts less. But the truth is, that hurts more. It pulls and pulls at your heart and wears you down until you feel just like you do right now. I bet I could blow you over like a feather," she said.

Tommy smiled.

"Maybe you could."

"Of course, I could. Keep eating, Mr. Livingston, even if it's just something you do mechanically."

Tommy nodded and lifted the spoon.

"Yes, ma'am. I guess I do need someone like you around right now," he confessed.

"Of course you do. It's what I do best, too."

"Oh? And what's that exactly?"

"Help grieving people deal sensibly with their grief. Faye says it's a logical thing for a nurse's sister to do, when you think about it. For hours and hours after she returns from her nursing work, she talks about her patients and the doctors and all that goes on. I've learned a lot about medicine and treating people just by sitting and listening to her.

"And what is grief? Grief is like a sickness, like a disease. It debilitates, tears down the body, has symptoms like . . . like the flu. It fatigues you, ruins your appetite, fills your stomach with butterflies."

"Yeah, I suppose you're right," Tommy said, impressed

with how vehemently she spoke about it. He ate some more of the oatmeal and drank some of his coffee.

"Grief over a lost loved one, especially a wife, turns grown men such as yourself into little boys again," she continued. "Our daddy was like that. It got so I had to remind him to brush his teeth. I stood over him and forced him to eat, just like I'm hovering over you and forcing you to eat. He became forgetful, too, and left things everywhere."

"Sounds like he was quite along in years when your mother passed away."

"No. He was your age. Don't underestimate what's happened, Mr. Livingston. Your wife was a much bigger part of your life than you realize even now."

Tommy stared at her for a moment. She looked so confident and sounded so positive. He began to wonder more about this young woman. Where were she and her sister from? How long had they been in Palm Springs? What sort of a childhood had she and her sister had?

"You're from L.A.?"

"Pacific Palisades, originally, but Faye and I have lived in a lot of places."

"Don't say? You seem too young to have lived in too many places," he said.

"Faye's work has taken us all over the country."

"How long you been here?"

"A few months. I like it here," she said quickly. "My father would have liked it here, too."

"What happened to him? After your mother's passing, that is."

"He . . ."

"Yes?"

"Took his own life eventually," she said and looked away. She sighed and turned back to him with a soft smile. "It was sad, but I understood."

Tommy continued to gaze at her for a moment. He had half suspected something like this.

"How did he . . . ?"

"He swallowed a bottle of sleeping pills. But when Faye and I found him . . ."

"Yes?"

"He was smiling. My mother must have been waiting for him, don't you think?"

For a long moment, Tommy said nothing. Then he shook his head.

"I'm afraid I don't believe in much after this life," he replied finally.

Susie was devastated. She sat back aghast.

"But if you don't believe in anything after . . . how will you ever . . ."

Tommy looked up sharply.

"Ever what?"

"Be with your wife again?"

"I don't expect I will," he confessed and rose from his seat, obviously anxious to end this topic. "Thanks for preparing my breakfast. I'd better go call some of these people back," he said referring to the list. Susie watched him go to the den to use the phone and then she rose slowly.

"It's just his way of dealing with his sorrow," she muttered. "He didn't mean it. Daddy would never have said anything like that.

"Never."

She brought the dishes to the sink and thought for a moment. Then she turned and stared angrily after Tommy Livingston.

"She's waiting for you. You can't leave her waiting. You won't," she vowed, and she vigorously sponged down the bowl, the glass, and the cup as if Tommy Livingston had some infectious disease. "You won't."

6

Corpsy Ratner followed the gas pump attendant's suggestion and took the Ramon Avenue exit off the I-10 freeway into Palm Springs. Once on Ramon, he lifted his foot slightly off the accelerator to hover closer to the speed limit. Corpsy, so nicknamed by his associates in the pathology department at the hospital in Phoenix because of his enthusiasm for his work, had an obsessive need to obey all laws, especially traffic laws. He prided himself on the fact that he had not gotten so much as a parking ticket his whole driving life, nearly twenty years, to be exact. What other man in his mid-thirties could claim so spotless a record? If nothing else, Faye Sullivan should have been impressed with that, he thought ruefully.

Instead, on every occasion, she had rejected him firmly, once even reinforcing this maligning of his image by claiming he reeked of the odor of formaldehyde.

At nearly six feet tall, Corpsy was as lean and awkward as a young Abe Lincoln, with the same soulful face cut deeply by premature wrinkles around his cheeks and etched in his wide forehead. He was hairy: the same dark strands that streamed down his forehead unevenly also curled up his spine and even over his shoulders. His eyebrows were bushy and thick like near-term caterpillars, and no matter how closely he shaved, his face was haunted by a five o'clock shadow mere hours afterward.

When he was a teenager, Corpsy would beg his mother to shave his back during the summer months; otherwise, he would never take off his shirt, never go swimming. Of course she would do it; she would do anything he asked of her. His mother was a simple, soft-spoken, meek woman who dwindled rapidly after his father's truck accident and death until she resembled a bird with a broken wing, denied song and flight, its eyes vacant, waiting for the inevitable end.

Corpsy was her reason to go on. He was Lillian Ratner's only child, and as such was babied and spoiled. Corpsy was the first to admit this, but he rationalized that he suffered his mother's indulgence for her benefit more than for his own. I'm all she has, he thought, which was especially true after his father's smashup returning from a haul to Texas.

No two people looked more mismatched than Bret Ratner and Lillian. Corpsy's father was a muscular, hard, gruff six-foot-three-inch man with sinewy arms and wide shoulders, a trucker who wolfed down his food even when he was on a week's layover. Corpsy had his long arms and legs and long fingers, but it was as if his mother's daintiness and fragility had interfered during his formation to prevent him from inheriting any of his father's strength. No matter how much he exercised, his body refused to become anywhere as hard as his father's, and his muscle structure remained mediocre, if not downright underdeveloped.

He gave up trying to be like his father and withdrew, feeding his ever-festering interest in the internal nature of things, from mere insects and flowers to animals and people. Not bright enough or rich enough to become a doctor, he became a lab technician and eventually got a job in the pathology department at the hospital. He had been at the job most of his adult life, devoting himself to his work with a religious intensity that rivaled monks' and priests' and that earned him the notoriety that resulted in his nickname.

But he no longer minded. In fact, Corpsy saw the outside world as a world populated by envious people, people who wished that they cared about something as intensely as he did, people who wished they had his capacity to love something other than their miserable selves.

To say he was obsessive was to understate. Corpsy wouldn't deny it. When he found something that interested him, he pursued it with a passion that threatened to kill him. It was true about aspects of his work, but it was also true about his hobbies, the latest being collecting the kidney stones and gallstones he found in the corpses he dissected. He kept them in jelly jars on the shelves in his bedroom, each jar labeled with the age and sex of the deceased. His mother was upset about it, but she rarely went into his room anyway. In fact, other than his mother, no woman had ever been in Corpsy's room.

Women, unless they were stone-cold dead, terrified him. Invariably, he would lower his eyes when a woman spoke to him, unless that woman was someone in authority, especially someone who wore a uniform. The uniform had the effect of neutralizing her sexuality and emphasizing her authority. He had deep respect for authority, which was why he was obsessive about obeying traffic laws.

But Faye Sullivan had been different. She had been the first woman in uniform who had touched him deeply, maybe because he had seen something in her eyes, a second set of eyes, the eyes of the woman beneath the white dress and within the white slip and white panties and white bra; the woman who pulled on those white socks and stepped into those heavy black shoes. He heard a warmer tone under the orders she snapped to underlings and he saw another pair of hips swing under the skirt of her uniform when she marched down shiny corridors.

He had learned her schedule, and when he was able to, he would sit in the parking lot by the hospital and wait for her to arrive just so he could watch her get out of her car and walk to the entrance. Often he was there at the end of her tour of duty to watch her emerge and get into her car. He had done this for weeks before gathering up enough nerve to say his first words to her, which were merely, "Good morning."

She returned the greeting with a perfunctory smile, but it was enough to encourage him. He decided to follow her home one day and that was when he discovered she had a twin sister. At first, that confused him, threw him into a fluster because he was both excited and discouraged by the revelation. He had been fantasizing about Faye, imagining that she was really just as lonely as he was, and just as particular about whom she associated with and befriended. That was why she was a loner at work and why the others resented her. Just as they resented him.

But a sister . . . this meant she did have someone close, someone in whom to confide her troubles, her secrets, her dreams and fears. And a twin sister to boot! They shared more; they had to.

However, when he saw Susie hobble down the stairway and he realized she had a handicap, his ambitions were once again kindled. There was a real loner in this family, someone with whom he could commune, someone who would understand his deeper feelings. But he didn't try to make any contact with her that day.

Always the gentleman and always respectful of authority, he finally gathered his nerve and approached Faye Sullivan while she was alone in the nurse's quarters at the hospital. He had waited for her to have the sort of patient whom he knew would not be a constant worry. He studied her pattern and then, when he felt confident, he approached.

"Excuse me," he began. She looked up from her magazine with surprise, but she did not smile. He swallowed hard, his Adam's apple almost freezing in place and refusing to bob. "My name is Cor . . . Arnold Ratner. I work in pathology."

Faye folded her magazine and sat back, her eyes becoming small and fixed, the pupils darkening.

"Yes?"

"Um . . . I've said hello to you on a number of occasions and you've returned my greeting," he continued.

Faye looked as if she didn't remember, but she nodded.

"I know you're not on staff here, that you only special, but I thought since we both work at the hospital . . ."

"What?" she demanded with growing impatience.

"I . . . I just thought I could come by one day and say hello."

"Come by? Come by where?"

"Your home . . . your apartment. The truth is," he continued, finally building up enough courage to say it, "I'd like to meet your sister."

"My sister?"

"Uh huh. Properly, of course. That's why I came here to ask your permission to drop by and pay you two a visit. Whenever you think it would be a good time," he added. Faye stared at him silently.

"How do you know about my sister?" she asked.

"Well, I just happened to see her one day and I was quite surprised at first . . . being you two are twins . . ."

"Have you called our house and spoken to her?" Faye demanded.

"Oh no," Corpsy said, shaking his head vigorously. "I would never do that."

"Did you speak to her in a store or . . ."

"No, ma'am."

"Susie is a shy girl. I don't think your paying us a visit would be wise," Faye said sharply. "And I wouldn't advise you to call or try to speak to her if you should see her out and about. She is a fragile person, Mr. . . ."

"Ratner."

"Ratner. I have a special responsibility to look after her. I'm sure you understand," Faye said and snapped the magazine open again. It was as good as her saying "Dismissed."

Corpsy's naturally pallid complexion turned crimson. He started to stutter another explanation and then quickly retreated, hurrying down to the sanctity of his lab, where he paced between two dissected male bodies and berated himself for making himself look so foolish.

But he couldn't erase Susie Sullivan from his mind. The image of her hobbling down those stairs lingered and tormented him. He had caught her angelic smile and he dreamt that smile was for him. Of course, he understood and appreciated Faye Sullivan's reaction to his request. In her shoes he might very well have responded the same way, but she just didn't know him, he thought. If she did, once she did, she wouldn't see him as any sort of threat to her sister.

And so, with the same sort of monomania he brought to all his obsessions, he began to pursue Faye Sullivan, seeking ways to ingratiate himself with her. He followed her every assignment and made it his business to be there whenever she arrived at the hospital to greet her, and whenever she left, to bid her a good evening. He tried to expand his hellos and goodbyes with small talk about her patients, the hospital, her work, even the weather, but she resisted.

And then he thought he would approach her through her patients and their families. He began to visit her patients whenever she wasn't on duty. With those who were able to talk, he spent time, always turning the discussion to Faye and praising her on her abilities. When the patients were too sick to talk, he spoke to the lingering spouse or daughter or son, if there was any. That was how he learned that Susie Sullivan cared for some of them.

When the first corpse of a dead spouse appeared in autopsy, it was as if he were greeting an old and special friend. This was someone Susie Sullivan had known and touched and cared for with affection. He treated the bodies the same way, taking extra care, extra interest, and that was how he discovered what the chief of pathology had missed: amyl nitrate. Taken in these dosages, it would bring on a heart attack.

He had every intention of pointing it out. He imagined Faye was somehow responsible, but then he envisioned Susie Sullivan's angelic smile and fantasized her beside him. Any investigation mostly like would begin with her, and he could do nothing to hurt her, nothing to put suspicion on her. However, armed with his knowledge he found new courage and became far more brazen when he approached the stern Faye Sullivan. He lingered longer when he greeted her and he saw she noticed the way he looked at her. There was curiosity in those blue eyes now, curiosity and not just annoyance.

One evening he waited two hours in the parking lot for her

to complete her tour, and when she appeared, he got out of his car and approached.

"I'd like to meet your sister," he said firmly.

"Now look, Mr. Ratner . . ."

She remembered his name, he thought smugly.

"Arnold."

"Arnold. I've already told you . . ."

"I thought she and I could talk about Mr. Brofenberg," he said sharply.

"Pardon?"

"Amyl nitrate," he said. She stared at him a moment and then pivoted and marched to her car, her heels clicking sharply in the night.

A few days later, Corpsy drove to the apartment Susie shared with Faye. He noted that her car wasn't in the parking lot, but he remained there for hours until he saw the complex superintendent come along and go into the Sullivans' apartment. Curious, he got out and approached. The door had been left open, and when he gazed into the unit, he saw how empty it looked.

"Can I help you?" the superintendent asked.

"I . . . I was looking for Faye Sullivan," he said. He couldn't bring himself to say Susie.

"Gone," the superintendent replied.

"Gone?"

"Checked out without asking for her security back, and after she had just paid a month's rent. Got to admit," he added when Corpsy didn't utter a word, "it surprised me. I thought she and her sister were more reliable than some of the dips I get renting units in this complex."

"But did she leave a forwarding address? Are they somewhere else in Phoenix?"

"Hey, I was lucky she left the keys with my wife. Place is in good shape, though," he added gazing around. "Not a scratch, and pretty damn clean, too. I can turn this around tomorrow."

"What about her mail?" Corpsy demanded.

"I'm not the post office, mister. I guess you weren't such close friends," he said with a wry smile.

"No, actually, I'm very close to her sister."

"Not now, you ain't," the superintendent said and laughed.

Corpsy glared at him for a moment and then rushed out. He drove around in a daze for a while, trying to come to terms with the reality before returning to the lab, but the frustration and the disappointment he suffered was so great, he couldn't work. When he gazed at himself in the mirror, he did see a resemblance to a corpse. I deserve my nickname, he thought. It riled him and he made a major decision. He decided he would pursue his fantasy. Nothing he had was as important. Eventually, he discovered where Faye Sullivan had gone by tracking back her requested letters of reference, and then he packed all that was of any importance to him, even some of the jars of kidney and gallstones, thinking they just might interest Susie.

"Where are you going?" his mother asked when she saw him carrying his things out to the car.

"To see someone."

"Where?"

"Palm Springs, California. Don't worry, I told the hospital, and I took my accumulated vacation days."

"But how long will you be away, Arnold?" she asked, her face troubled. He had never so much as left for a weekend before. Even going out for the evening was a major undertaking.

"I don't know," he said honestly. Then he smiled. "Until she says yes, I suppose."

"She? Who?"

"Susie Sullivan," he replied. "She's a nurse's sister and she's the woman I love."

His mother was astonished. When had he courted her? Why hadn't he mentioned her before?

"She's very shy," he explained, "but she's waiting for me . . . just sitting by a window gazing out and hoping I will come. It's going to be a surprise," he concluded.

His mother shook her head and fumbled for words.

"You're . . . going to marry . . . marry this girl?"

"Of course," Corpsy replied. "And live happily every after," he added. He kissed his mother on the cheek and hurried out to his car. She stood on the steps and watched him drive away.

He had a game plan. He would find a place to stay first and then he would go to the hospital and park and wait to spot Faye. He would be as inconspicuous about it as he could. He would follow her home and then . . . then she would be impressed with his determination and finally invite him in to meet Susie. It seemed so logical, so easy.

Now he was approaching Palm Springs, but he didn't see the wide streets lined with beautiful palm trees and colorful vines of bougainvillea, nor did he see the velvet green golf courses and the sparkling fountains, the new homes and town houses, the comfortable condominiums in their peaceful settings. He saw only an angelic smile on a beautiful young woman as she hobbled along, alone, waiting for him to come into her life.

7

Frankie paused before opening his car door. For a moment he just sat in the vehicle in the police station parking lot and stared at the building that had been his second home for so long. Of course, he had realized it would someday come to this, but he had hoped it would have been on his own terms: when he could admit to himself that he was tired and ready. This wasn't fair. He felt as if he had been driven here by a malicious chauffeur, shackled and carted like some suspect and dragged into his supervisor's office to turn over his pistol and badge. Reluctantly, he stepped out of the vehicle and slowly started toward the entrance.

As he walked he realized it was one of those magnificent Palm Springs days, with the temperatures warm but made tolerable by a gentle breeze, the sky a deep blue, peppered with dots of cotton-candy clouds. This shouldn't be the day a large part of him dies, he thought. It should be cloudy and overcast or at the least, dreary and miserable, as dreary and miserable as he felt on the inside.

Imagining himself as a retired person, even in Palm Springs, which was one of the retired person's paradises, was a tough pill to swallow. If we're lucky enough to live a full life, he thought, we really die a few deaths and experience re-births. The person I'm about to become would be a stranger to the young man who first set foot in this building to apply for the job. For a moment he envisioned his younger self standing in the doorway watching him approach, a faint, almost sardonic smile on his younger face.

"About time," his younger self said. "About time you made room for new blood. Too bad you had to be brought to the brink of death before considering it, but that's you, stubborn until the end."

"What do you know about me?" he fired back at this imaginary second self. "You're too young to have that much wisdom."

"I'm not too young to know an old fool when I see one. I'm not surprised at your attitude. Look at how you and your daughter bark at each other. You ever give her a chance, a real chance, to get close to you?"

"Don't bring my daughter into this. She makes her own problems."

"Just like you," his younger self quipped and then popped like a soap bubble, leaving him staring at himself in the glass of the door.

Ironically, aside from that deep depression that had seized him in its unflinching, viselike grip, he didn't feel that sick. The doctor had explained to him that as long as he didn't exert himself strenuously, he wouldn't notice all that much difference, except for the occasional shortness of breath. Of course, his condition would worsen with time, and that was a good reason to go ahead with the pacemaker, but the thing of it was, he didn't look pale and infirm. He didn't limp or grow weak. On the surface he didn't appear even slightly changed. He had to believe the doctor's word and the analysis the doctor derived from his medical crystal balls: he was a sick dude.

"What about after the pacemaker?" he had asked the doctor when Jennie wasn't around. The doctor shook his head.

"We'll see, Mr. Samuels, but at your age, you should think in terms of retirement, especially in light of the physical stress your job demands."

There wasn't much room for hope. He couldn't turn back the years.

Rosina turned from the desk she was at and spotted him as soon as he entered. She handed her paperwork to Derek Simpson, a young detective who had recently joined the force, and hurried across the room to greet Frankie.

"Didn't know you were coming in today," she said, hugging him.

"Me neither. Nolan called to ask if I would stop by. I guess he figured I had had a chance to catch my breath. Now is as good a time as any to punch me in the stomach."

She nodded with a smirk.

"We busted that pump station," she said. "They were selling drugs out of it. I'm just finishing the paperwork now."

"You worked with Simpson?" he asked, nodding toward the tall, dark-haired twenty-six-year-old man who in many ways reminded Frankie of his younger self.

"My new partner. His youthful enthusiasm bowls me over," she added, and Frankie laughed. It was the way he had first characterized her when they began their partnership.

"Be careful, Flores. You're going to become one of the old-timers here faster than you think."

"You're right. Anyway," she said leaning closer to him, "I just wanted to tell you I did some follow-up of my own on that Murray suicide."

Frankie raised his eyebrows.

"My urban cynicism is catching?"

"Let's just say I don't like loose ends, either."

"And?"

"I called the coroner like you suggested. He said there was enough Dilantin to put him out, but he couldn't swear to when he injected himself with the insulin."

"If he did inject himself," Frankie corrected.

"He did. Prints were all over the insulin bottle and hypodermic." She paused, and he sensed her hesitation.

"What?" Frankie asked. "Come on, there's something bothering you, Flores."

"However," she said, closing and then opening her eyes, "I went back to the apartment and checked every cabinet in the kitchen. No Dilantin anywhere, and their doctor here never prescribed any for Sam Murray."

"Go on," Frankie said, knowing there was more.

"They were snowbirds, here for the season, so I even called their physician back East."

"And?"

"Sam Murray had been prescribed a sleeping pill at one time, but it wasn't Dilantin."

"I see. Very interesting. You didn't tell Nolan, did you?" Rosina just stared. "You did?"

"Yeah, I thought I should. He has a way of finding out everything everyone does around here anyway. Company spies or whatever."

"Ass-kissers. So? What did the general say?"

"First, he was pissed I spent any time on it, personal time or otherwise."

"But what did he say when you told him about the Dilantin and their doctors?"

"He wasn't impressed. He said old people are always lending each other medicine. The way he put it," she said lowering her voice to imitate Nolan, "was 'instead of knocking on the neighbor's door to borrow a cup a sugar, they knock to borrow blood pressure pills and sleeping pills.'"

"Possible, but not conclusive until you interview a neighbor who did," Frankie said.

"To him the Murrays were just another couple of retirees struggling to live on a fixed income. So he sees no motive, no reason to go any further."

"There are other reasons why people kill people," Frankie said, "besides attaining something of material value."

"Herr Nolan doesn't see it that way. He spoke with the coroner, who is convinced it was suicide."

"Where did they live?"

"That low-income apartment complex east of the Tram on Vista Chino, the Palm Court."

"So you didn't get to speak to any friends, neighbors?"

Rosina shook her head.

"Not really."

"Not really?"

"No, to be exact. I ran up there and ran back. Besides having me finish up the pump station investigation, Nolan's got me and Derek staking out a car wash off East Palm Canyon. There's a body shop attached, and people who have had their cars washed there lately have also been ripped off soon afterward. Latest is a guy on Laverne who had the two front seats of his late model Honda Accord swiped."

"The seats?"

"Cost about four thousand to replace. Hey, this is a busy place, Samuels," Flores said.

"I seem to remember," he said and looked toward Nolan's office. "All right, I'll go face our Führer."

"Don't forget to salute," Rosina quipped as Frankie started away. "How about lunch one day this week?"

"I don't know if I can fit it in, but I'll try," he said. She laughed, and he turned toward Bill Nolan's office.

Chief of Detectives William Nolan never tolerated being called Bill, and especially hated Billy. Even in grade school, when one of his teachers tried for some informality and referred to him as Bill or Billy, William Nolan would correct the teacher in no uncertain terms.

"My name isn't Billy. It's William," he would say firmly, with not the hint of compromise in his dark brown eyes. It was something his mother had ingrained in him from the first moment he could understand its significance. His father had deserted her shortly after he was born and she was sensitive about their family image afterward. Her stern attitudes and unbending standards molded him into a coldly impersonal young man, intelligent but arrogant, ambitious but selfish. He was unpopular with his fellow students in school and in college, but being liked by his peers was far lower on his totem pole of values than being respected by his superiors.

Consequently, he was better at individual sports such as wrestling, track and field, and tennis than he was at any team sport. But he excelled athletically as well as intellectually. Everything he did, he did with a fierce determination, no matter how insignificant the activity seemed at the time.

A military career came naturally to him. He felt far more comfortable in an organized setting with a definite code of behavior and a clear pecking order. He was an ideal candidate for officer's training and chose the military police as the logical next step. He was promoted rapidly and got into high-tech surveillance.

He didn't marry until shortly before he retired from the military. His wife came from an orthodox Catholic family that found a religious significance in the fact that they were related, however distantly, to Cardinal Spellman. Mary Spellman was a mousy little woman who was compliant and obedient, the perfect mate for William, who had simply decided that he had reached the point when he should be married and have children. It almost didn't matter what Mary looked like. He found her working as a receptionist on the military base, courted her formally and quickly, and proposed marriage by stating it was the most sensible step for them to take. She accepted, but all their attempts to have children failed.

After his military retirement, William made a quick reputation for himself in civilian police work and when the opening in the Palm Springs Police Department was advertised, he applied with an impressive, arm-long list of references and was hired, much to the chagrin of some of the old-timers like Frankie; but the city fathers wouldn't appoint anyone on the inside. They wanted an outsider because they thought an insider would play favorites. They were right about one thing: Nolan didn't play favorites, he treated everyone equally, in the same condescending manner.

Frankie knocked on Chief Nolan's office door, waited for the command to enter, and did so. His superior was seated behind his desk initialing some reports. As always, his pecan brown hair was clipped short. What few gray hairs he had were only at his temples, managing to give him a distinguished look. In his suit and tie, William Nolan appeared immaculate, but then he always did, no matter what the time of day. Somehow, the nitty-gritty part of police work left him unscathed. In a suit, Nolan could easily be mistaken for a businessman, not someone on the hunt—for drug dealers, prostitutes, burglars, and other street riffraff.

He gazed up. Seeing Frankie, he indicated the empty chair across from him with his pen. "Take a seat."

Frankie sat down. Nolan continued to initial the documents in front of him before looking up again. When he did, he pushed back on his chair and straightened his shoulders.

"So, how are you feeling?"

"Good," Frankie said quickly. And then added, "As good as I can under the circumstances."

Nolan nodded.

"I had a long talk with your doctor and he's making a strong recommendation that you retire. You've got the years in, so you can claim full benefits."

"Why don't we wait to see how I am after the implant?" Frankie suggested. "The doctor wasn't a hundred percent sure when I asked him."

"Why, what do you think you'll become when you get your pacemaker implanted, the Six Million Dollar Man, a cyborg cop?" Nolan quipped. His smile lifted only the right corner of his mouth and was really indistinguishable from a sneer.

"No, but with the pacemaker in, I might be able to resume normal activities."

"Normal layman activities. You're not going to be able to give me a hundred percent, not that you were doing so in all departments anyway. I've been warning you about your health, but I'm not here to say I told you so."

"Let's be grateful for little things," Frankie retorted. Nolan showed little emotion. There was just an icy twinkling in his cold eyes. Otherwise, his face remained its granite-solid self.

"You're the oldest detective in the department, for chrissakes," Nolan said. "It's time you hung it up anyway, but if you force me to, I'll have a second doctor confirm everything the first says and enforce your retirement. Your choice."

"Everything isn't always black and white, Nolan."

"Most is."

"Not even most."

"Some day after you've recuperated, we'll have lunch and philosophize, but right now . . ."

"I'm not having the procedure for a week, maybe eight, nine days," Frankie said quickly.

"So?"

"I'd like to wrap up some things, remain on full-time duty."

"You just came out of the hospital, for crissakes, and you fell on your face pursuing a suspect. You could have endangered the life of another police officer and you want me to let you hang around? You just use your sick leave and do what your doctor tells you to do.

"I had Maggie prepare all the papers for you to sign," Nolan added. "I only want to make things easier for everyone."

"I bet. Look. Let me take a few days to clean up my things, tie up some loose ends."

"What loose ends?"

"I don't know. Loose ends. What's the difference? You won't give me any assignments that will endanger another officer," Frankie snapped. His face felt hot, as if he had walked into a steam room. Nolan stared at him.

"You got to know when it's time to let go, Samuels."

"I'll know."

"I want your badge and gun on this desk by the end of the week," Nolan concluded and started to peruse the documents on his desk again. Frankie didn't move. Nolan looked up, surprised. "What?"

"This suicide Rosina investigated, Mr. Murray . . ."

"So?"

"Sounds screwy, Dilantin, insulin, but no trail on the Dilantin."

"This one of those loose ends you mentioned?" Nolan looked like he was ready to burst into laughter, but Frankie held his ground.

"Could be."

Nolan stared and then gave Frankie that corner-lip smile again.

"All right. Go visit with the senoir citizens. See how retired people live. Get some pointers." His smile faded. "But don't so much as tug too hard on a stuck door, you hear. I don't want you setting up this department for some kind of lawsuit."

"What?"

"Go on. Tie up your loose ends." Nolan waved at the door.

Frankie rose slowly, his heart pounding, his blood pressure surely sky high. That shortness of breath came over him, but he turned quickly so Nolan wouldn't see him gasp. He hurried out of the office and went directly to his desk, where he sat down, turned his back to Nolan's office, and counted to ten. Gradually, his heartbeat slowed.

When he felt relaxed enough so that his voice wouldn't reveal the knots tied inside him, he dialed his home.

"Just checking in, Mommy, like you told me," he said when Jennie answered.

"Very funny, Frankie. What happened?"

"You'll be happy to know Herr Nolan and I discussed my upcoming retirement," he said. It wasn't a lie.

"Upcoming?"

"Well, I can lollygag about and clean up my desk, gossip with the boys."

"You mean give some of the younger ones advice, ride along with them . . ."

"No, absolutely not."

"Frankie."

"I swear. I'm not going on any investigations with anyone. You've got my word on it, Jen. I can sit around here just as easily as sit around at home, right?"

"Why don't I believe you?"

"You just can't get used to the new me," he kidded.

"Will you be coming home for lunch?" she asked in a dry voice.

"Probably."

"But not absolutely. There's nothing new about you yet, Frankie Samuels."

"I'll be all right, Jen," he said firmly.

"Don't forget Stevie and Laurel are driving down for dinner. They'll be here early," she warned.

"Got the message," he said.

After he hung up, he took a deep breath. Then he got up quickly and left like a little boy who had been given too many lollipops and wanted to leave before the clerk discovered his mistake. When he got into his car, he drove off toward North Palm Springs and the Palm Court apartments.

He smiled to himself as he drove. Somehow, he had pulled it off. He could be a policeman awhile longer. Of course, he wasn't going to describe it exactly that way to Jennie. She'd be far worse on him than Nolan could ever be.

8

Corpsy Ratner drove up to the office of the pink stucco motel and parked his car. The property looked just run down enough to be one of the more inexpensive ones in Palm Springs, but not quite seedy enough to cause him to pass it by. There was no sense in investing a fortune in a place to stay. He didn't intend to be in the room for much more than sleep. He expected to spend most of his time hunting down the Sullivan twins and then courting Susie. Once he was properly introduced, he was positive they would hit it off. From then on, he would practically camp on her doorstep until she accepted his proposal of marriage and he carted her back to Phoenix, where they would live.

Corpsy began to consider how he would approach Susie when he did see her. He felt he should be serious, but not too serious.

He had to find a successful middle ground. Suddenly, now that he was actually here and contemplating their initial meeting, he became very nervous. What if he made a total fool of himself? Would she give him a second chance? She had to; he would plead, beg if necessary. She would see how sincere he was and she would accept him.

He wouldn't go too fast, but he wouldn't linger. He had to convince her that he wasn't interested in a quick affair. She had to see he wasn't that sort of fellow. He would sweep her off her feet quickly, completely, and then he would propose and take her home. How long should it take? he wondered: a week, two weeks? Two weeks seemed long, and besides, he didn't want to live in this motel for two weeks, even though he would only spend a small part of his day here. She would understand. They had a life to start together. Why delay it more than they had to?

But what about her sister? he wondered. Would Faye put obstacles in his way? Maybe she would be jealous that Susie had someone who loved her and she didn't. Sisters could be mean and jealous of each other. Well, he wasn't about to let that happen. If she got too nasty, he would simply whisper "Amyl nitrate." After all, that had frightened her enough to send her packing, hadn't it?

Confident, eager, and very buoyant, he stepped out of his vehicle and walked to the motel office. There was a short, plump woman behind the desk, who didn't look more than twenty-eight or -nine. Her dull brown hair hung down listlessly along her ears. She was chewing something and reading the *National Enquirer,* so fascinated with whatever story she was on that she didn't hear or see him enter. He stood at the desk a moment, and then she felt his presence and looked up with surprise.

"Oh! I'm sorry," she said, rising. Her one-piece faded blue dress hung over her chunky body like a sheet of drapery, but he could see the movement of her heavy, braless bosom against the cloth. To Corpsy, she had a face without much light. He liked to think of living people as bodies with a glow. It was almost measurable in watts. The dead on whom he worked had literally had their lights put out. Their eyes resembled blown bulbs.

This woman's eyes were dim. She didn't know, but he did: she wasn't long for this world. Only someone who dipped his hands into the bodies of the dead would be able to see and predict as well as he could. It made him feel . . . godlike.

"I need a room, nothing special," he said quickly.

"Uh huh. You want a double bed or queen size or king size?"

"I just need a single," he said, annoyed with the implication.

"A single? Well, do you like sleeping in queen size or king size? King size is ten dollars more a day."

"I'll take queen."

"Uh huh. How long are you going to stay?"

"I don't know. Maybe . . . two weeks."

"Really? Okay. Please fill this out," she said handing him a card. He read it first and then began to fill in the information. She stood watching him and chewing like a cow. It annoyed him, made his insides tumble and turn, but he swallowed and continued scribbling.

"Credit card," she said when he handed her the form. He dug into his wallet and produced it. She made the imprint and handed it back. "I've got a queen on the far end or one right near the office."

"Far end," he said quickly. She handed him the key. "Unit 31. You just drive down to the end and park in front. If you need anything, just call."

"Where's the hospital here?" he demanded.

"Hospital? Oh. It's not far. It's . . . um . . . three streets over and then one, two, four streets up. You can't miss it. Is there something wrong?"

"What? Oh, no. I work in a hospital and I'm here to see some friends who work in this hospital," he told her. "Thanks," he said and left quickly before she asked any more of the questions he saw lingering in her dull eyes.

His room looked worn, tired, but clean. The rug was faded and even torn in spots. The bathroom fixtures were a bit rusted, but it was tolerable. He didn't envision bringing Susie here anyway. They weren't going to have sex until after they had exchanged their vows. He was determined about that and he was sure that once she saw how he felt and what he believed, she would be even more impressed with him. Respect, he would tell her, must come first. Love follows on its heels.

He liked that; it was almost poetic: love follows on its

heels. It reconfirmed his faith in himself, his belief that he could be romantic enough to win the heart of the woman he loved. Full of renewed confidence, he brought all of his things into the motel room, then left to find the hospital.

The fat girl's directions weren't right. Instead of going north, he had to go south a few streets. At the hospital, the parking lots confused him. There was one near the emergency room and one near radiology and one on the other side. He cruised through each, searching for signs of Faye Sullivan's black BMW convertible, but he didn't see it. He pulled over across the street from the parking lot near the radiology building and waited.

But it was hot in his car, hotter than he had anticipated. Beads of sweat broke out on his forehead and behind his head, trickling down his neck and under his shirt, making him feel very uncomfortable. His stomach churned, too, and he realized he hadn't had any breakfast. He had been too excited about his arrival in Palm Springs and his proximity to Susie. He started his engine with the intention of driving toward the center of town to find a restaurant, when he realized he could eat in the hospital cafeteria. In fact, he could meld in real well, he thought, and maybe even learn about Faye and Susie quickly.

He returned to the motel and dug out his hospital blues. After he dressed in them, he returned to the hospital and found the cafeteria. He smiled when the cashier charged him staff rates, and then he sat himself down near three nurses. For a few minutes, he ate and pretended little or no interest. When one looked his way, he smiled and she smiled back, encouraging him.

"Excuse me," he said, and they all stopped talking and looked. "I met a nurse here the other day. She was having a problem with her car radio and I told her I'd look at it for her, but she left before I could help. Electronics is kind of a hobby of mine," he added.

"What's her name?"

"Faye Sullivan. I just met her and . . ."

"I don't know her," the first nurse said.

"Faye Sullivan? Didn't she do private duty for Dr. Stanley's patients?" the nurse in the middle asked. They all thought a moment.

"Now that you mention it, I think so. She doesn't do a regular shift," the first nurse explained. "She specials for the Palm Springs Nurses' Registry."

"Oh. Well, she probably had the radio fixed by now anyway," he added and shrugged. They went back to their own conversation.

After he had his lunch, he found the nearest pay phone and called the Palm Springs Nurses' Registry.

"I'm trying to locate a Faye Sullivan," he said. "She works through your agency, I understand."

"Yes?"

"Well, I'd like to find out where she lives."

"We don't give out that sort of information. Do you need some private-duty nursing care?"

"No, it's not that. I'm . . . her cousin and I've just arrived in Palm Springs, but I don't know her address."

"Why don't you call her?"

"I don't have her phone number and she's not in the book. She's just recently come to Palm Springs."

"Well, why don't you call information," the receptionist suggested with a tone of annoyance.

"I don't think they give out addresses, do they?"

"Well, we don't for sure, but they might."

"Oh. I'm sorry to bother you. I just wanted to surprise her. We haven't seen each other since we were both about five," he said, and he laughed. The receptionist softened.

"I'm really not supposed to give out our nurses phone numbers and addresses."

"I understand. I'm sorry."

"Wait a minute. You'll find it out anyway if you call information, I'm sure." A few moments later, she gave him the phone number and address. "But remember, you didn't get it from me."

"I will. Thank you. Boy, is she going to be surprised."

He cradled the receiver quickly and clenched the slip of paper tightly in his hand. It was as if he were clutching a thousand-dollar bill. To him the paper was far more valuable anyway. He hurried out to his car and started away. When he came to the first corner, he pulled over to ask a pedestrian for directions. The man was a tourist and knew even less than he did. Annoyed, he shot off and headed down Palm Canyon Boulevard into the heart of Palm Springs. As soon as he saw an open parking space, he pulled in and went into a photo shop to ask directions. These people were far more helpful. Minutes later, he was pulling into Faye and Susie Sullivan's apartment complex. He found an empty space in guest parking and turned off his engine.

Faye's car was nowhere in sight. He folded his arms and sat back. She had to drive in the same way he'd entered, he thought. It wouldn't be too much longer. Anticipating her arrival, he started to plan. Should he get right out and greet her? What if Susie was with her and Faye had a bad reaction to his sudden and unexpected appearance? That could get things off to a bad start. Even if Susie was alone, she wouldn't appreciate being surprised like this.

No, for now, he just wanted to know exactly where they lived. Later, he would let her set eyes on him in a casual manner. Then he would approach her politely and then . . . then she would be impressed with his determination and let him see Susie. That was how it all played out in his imagination. He nearly fell asleep dreaming about it, but he opened his eyes abruptly to the sound of a car passing and saw Faye drive in. She was alone. She parked in under the carport across the way and got out of her vehicle quickly. She was dressed in her nurse's uniform and looked like she was returning from work.

Must have done some private duty at someone's home, he thought. He watched her go down a walkway and up a set of steps. Just as she reached the patio, the door of another apartment opened and an elderly woman stuck her head out.

He watched Faye and the woman have a conversation and leaned forward when Faye opened her own apartment door, hoping he would catch sight of Susie.

But he didn't. He waited in his car for at least another hour or so before giving up because the elderly woman to whom Faye had spoken emerged from her apartment and gazed his way suspiciously. He had the impression she had been watching him from her front window.

Spooked, he started his engine and backed out of the spot. He drove off without looking back and returned to his motel. He was disappointed he had not seen his beloved, but he was happy he had found where she and her sister lived so quickly. That had to be a good omen. It was all going to go well; it was promising.

The fat receptionist was standing outside the door of her office when he pulled into the motel lot. She smiled at him and he smiled back. He had forgotten for the moment that he was dressed in hospital blues. The moment he stepped out of his car, however, she started toward him.

"You working in the hospital?" she asked.

"No, I'm . . . well, I did help a friend who works there," he said quickly.

"Oh. I got a friend working there, too. Her name's Samantha Logan. We all call her Sam for short. She's a black girl, about twenty-four."

"I didn't meet anyone like that," he said edging toward his room.

"What's your friend's name? Maybe Sam knows him."

"Charlie Goodwin," he said, holding in his smile. Dr. Charles Goodwin was the head of pathology back at his hospital in Phoenix.

"Goodwin. I'll ask her if she knows him."

"Fine. Oh, where's an inexpensive but good place to eat dinner?"

"What kind of food?"

"Just a hot turkey sandwich or something."

She thought a moment.

"Try the Village Deli of New York in the Sun Center, cor-

ner of Palm Canyon and Indian. Ain't you eating with your
friend Charlie?"

"No. He's got to work. Thanks," he said quickly, afraid she
might suggest he eat with her.

He stepped into his room before she could reply and
waited by the door to be sure she returned to her office. He
heard her footsteps over the gravel drive and then he turned
away and began to undress.

Faye looked tired, he thought. She must have had a difficult patient and a hard night. When he was naked, he sat by
the telephone and played with the numbers, punching out
the Sullivans' number without lifting the receiver. Then he
lifted it and pretended Susie had answered.

"Hi. Susie?" he said. He imagined her saying yes. "I'm Arnold Ratner. I work in the hospital in Phoenix in which your
sister used to special for patients. Maybe she mentioned me
to you. She did? What did she say about me? Well, that's
true. I was very interested in meeting you. I still am. Very interested and I happen to be in Palm Springs right now. Do
you think I can come by and see you, say tomorrow some-
time? Anytime. Two o'clock in the afternoon? Fine. I tell you
what, though. I would rather take you to lunch. Why don't I
come by at twelve? Is that all right? It is? Great. See you
then. Bye, Susie."

He cradled the receiver and sat back with a smile on his
face as if he had actually made the call. When he gazed down
at himself, he was surprised to see he had a thick erection.
His penis reminded him of a small rodent sniffing the air. He
gazed around helplessly for a moment. Then he got up
quickly and went to his bag of toiletries and took out his electric razor. He plugged it in beside the sofa and sat down. He
kept his eyes closed until he turned on the razor, placing the
rear side of it against his throbbing penis. The vibrations re-
verberated up and down the stem, making him quiver until
he had an orgasm that he thought would never end. His
hands and his wrist were soaked, as was the electric razor.

He quickly wiped it dry and put it away and then he took
a hot shower and lay down.

When Susie and he were married, this sort of thing would stop, he thought. He would have sex just the way he was supposed to and he would make babies in Susie's body just the way he was supposed to.

He fell asleep dreaming of her beside him, her bad leg draped over his hip.

9

Faye had parked her car in her designated space under the carport and had hurriedly stepped out and up the blue-and-white tile steps bordered in bright red bougainvillea to the front door of their two-bedroom apartment without spotting Corpsy Ratner. Her attention was on their daily newspaper, stuffed awkwardly in the newspaper pouch on the side of her door. The lid to her mailbox was up because there was so much mail shoved into it, mostly junk mail. Just as she paused to gather everything, the front door of the neighboring apartment opened and Tillie Kaufman peered out. The seventy-one-year-old woman with short blue-gray hair clicked her tongue and shook her head. She was tall and plump, with a remarkably cherry-white complexion for a woman of her age. Faye paused, anticipating.

"Your newspaper was lying on the sidewalk again. I knocked on the door to tell your sister, but she didn't answer. She's home?"

"No, she's on a job," Faye snapped.

"Well, I put the paper in the box before one of those young hooligans could come along to steal it. They usually do if they find one still lying here in the afternoon."

"Thank you, Mrs. Kaufman."

"I heard you go out during the night. An emergency?" her nosy neighbor inquired. Unless elderly people were sick or in mourning, Faye found them distasteful and annoying. She hoisted her small shoulders and pulled herself into a stiff posture.

"Why else do you think I'd go out that time of the night, Mrs. Kaufman?"

The old lady nodded and then shook her head.

"Somebody's always very sick."

"Of course somebody's always very sick. Especially in a community that has so many elderly inhabitants," she added. Mrs. Kaufman continued to nod as if her round head with its clipped hair were sitting on a small spring.

"Morris has the gout again. This on top of his high blood pressure."

"It doesn't surprise me, not with the food you feed him. You don't listen."

"I try, but he gets so angry. He says food's food. He's eating the same things he ate all his life."

"He's not supposed to eat the same things. He's older."

Mrs. Kaufman shrugged.

"He doesn't think so. I tell him to come out of the sun, but he doesn't listen. I tell him to stop smoking those smelly cigars, but he doesn't stop."

"He will," Faye said.

"When?"

"When he's dead," she replied, and jabbed the key into the door lock.

Tillie wasn't shocked. She continued to nod.

"I told him that, too, but he doesn't listen. So who was so sick?" she asked as Faye pulled the mail out of the box.

"You don't know her," she replied.

"It's very nice: you being a nurse. I wish I had become a nurse instead of a paralegal. What kind of a thing is a paralegal?" she asked in a self-deprecating manner. "You're not a lawyer, but you do a lawyer's work and get less money? At least, a nurse helps people and has self-satisfaction. A nurse is a dedicated person."

Faye paused just before entering her apartment.

"Not all nurses, Mrs. Kaufman. Some are no better than

anyone else who works only for the money. I'll stop by later and check Mr. Kaufman's blood pressure." She shut the door before her neighbor could ask another question or make another comment.

In the sanctity of their small, dark apartment, Faye Sullivan felt herself relax. The weight of responsibility lifted from her shoulders. With the window blinds drawn, the door shut tight, the lights still off, she felt a cool rush, an emotional cleansing. Here, she didn't have to be a nurse; she didn't have to worry about other people. She didn't have to be respectable, efficient, professional. She could succumb to any and all inclinations, desires, fantasies.

She dropped the newspaper and mail on the small table in the entryway and gazed around the living room. In the dim illumination from the sunlight that leaked around the blinds, the room was ethereal. In fact, the entire apartment had a hazy atmosphere. It was as if she had entered a dream. It made it all so much more beautiful. She closed her eyes and wished and wished . . .

"I'm home," she suddenly cried. A moment later, she heard his reply.

"It's about time. You're late for your appointment," he added. She smiled. Then, without taking another step forward, she began to disrobe. When she was naked, she moved forward slowly, her heart pounding. The gray shag carpet tickled the soles of her feet. She nearly giggled. At the doorway of her bedroom she paused and then slowly, ever so slowly, she peered into the room.

That young intern, the one who was so terrified when he was called to the emergency in Sylvia Livingston's room, Dr. Hoffman, was sitting up in the bed nude, wearing only a stethoscope around his neck.

"Doctor time!" he declared, and she laughed.

She ran to the bed and dove into the quilt, pulling it around her quickly.

"Come on, now," he coaxed. "Let's not be a shy little girl."

She peeked out of an opening.

"But I'm afraid, Doctor."

"There's nothing to be afraid of, young lady. I've done this hundreds of times before."

"You have?"

"But never to one as pretty as you," he added. Then he reached out and slowly lowered the quilt, exposing more and more of her naked body. "Just relax," he said. "Close your eyes and think of something nice. Think of ice cream."

"That makes me cold," she said, and she shivered.

"Then think of . . ."

"I'll think of a warm, bubbly bath."

"Good."

She felt the stethoscope on her breast. He slid it down gently over her nipple and then lifted her breast to get to her heartbeat.

"My, my," he said. "What a happy little heart." He moved the stethoscope down her chest, over her stomach to her belly button, and paused. "Gurgle, gurgle," he said. She smiled. "And now let's see if anyone's home."

He placed the stethoscope over her pubic hair and tickled the entrance to her vagina. She moaned and opened her legs a little more.

"Do you mind visitors?" he asked. She shook her head.

"Knock, knock, then," he said.

"Come in," she replied quickly. A moment later she felt him enter. At first it was like a gynecologist prodding, exploring, examining. Then it thickened and began to pulsate and soon her dream lover was driving her toward an ecstatic frenzy. Her body lifted and fell, lifted and fell. She moaned and began to claw the air, hoping to take hold of him and draw him down over her, but, as always, there was nothing to grasp. He had put all of himself into her. Suddenly he became a hot rush and with a thrust lifted her buttocks off the bed and drove her back until her head reached the head board. She screamed and dropped her eggs into his hot, white pool swirling within her. Then she began to calm down, withdrawing her passion with little cries and gasps until she was finally quiet, finally still.

She lay like that for nearly an hour. When she opened her

eyes, he was gone, of course. All that remained was the stethoscope. She sat up slowly and gazed around her bedroom. Loneliness, like the rancid odor of mildewed wood after a flood, settled in around her. Sitting naked like this brought back the memory of her father coming into her bedroom. He had been sleeping on the sofa in the den and he looked like he had been tossing and turning all night.

"It's cold," he said, embracing himself. "I've got to crawl into your warm bed before I get up and get dressed."

Before she could reply, he was crawling in beside her, his cotton pajama bottom sliding down over his love handles as he slipped under the blanket.

"I'll get up and make coffee," she said, but he had his hand on her thigh.

"No, not yet, sweetheart. Just stay here for a while and help Daddy get warm. That's it."

She had her head turned away so he didn't see the tears streaming down her face, nor did he hear her sobs. He was moaning too loudly.

Remembering made her grow nauseous and dizzy. The vertigo was coming, so she quickly closed her eyes and took deep breaths until it subsided.

Then she thought she heard the front door open and close.

"I'm home," Susie called.

"In here."

Susie came to the doorway and peered in. Her face looked radiant, as radiant as it always did when she was involved with a new widow or widower.

"Are you all right?" Susie asked quickly.

"I'm fine. How's he doing?"

"He slept well."

"Was he surprised to see you there?"

"And how! But he was very nice and so . . ."

"Vulnerable?"

"Yeah, I think so." She paused. "What does that mean again?"

"Easy to hurt."

"Yes, that's it. He's like a little boy, just like Daddy."

"Daddy was never a little boy, not the way you mean."

"Of course he was. He was always forgetting to put the toilet seat down. And remember when he left the house wearing two different shoes and you had to run out and bring him back?"

"That was different. I don't want to talk about it anyway," Faye said quickly. "Did you get him to eat?"

"Uh huh. And I tidied up."

"Good. Aren't you tired?"

"Yes."

"Me too."

"So we'll both sleep."

"Are you going back?" Faye asked cautiously.

"Of course. We just left it kind of vague for now, but he knows I'll be back. He's going to his son's for dinner tonight. I tried to talk him out of it. I offered to make him dinner. He belongs at home, resting," she added with a smile.

"Don't push. If he wants his family and they want him, he'll be all right."

"He doesn't want his family; he wants his wife and she wants him. They were in love," Susie insisted.

Faye sighed.

"I'm tired," she said. She lowered her head to the pillow and closed her eyes. She felt Susie standing there watching her for a few moments, and then she heard her go into her own bedroom.

Faye didn't wake up until midafternoon. When she did, she went to Susie's room and peeked in and saw she was still fast asleep. Poor thing, Faye thought, exhausted emotionally. She always gets that way. Faye closed Susie's door softly and then went to take a shower. She put on a pair of jeans and a short-sleeve cotton blouse and went into the kitchen to warm up some of the pasta Susie had made earlier. While she ate, she read her mail and perused the papers. She turned to the obituary page in the most recent edition and shook her head when she saw that Susie had cut out the article about Sylvia Livingston. Sure enough, when Faye looked in the living room, she found the article already pasted neatly in Susie's album beside the obituary for Dorothy Murray.

She thumbed back a few pages, gazing at the obituaries from the newspapers in Palm Beach, Florida, and Phoenix, Arizona. Then she closed the album and ran her palm over the soft velvet cover. The album was getting very thick. Susie was very proud of it, very proud of the contents. Faye placed it back on the coffee table and returned to the kitchen to make herself some coffee just as Mrs. Cohen from the service called.

"Motorcycle accident victim," she began. "Twenty-year-old. Dr. Enker operated on him this morning. Parents want private nursing around the clock. He's still in a coma, bad head injuries. How about the night shift? It's a milk run."

Faye shook her head without answering.

"Hello? Faye?"

"No, I . . . I'm exhausted from my last two cases, one after the other."

"So?"

"I'd like a couple of days off first," she said firmly. Mrs. Cohen grunted.

"Suit yourself, but you're passing up easy money."

"I'm not in it for the money," Faye snapped.

"What are you in it for, the boxes of candy? Jesus. All right. Take a few days off. I just love you independently wealthy single women," Mrs. Cohen said and then hung up.

"Who was that?" Susie asked from her bedroom doorway. Her eyes looked sleepy.

"The service."

"Oh."

"I ate your pasta. It was still great."

"Thanks. Where are you going?" she asked when Faye started away.

"To take Mr. Kaufman's blood pressure. I promised Tillie."

"She's such a damn busybody."

"I know, but I treat the patient, not his wife."

She fetched her bag and went next door. As she expected, Morris Kaufman's pressure was high.

"You must stay away from those salty foods," she told him.

"I told him that," Tillie Kaufman said. "But he won't listen."

"What are you trying to do to yourself?" Faye demanded. "Don't you know how terrible it is to die and leave your wife alone?"

Morris Kaufman was an inch or so shorter than his wife and much thinner, but his face was sallow and his eyes a tired, dull brown.

"With her friends, she'll never be alone. You see how those busybodies are here night and day, mooching," he kidded. Faye didn't laugh.

"Friends," Tillie said. "All they do is make a mess. My apartment doesn't always look this bad, Faye. But with Morris so sick . . ."

Faye understood.

"I'll ask Susie to stop by and clean up a bit for you."

"Will you? Thank you. She's such a delight whenever she comes to see us. Isn't she, Morris?"

"Yes, she is."

"Never mind all that. You better start following your dietary restrictions, Mr. Kaufman."

"You should listen to her, Morris. She knows what she's talking about."

"I'm listening. So tell me," he said, leaning toward her, his breath stale from his last cigar, "you had a visitor today?"

"What?"

"I'll tell you what he listens to—he listens to the walls," Tillie Kaufman said.

Faye reddened.

"I had no visitors, Mr. Kaufman, and I don't like being spied on. Don't do it again," she warned.

"See," Tillie said. "I told you you just heard her television set."

Morris Kaufman shrugged and smiled conspiratorially. Faye glared at him. Then she wrapped up her blood pressure cuff and stethoscope and marched quickly to the door of the Kaufman apartment. Tillie followed.

Still fuming, Faye looked back in Morris Kaufman's direction. "Take him to the doctor and have him prescribe some stronger medication for the high blood pressure. He could have a stroke any moment."

"You mean it?" Tillie said, alarmed. Faye paused, deciding whether or not to continue and punish her old neighbors. The fury inside her was like a fist closed so tightly it would never open. It made her stomach ache and sent a ring of fire around her heart.

"Yes," she said firmly.

"Oh God. Morris," Tillie Kaufman muttered. She turned to go back to her husband.

"What's the matter?" Susie asked as soon as Faye closed the door behind her in their apartment.

Without answering, she went into the bedroom. She looked at her bed and the stethoscope and then stared at the wall between her apartment and the Kaufmans'. She hated those thin walls, but he had no right to put his ear against them and listen to her while she . . .

She brought her hands to her face. Sick as she was, Mommy had heard her moans through the walls, too. Mommy had gotten out of bed and come to the door, and when she looked in and saw Daddy . . .

Would she ever forget that ear-shattering scream, the way her body folded to the floor while she clutched at her broken heart?

"What's wrong?" Susie asked, coming up behind her.

Faye lowered her hands and took a deep breath. Susie didn't know; Susie never knew.

"That Morris Kaufman," Faye replied and nodded toward the wall. Susie understood.

"You had someone here?"

"Yes."

"And he listened in?"

"Yes. Elderly people can be so insensitive," Faye said. "Unless they're dying or suffering."

Susie nodded, her eyes suddenly growing smaller. "Maybe," she said slowly, "maybe he's taking the wrong pills."

Faye stared back at her. She understood what Susie was saying.

"Tillie would like you to stop by when you get a chance and tidy up their place."

"Okay."

Faye looked at herself in the mirror and then Susie stepped up beside her and smiled. Their smiles were so much alike, they seemed to have the same face.

She could hear her sister's thoughts. It wouldn't be too difficult for her to substitute a decongestant for his blood pressure pills, an antihistamine that when taken liberally would raise his blood pressure.

Then he wouldn't be listening to things that weren't any of his business.

10

The Palm Court apartment complex was a property on the north end of town, where it could be very windy at times. Consequently, the rents were cheaper and the tenants were lower-income people and retirees who could economize and afford to spend a season in Palm Springs. From the superintendent, a short, stubby bald man with small gray eyes, Frankie learned that the Murrays had been coming to the Palm Court apartments for the last five years. He called them two of his regulars. While he spoke, he worked an unlit cigar in his mouth, savoring the tobacco juice.

"Nice couple, got along with everyone, hated to call me to fix something. Whenever they did, Mrs. Murray would apologize like crazy. I told them, it's my job. Don't hesitate to call, but they were the sort who never wanted to impose. A lot different from most of my tenants. Some will call in the middle of the night if a door squeaks, know what I mean?"

Frankie nodded.

"They make a lot of friends here?"

"Not really. Most of their friends live in other areas in the desert. I do have another elderly couple in 14C who were their closest friends in the complex, the Stuarts."

"Did you notice anyone visiting him the day or night before he was found?"

"I wasn't here that day. Went up to Hot Springs to visit

with my cousin and didn't learn about Sam Murray's death until I returned in the afternoon. I didn't even know the old lady died."

"Point me toward 14C," Frankie asked. He followed the walkway around the building and knocked on the door. The desert winds had started up, kicking sand and dust around. The sky had thin, wispy clouds brushed across the sea of light blue, but the roar of the wind made it seem as though he were about to encounter a hurricane.

Mrs. Stuart, a small blue-haired lady in her early seventies, opened the door cautiously and peered through the opening, the chain lock still in place.

"Yes?"

Frankie showed her his identification.

"I'd like to ask you and your husband about the Murrays," he said. "I understand you were friendly."

"Just a minute." She closed and opened the door to let him in, stepping back just enough to permit his entry, her eyes still full of suspicion. "My husband went to the supermarket," she explained.

Frankie thought she had the sort of aged face to which still clung what had once been youthful beauty. Her eyes, although revealing the sort of paranoia he frequently saw in older people, were still quite blue. She was an elegant woman, concerned about her appearance, dressing herself in her jewelry and hair combs even though she would only spend the day in her apartment watching television.

He looked around the simple apartment with its thrift-shop furnishings and simple decor. The windows had slim wooden blinds and flower-print curtains, but the ceiling showed evidence of an occasional leak. He took out his notepad and smiled at Mrs. Stuart.

"That's all right. Maybe you can help. Were you surprised to learn Mr. Murray had committed suicide?" he asked.

"Me, not so much, but my husband still can't get over it. It's made him sick."

"You knew Mrs. Murray was sick?"

"Sick," she said disdainfully. "Everyone we know these

days is sick. She was a diabetic, but she didn't watch her diet. Every year they returned, she looked worse and worse to me. I gave her many a lecture, but older people can't shake their old habits as quickly as younger people."

Frankie smiled at her reference to the Murrays as old. What was she, a spring chicken?

"Did you or your husband see Mr. Murray after his wife passed away?"

"Of course. We went right over."

"How was he taking it?"

"He was very upset. He was concerned that she had died here and he would have to ship her body back East."

"So he was planning on doing that?" Frankie asked quickly.

"Why shouldn't he plan it? That's where they had their plot."

Frankie nodded.

"And he didn't say anything to you or your husband about killing himself?"

She sat down on the sofa.

"He said he wished he was dead, too. My husband was worried, so he went back to stay with him, but he didn't stay long."

"Why not?"

"He was asleep and the maid said she would stay there, maybe even spend the night."

"The maid? What maid?"

"He had a maid come . . . to help with things right afterward. Dorothy was a stickler when it came to keeping her place clean, so Sam got it in his head that he better get a maid. People do funny things when they suffer deep grief," she said, reaching back into her pool of wisdom.

"Did you or your husband know this maid?"

"No. I think he got her from some agency. Most people here don't have maids. These aren't big apartments and it's an expense they can't afford. When I can't clean for myself, we'll check into a home," she added dryly.

"Do you remember this maid's name?"

She thought a moment and then shook her head.

"You think your husband might remember?"

"Maybe."

Frankie thought a moment.

"Do you know how Mr. Murray killed himself?" he asked. She grimaced.

"I heard he used her insulin."

"That's true. He also took some sleeping pills. Dilantin. Could you have given him some sleeping pills?"

"What?"

"I mean, only to help him sleep."

"No, I didn't give him any pills. My pills are all prescription pills. You don't give someone else your prescription pills. They have to get a prescription from their own doctor. We're old, but we're not stupid," she added bitterly.

"I'm sorry. I had to ask."

"I'm sorry, too," she said and stared wistfully at her hands. "This will be our last season here. We got to find someplace else. It's too depressing now."

"Can I have your phone number? I'd like to call your husband later and see if he remembers the maid's name."

She gave it to him and then got up to show him out. After she opened the door, her eyes brightened as if she just had realized the possibilities.

"The police don't think Sam killed himself?"

"What do you think, Mrs. Stuart? Why did you say you weren't as surprised as your husband?"

She shrugged.

"You can't help thinking about yourself and what you would do. Poor Sam. He woke up, looked at his four walls and decided he was too tired to go on. You're still a young man," she said, "but when you're older and retired and you're doing the same things day in and day out with the same person and you have only yourselves . . . you get tired, especially when you find you're alone."

Her words drilled deeply into his own self-awareness as her eyes filled with tears. How true was the prediction? What was he more afraid of . . . living with a time bomb in his chest or retirement?

"Thank you. You've been very helpful. I hope you find a brighter, more cheerful place to stay next year."

"If it's near the Fountain of Youth, I'll let you know," she replied. He laughed.

"Please do."

He left and considered going home for lunch just to reassure Jennie, but he wanted to spend more time on this. He decided to call her and tell her he was having lunch with Charlie Porter, the only other member of the Palm Springs Police Department who came close to him in age. Charlie was a patrolman who had never developed interest in plainclothes. He did find him at the station and they went to their favorite Mexican spot, a small hole-in-the-wall on South Palm Canyon.

After lunch he called the Stuarts and spoke to Mr. Stuart, who remembered the maid's name was Susie.

"I don't remember her telling me her last name."

"What did she look like?"

"Pretty girl. Not too tall, not fat."

Frankie smiled. With that description, he would go far.

"Do you remember the color of her hair?"

"I think it was brown, maybe light brown. I don't think it was black. Hey, when you get to be my age, you don't look at girls the same way."

Frankie laughed.

"Anything else you can remember about her?"

"No, I don't . . . oh, wait. Yes, she limped when she walked."

"Limped?"

"She wore something on her leg . . . not a bandage . . . a metal contraption."

"A brace?"

"Yeah, a brace."

"Okay, that's very helpful, Mr. Stuart. Your wife told me when you went back to see Mr. Murray, he was asleep."

"Yes, and the maid was straightening up in the kitchen. She said she would be there awhile longer and if there were any problems, she would call me. But she never called and . . . well, you know the rest, I guess."

"I do. I might come by to see you, Mr. Stuart."

"I'll be here most of the time," he said sadly.

"Thanks."

Frankie began by looking up every cleaning agency listed, but none of the agencies had any Susie working for them and certainly not a young woman wearing a leg brace. Perplexed, he sat back and wondered how to follow up this lead. A short while later, Rosina returned from her stakeout at the car wash with Derek.

"You're still here?" she asked with surprise.

"Nolan and I have come to a sort of truce for the moment," he said. Then he grew serious.

"Did you know the Murrays had a maid at the apartment the day before Mr. Murray was found?"

"A maid? No."

"I've been trying to track her down. All I have is a first name, a skeleton description with one big identifying characteristic."

"Which is?"

"She wore a brace on one leg and limped."

Rosina smirked.

"A handicapped maid. Interesting."

"Isn't it?"

"And you found all this out by . . ."

"Questioning a neighbor. It's called follow-up," he kidded. "Anyway, I've called every agency listed and no one of that description is employed by any of them."

"Sounds like a lot more follow-up is required."

"Yeah, well . . . it will keep me from thinking about my immediate future, I suppose."

"What does Jennie say about all this?"

"I haven't exactly . . ."

"Told her everything. She better not ask me. I tell the

whole truth and nothing but the truth," Rosina warned.
Frankie rolled his eyes. He gazed at the clock.

"I'd better get home. My son and his wife are driving in
from L.A. for dinner. If you come up with any ideas as to
how I can locate this limping maid . . ."

"Call you at home?"

"Disguise your voice if Jennie answers," he half kidded.

"Frankie, just go home, will you."

"Why is it everyone says the same thing? Even Charlie
Porter thinks I'm nuts hanging around here."

"Think about it," Rosina said. "Maybe you are nuts. I gotta
go report to Nolan. Have a nice dinner."

"Flores," he called after her. She turned. "Your biological
clock is ticking."

"*Vamos,* git," she said, waving toward the door. He laughed
and left.

He was surprised when he turned into his street and saw
Beth's car parked in their driveway. The white LeBaron convertible was caked with mud and grime. She had obviously
driven through some storms. The backseat was covered with
signs and posters denouncing antiabortionists and pro-
claiming the basic right of a woman to choose.

Beth and Jennie were sitting in the living room talking
when he entered. Beth took after Jennie when it came to her
looks. She had Jennie's beguiling green eyes, eyes that could
take a strong grown man prisoner in a twinkle and get him to
relent or promise and obey. She had Jennie's soft, sensuous
lips that turned up just a smidgen at the center when she became thoughtful, curious, or skeptical and pressed them together; and she had the same cute small nose, the kind that
would give a plastic surgeon a wet dream.

But her thoughts and her attitudes and her steel-vise determination made her assume Frankie's authoritative demeanor, especially these days when she was being driven by
her feminist causes. She was about two inches shorter than
he was, but somehow she always seemed taller to him whenever they got into one of their frequent political arguments.

The old adage about like poles repelling never seemed as true as it was in their case. How he wished she didn't have his stubbornness and his grit sometimes. And then there were times, times he never openly acknowledged, when he stood off to the side and proudly watched her in action with others, plowing over their prejudices and narrow vision and trampling them into the ground with her bulldozer of facts.

"Hi, Dad," she said. Since he had last seen her at the hospital, three days earlier, she had gotten her hair cut severely just below her ears, the bangs clipped back to reveal almost all of her forehead with its sprinkle of rust-colored freckles.

Her well-proportioned figure, shaped by an almost religious devotion to exercise videos and sensible eating, was buried under a NOW sweatshirt and a pair of those loose-fitting jeans he hated so much because they made her waist and rump look wider. He once had had the audacity to say they weren't feminine, a remark that led to half an hour of accusations in which she compared him to a Neanderthal and finally to Dan Quayle, whom she considered the twentieth-century version of a caveman.

"Car looks like you went through hell," he said.

"There was a terrible rainstorm in Arizona and so much road construction all along the way. If you want to get an idea how bad the infrastructure in this country is, just take a ride across it."

"Oh, honey. Why did you drive all night?" Jennie moaned.

"I was juiced up, Mom. We had a great protest. They thought they'd close down the clinic, but we were right there to stop them and protect any woman who needed it. Not one woman scheduled for an abortion had to cancel," she said proudly.

"It's a waste of time," Frankie said. "The Supreme Court's probably going to make it illegal someday."

"Only for the poor," Beth retorted.

Frankie shrugged.

"Nothing new about that."

"And that makes you happy? You can live with that?" She looked poised, ready to pounce like a cat.

"Please," Jennie pleaded. "No discussions. Let's have a truce. No politics in the house tonight, okay?"

"You can't cut it out of your life, Mom. You can't ignore what's happening out there by turning on a soap opera."

"How about what's happening in here?" Frankie snapped.

Jennie bit down on her lower lip and her eyes started to moisten.

"All right, all right," Beth said quickly. "I'll keep my mouth shut."

"That will be a first," Frankie muttered. She reddened, but stifled any retort.

"I was going to ask how you were feeling, Dad, but I see you're the same old Dirty Harry."

"Frankie," Jennie warned him before he could respond. He nodded.

"All right," he said, plopping into his easy chair. "I'll be good. I'll sit here and read my paper and drink my Geritol cocktails and reminisce about the good old days."

"As you see, your father is not taking his situation well. He's not," Jennie said, emphasizing with her widened eyes, "rolling with the punch the way he always advises other people to do."

"I'll teach you how to meditate, Dad," Beth said in a softer tone. "Mark says most nervous conditions and even some mental problems could be cured easily if people would learn to meditate."

"Sure, you and your mother will turn me into a card-carrying senior citizen," he said.

Jennie and Beth gazed at each other and laughed.

"Yeah, what's so funny?"

With a second conspiratorial glance at Beth, Jennie replied, "Beth's bought us some presents."

"Presents? You had time to shop on this protest trip? I thought that would be considered blasphemous."

"It's not a twenty-four-hour thing, Dad. We do get time to be real people," Beth said. Jennie kept smiling.

"All right, what's the joke? What did she buy?"

"She bought me a nice house gift, that clay vase on the hutch."

Frankie looked and nodded.

"It is nice."

"And she bought you something nice, too. Go look. Your present's in the bedroom," Jennie said. He gazed suspiciously at Beth and then got up and gingerly entered the bedroom to see the neon green Bermuda shorts and matching polo shirt laid out on the bed. Beside them was a pair of matching green knee-high socks.

"Very funny," he called from the bedroom. His wife and daughter roared. He returned to the living room, the garments in hand. "And exactly where am I supposed to where this?"

"Anywhere, Dad," Beth said. "It's your new undercover uniform."

"I'll give you undercover," he said. He couldn't help smiling, however. He held up the shorts. "Right size at least."

"I know your sizes, Dad," Beth said, suddenly growing serious.

"Aren't you going to thank her, Frankie?"

He smirked.

"Thanks," he said. "Did your mother put you up to this?"

"No. I just picked up a recent copy of *Palm Springs* magazine and looked at some of the pictures."

"Great. You know what I'm going to do?" Frankie threatened. "I'm actually going to put this on. How's that?"

"Doesn't scare me, Frankie Samuels."

"I'm not so sure about me," Beth said.

"Stevie called from the car phone," Jennie said. "They're about forty minutes away."

"Great," he said.

"So where were you all this time, Frankie?" Jennie asked with abrupt directness.

"What d'ya mean, where was I? I called you from the station."

"And I called back just after you left the first time," she said, her eyes small with suspicion.

"Jesus. Who's the detective in this house anyway?"

"Never mind all that. Spill it."

Frankie looked at Beth, who was smiling from ear to ear. She just loved to see Jennie handle him.

"An old man committed suicide. I did a simple follow-up," he confessed. When it came right down to it, he couldn't lie to Jennie face-to-face.

"Why did he kill himself?" Beth asked.

"Wife passed away and he couldn't face life without her."

"Oh, the poor man," Jennie said.

"Doesn't surprise me," Beth said. "Not with the way the elderly are treated in this country. The richest country in the world, and we have a segment of our older population eating pet food to survive. A couple of F-15s would probably end hunger in a dozen states, and vastly improve the health care they get . . ." She laughed. "I know people who get better care for their dogs and cats. No, what surprises me is more don't commit suicide. In fact, it might do some good."

"What good would that do?" Frankie snapped.

"It could bring more attention to the problem. One mass suicide . . ."

"Oh, Beth," Jennie said, grimacing.

"I'm sorry, Mom, but sometimes, most of the time, unfortunately, the only thing that moves the power brokers in this country is a violent or dramatic action."

"So a few dozen old people should be bused to the White House lawn and left there to cut their wrists?" Frankie said.

"No, leave them here and let the indifference cut their wrists for them," Beth shot back.

"Can't we change the subject?" Jennie begged.

Frankie pressed his lips together.

"Yeah, sure." He looked at the Bermuda shorts. "I'll just change into my new uniform and take my place in my assigned rocker on the patio and wait for the suicide march on Washington."

In his bedroom he stood before the dresser mirror staring at himself. He recalled standing before the mirror after he had hit thirty, searching his face for the telltale signs of age. It was terrifying then, but something happened when he reached forty and fifty: he started to think of himself as well-preserved, one of the lucky ones who didn't show age. Even now, even after all that had happened, he didn't look his age.

But he had to live a different sort of life now, and he was afraid that it had been the work that had kept him looking and feeling young. As long as he remained around younger people, around activity, as long as he had to be sharp and strong and quick, he would be so, but like a wild animal in the zoo, he could lose that edge, forget how to hunt, forget all that had to be done to survive, and before long, he would look his age, look like a man who carried a pacemaker and then . . .

That's what growing old means, he suddenly thought. It means hating the truth. No wonder that old lady could understand Sam Murray committing suicide. The truth was too heavy a burden. Was he plodding along looking for some evil force, maybe just to give himself something to do? Perhaps the truth itself was the evil force and the truth could be hunted and cornered but never captured, never locked away. It was the one monster from which everyone wanted to flee at one time or another. He was fleeing it now, pretending the heart problem hadn't occurred, wasn't he?

He sighed. Then he slipped into the Bermuda shorts and polo shirt and put on his sandals and his sunglasses. Maybe he would take up golf after all, he thought. He went out to wait for the arrival of his son and daughter-in-law.

11

Susie paused at the Kaufmans' door and checked again to be sure the pills were in the left pocket of her uniform. Then she pressed the buzzer and waited.

"Coming," she heard Tillie call. The Kaufmans had just finished their early dinner and Tillie was still tidying up. She came to the door with a dish towel in her hand. "Oh, Susie, hello," Tillie said. Susie eyed the towel.

"Faye told me that you needed to have some cleaning done. You're not doing it yourself, are you, Tillie?"

"Oh no. Just finishing my dishes. I can't do the heavy cleaning. It's so hard for me now with Morris sick. He runs me ragged as it is and by the time . . ."

"It's okay. I have a little time now," Susie said quickly as she stepped into the apartment. She had been in here before to clean. She knew where everything was kept and went directly to the closet in the kitchen, Tillie trailing behind.

"I heard your sister go out last night. By the time I looked out, she was already in her car and backing away. Was it an emergency?" she asked.

"Yes," Susie said, not offering any more information.

"I thought so. I told Morris, but he said I exaggerated. An accident? A heart attack?"

"If I've told you once, I've told you a hundred times, Tillie,
I don't discuss my sister's patients. Medical information is
personal. Some people don't like other people knowing what's
wrong with them."

"Sickness makes you ashamed," Tillie Kaufman agreed,
nodding.

Susie took out the sponge mop and pail and went to the
sink.

"You think the floor needs it?"

"Of course it does," Susie said. She paused and grimaced
when she looked at the counter and saw the remnants of a
pastrami on rye.

"Who ate that?"

Tillie looked away guiltily.

"Morris?"

"He ordered it and had it delivered before I even knew,"
she confessed. "He ate so much, he had to go lie down a
minute. Don't tell your sister. She'll yell."

"She might; she might not. I know she's disgusted with
him," Susie began to do the floor. Twenty minutes later, she
was out in the living room dusting and straightening up. Before she was finished, Morris came out of the bedroom and
plopped himself down in the La-Z-Boy.

"I can watch television while you work?"

"I'm finished in here," Susie said. "I'll do your bedroom
now."

"When I was a young man, I had beautiful girls like you do
my bedroom all the time," he said under his breath, and he
laughed. Susie turned on him.

"What kind of talk is that with your wife in the apartment,"
she snapped, her face flushed.

"Just talk," he said, shrugging. "What do you think I can
do now, more than talk?"

"You're incorrigible," Susie said. Morris laughed.

"When you're my age, you can't be anything else."

Susie left him and gazed in at Tillie, who was shining sil-
verware in the kitchen.

"I can do that for you when I'm finished with the bedroom and the bathroom," Susie said.

"It's all right. I've got to keep busy," Tillie said.

Susie left her and went to the bedroom. She started to vacuum the rug and the windowsills and then paused when her gaze fell on Morris Kaufman's pill bottle beside the bed. She listened for a moment and then took the pill bottle and went into the bathroom. She dumped the contents into the toilet and replaced it quickly with the pills in her pocket, pills that were too close in appearance for Morris or Tillie to note the difference. Then she returned the pill bottle to the table and went back to her work.

Nearly two and a half hours later, she returned to her apartment to take a shower. Faye had gone out to do some errands, but Susie suspected she was making plans for them to leave Palm Springs. It saddened her. Just when she finally got used to a place, Faye would decide they had to pick up and go. And she always blamed it on her, blamed it on her good work. But then Faye had a way of making her feel guilty for anything that went wrong in their lives, even Mommy's death, although she never had come right out and said it, exactly. She didn't have to; Susie understood what Faye was implying all the time—that she was a big burden for their parents because of her handicap and her introverted personality.

"All they did was worry and worry about you," Faye once told her when she was angry. "It was like having a daughter who never grew past twelve."

She sighed and sat thinking about her life and all of the places they had been together. She wasn't stupid. She knew she was the main reason why Faye hadn't ever found someone to love her and marry her. Her husband-to-be would have to be willing to marry Susie as well, take her into their lives, too. She thought it was going to happen years ago when Faye began dating that young doctor, Daniel Matthews. He didn't even know she was around because she never interfered, never burst in on them when they were together. She kept herself in the background and gave Faye a chance. Faye admitted she was in love with him. She wanted to marry him.

But then he found out about Susie and he started to retreat from Faye. Before he could actually come out and tell her he was no longer interested in her, he had that terrible automobile accident and they discovered he had taken too many amphetamines. That was just another thing Faye blamed on her.

She sighed. It really wasn't fair to Faye. One day, someday soon, I have to pick up and leave, Susie thought, so my sister can have a normal life.

"Let's take a walk," Frankie suggested after dinner.

"After what you ate, Frankie Samuels, you'd better take a walk," Jennie said.

Everyone got up and the family sauntered out, Frankie and Stevie in front, Jennie, Beth and Laurel holding up the rear. Frankie felt good with his family around him like this. Maybe Jennie was right; maybe he would grow used to a calmer, slower pace and in doing so begin to enjoy the things only civilians enjoyed.

A pleasantly warm breeze enveloped them. Above, the desert twilight sky was painted with long strokes of pink and light blue. There was barely any traffic on their street and what there was moved at a relaxed pace. Occasionally they came upon other pedestrians walking their dogs or themselves as if they had eternity at their disposal.

"Mom pulled me aside before," Stevie said.

"I saw. Another conspiracy."

"She's very worried that you're not taking all this well. She wanted me to tell you that a branch that doesn't bend . . ."

"Breaks, I know." Frankie sighed. "You know what it's like, Stevie? It's like getting into a hot bath. You don't just jump in. You ease yourself in. That's all I want to do. She doesn't have to worry."

"You've got nothing to be ashamed of, Dad. We're very proud of you."

"Even Beth?"

"You'd be surprised at what she says behind your back."

Frankie laughed and paused to look back. He watched Beth and Laurel saunter along behind. Beth had put on one of her simple print dresses, but one piece still hung wide and loose, reminding him of something his grandmother used to wear. She wore no make-up, save a thin layer of lipstick, no earrings, no necklaces or bracelets. Her watch was one of those big-faced, masculine-looking timepieces, and she clumped along in a pair of thick-heeled black shoes. Could she possibly look at herself in the mirror and think she was attractive? he wondered.

Beside her, Laurel strutted with a model's elegance. Her shoulder-length blond hair lay softly over her shoulders. Its rich, thick strands were alluring, filling him, as he imagined it did most men, with an urge to run his fingers through the golden locks for what would definitely be a most pleasing tactile experience. Every once in a while, Laurel raised her cerulean eyes toward him and flashed that gentle smile that warmed his heart. Stylishly dressed in a close-fitting light-blue cotton-knit dress and matching shoes, she drew glances and gazes from nearly every driver and passenger in the cars cruising down the street, as well as from every other pedestrian. She wore a pair of pink and turquoise native American handcrafted earrings and a matching necklace. Her watch was a woman's Rolex.

Remarkably, despite the differences in their lifestyles, Beth and Laurel got along pretty well. Although Laurel never joined Beth in her protests, she sympathized and agreed with most everything Beth believed and said. Laurel was the one Beth had turned to when her marriage fell apart. Stevie handled the divorce, but Laurel handled Beth.

Frankie and Stevie walked on.

"So what's this case you started the moment you got home from the hospital?" Stevie asked, quoting Jennie.

"No big deal. A man in his sixties allegedly committed suicide."

"Allegedly?"

"Everything's allegedly to me until I'm positive beyond a doubt."

"What's your supervisor think?"

"You know what I think of him and what he thinks."

"Yeah, but?"

"You don't want to draw attention to suicides committed by older people, especially here in one of America's prime retirement communities, but I told him I thought it warranted a more thorough investigation."

"You really think so?"

"Looks odd to me," Frankie said.

"That old policeman's instinct?"

"Maybe. It's rarely led me on a wild goose chase," Frankie bragged.

"Maybe you could become some sort of a consultant for the Palm Springs Police Department after you retire, Dad. Nothing heavy, just a little part-time."

"I don't know. Your mother watches every move now."

Stevie laughed.

"You'll get used to retirement, Dad. Eventually." Frankie nodded and looked back at the women again.

"Actually, I'm worried about Beth," Frankie confessed. "I wish she'd find someone soon."

"I know. I'm working on it subtly with Laurel. We hope to connect her with a few of our single friends."

"Make sure, whoever it is, he's a lot more stable than the piece of work she married," Frankie warned.

"You never know who's stable and who isn't these days, Dad, but we're being as selective as we can be. Only thing is, Beth considers our friends part of the power structure oppressing the poor and the downtrodden, as well as polluting the environment."

"Whoever it is, make sure he's dressed in jeans and sneakers when he comes to take her on the first date."

Stevie roared.

"What are you talking so much about?" Jennie asked.

"Hey, can't we have any secrets?"

"No, because your secrets usually mean more problems for us women," Jennie replied.

"This is a taste of what retirement is going to mean," Frankie said, nodding. "Twenty-four-hour abuse instead of four or five."

"Come on, Dad," Laurel said scooping her arm through his and standing him up, "I'll protect you."

"Are you sure you're not embarrassed to walk with a stubborn old man?" He looked back at Jennie. She absolutely glistened with happiness. His gaze shifted to Beth, and for a moment he felt like rushing to her and wrapping his arms around her the way he used to when she was a little girl. She looked so lost now, so lonely and forgotten, and so afraid that he no longer cared for her.

"Hey," he said reaching for her hand, too. She widened her eyes with surprise. "Come on. I need protection on the left." She took his hand and moved up alongside him.

"Figures it would be on the left," Stevie quipped.

"Mr. Republican speaks again," Beth returned.

"Let's turn back soon, Frankie. I don't want them heading back to L.A. too late," Jennie said.

"Right, dear."

Bathed in laughter and smiles, Frankie and his family finished their walk.

Later, soon after Steve and Laurel had departed for L.A., Frankie retired to the patio with the newspaper in hand. The sun had fallen behind the mountains and the temperature had dipped to a comfortable seventy-four. The long shadows cast by the San Jacinto mountain range changed the bright red of the bougainvillea blossoms into more of a ruby. He relaxed, admiring the setting. From inside the house, he could hear Jennie moving around the kitchen, still cleaning up from dinner. Beth worked with her, having decided to remain one more night in Palm Springs before returning to L.A. herself. A few minutes later, he sensed someone behind him and turned to see Beth standing there and staring at him.

"What's up?"

"Nothing. I just thought I'd come out a minute and see what you were doing. How are you really feeling, Dad?"

"I'll be okay. The doctor assures me once the pacemaker's in, I won't see any real difference."

"Mom's afraid you're going to find a way to do something strenuous anyway."

"I know. She insisted I get an electric toothbrush."

Beth surprised him by laughing.

"What?"

"It's been a long time since you told me one of your jokes, Dad." She flopped in the chair beside him and gazed up at the mountain. "It is pretty here."

"Yes."

"And meditative."

"That it is," he said.

"You're not really going to take up golf, are you?"

"Might not have a choice. Another fellow who resisted was found stuffed in his mailbox one morning."

"Stop," Beth said laughing. Suddenly her smile evaporated and she sighed deeply. "I wish we could be friends," she said.

"Friends? We're friends. How can we not be friends? We're related."

"I mean it, Dad. I wish . . ."

"I know," he confessed. "It's not all your fault. Oh, maybe ninety-five percent."

She smiled.

"I can't help believing strongly in the things I want to see happen and see corrected."

"I'm not against any of that. I just wish you . . ."

"Were married and living in a house with a dozen kids. I know."

"Not everyone wants the same things. I realize that. I'm not pushing you into anything. It's just that my experience tells me we're sort of made to go through life in pairs."

"What frightens you the most, Dad? Is that it, being alone?"

"Yep," he confessed after a moment. "Always thought it would be easier if I went first."

"Easier for whom? Not for Mom."

"Women are survivors," he said, thinking about Mr. Murray's apparent suicide.

"She wouldn't know what to do without you to look after. It's nice to have someone to look after," Beth admitted softly.

"Don't ever tell her I said so, but I like it," he said. Beth smiled and looked at the mountains again.

"Laurel is so perfect, isn't she?"

"She's perfect at what she does, what she chooses to do, and I suppose you're perfect at what you choose to do."

"She's perfect," Beth insisted. "She's just what every man dreams a woman should be. I should hate her, but I don't. I envy her because she's happy."

"I thought you liked what you do."

"I don't like it. I do it because it has to be done. I'm a lot like you . . . doing things you don't like to do, but things you know have to be done."

"I suppose you are," Frankie said, seeing it from that perspective for the first time. "It's not a good thing to do forever, though, Beth. It consumes you, takes its toll. Maybe you paid enough dues and you can be a little more selfish now, huh?"

She shrugged.

"How about you, Dad? You think you'll like being a little more selfish?"

"I'll get to like it," he promised. She shook her head.

"You know why we fight so much, Dad?"

"Why?"

"We can't lie to each other as well as other people can lie to each other."

He nodded. There it was again, the lesson: truth was a hard burden to bear and when you were confronted with it, you often chose to ignore it or run from it.

"Then let's stop it," he said.

She smiled and he put out his hand. She seized it eagerly, stood up, and leaned over to hug him.

In his arms she felt like his little girl again, and just for a moment, he thought all that had happened since, all the years, had been merely a dream.

12

When Faye returned to their apartment, she found Susie in her bathrobe still sitting on the sofa. She gave Faye a big smile and Faye closed the door softly.

"What?"

"You have visitors. They came here," Susie said. She tilted her head toward Faye's bedroom.

"They're here?"

"Waiting patiently."

"Why?"

"To show their appreciation, silly. It's not the first time such a thing happened, is it?" Susie asked with a licentious smile on her face. Faye blushed. "They're waiting for you," Susie sang, playing with the open collar on her robe. Her breasts were visible nearly to the nipples. She grimaced. "They wanted only you."

Faye took a deep breath. Her heart was pounding. If Susie were lying . . . She walked slowly toward her bedroom, a cautious smile on her face. Sure enough, when she opened her bedroom door and looked in, she found them there, waiting, both stark naked.

"Perry said we should thank you for being a big comfort to Dad yesterday," Todd told her. "We know you were as saddened by Mom's death as we were. You really care for your patients."

"There is only one true remedy for the way you feel," Perry added.

Faye widened her smile.

"This is so nice, so considerate."

"Well, we must admit," Todd said, flashing a look at his brother, "it isn't only for you. We need it, too, and our wives . . . well, our wives aren't in the right frame of mine at the moment. You understand, don't you?"

"Of course, I do," she replied. They both grinned.

"I told you she'd understand," Todd said. Perry nodded.

She entered the bedroom and placed herself between them, turning to face Todd because he was more aggressive, more apt to take action. He did. He began to unbutton her uniform. As he did so, Perry stroked her hair and then leaned in to plant a soft kiss on her neck. She closed her eyes and moaned. Todd worked her uniform over her shoulders and down her arms to let it fall to her feet. Instantly, Perry inserted his fingers under the elastic of her panties and slipped them down her legs. Todd took off her bra.

"I hate those aseptic-looking white socks and white shoes," Todd said. He squatted to untie the laces and she lifted each foot to permit him to take off the shoes and the socks. All of them were naked now. She waited as they drew closer, sandwiching her between them. She felt their erections prodding, Perry's lips moving over her neck and her shoulders, Todd's lips sucking and kissing her face, her mouth, her breasts. She was too weak to stand and began to sink to her knees, but Perry lifted her from behind and gently brought her to the bed. He put her on her left side at first and continued to make love to her from behind while Todd made love to her from the front, fondling her breasts, running his fingers down the center of her stomach until he reached her pubic hair. She moaned and shifted her legs.

Then Todd pulled her on top of him. She straddled his body, her hands on his shoulders and he entered her quickly. She subdued a cry by biting so hard on her lower lip that she tasted the salty taste of blood. As Todd worked himself farther and farther into her, moving with a rhythm that reached

into her deepest and most quiet places, Perry suddenly took
hold of her shoulders and brought himself in from behind.
Her whole body sung. It was as if she had fallen into some
pit of sexual ecstasy that turned each and every cell of her
body into an erogenous zone.

The two brothers worked with a harmony that bore out
her suspicion they had done this often before. Never did
one move against the other. Their rhythms were perfectly
coordinated. She barely caught her breath after Todd's
thrusts when Perry's overwhelmed her. But it was wonderful and when they all came together it was an explosion
of orgasms the likes of which she could never dream to
duplicate.

Perry rolled over first, and then she did and Todd fol
lowed. They all lay there, breathing hard and fast, happy with
the feeling of exhaustion and the way their bodies cried for
air. It was an exquisite agony.

"That was . . . wonderful . . ." she gasped. "Wonderful."

"You deserved it."

"Every moment," Todd said.

"Just lay there, rest. Close your eyes," Perry said. "Relax.
That's it."

He planted a kiss on her right nipple and Todd planted
one on her left. Then she felt them lift off the bed. She remained on her back, her eyes closed, savoring the delightful
cooling down of her skin, the quieting of her sex, the slowing
down of her heartbeat. She even fell asleep for a few mo
ments.

"Can I open my eyes now?" she asked. There was no response, so she did.

They weren't there.

"Todd? Perry?"

She rose from her bed and went out to see if they were
still in her apartment. Maybe they were having a cool drink.

"They're gone," Susie said. She was standing by the cur-
tain, looking toward the parking lot. She turned slowly. "They
said they had to get home to their families." Susie smiled li-
centiously. "How was it?"

"I'm sure I don't have to tell you. I'm sure you had your ear to the door."

"I did no such thing," Susie replied with indignation. "I don't spy on you. I leave that to Mr. Kaufman next door. But," she added with a laugh, "he won't be doing that too much longer."

Faye stared.

"What did you do?" she finally asked.

"I went next door like you told me to and cleaned their place."

"And?"

"And changed Morris's prescription," she said.

"You didn't do that," Faye said, a look of surprise on her face.

"You wanted me to do it."

"I didn't."

"Yes you did. Don't say you didn't now that I have. Don't start doing that again. You always want me to do it and then when I do, you pretend you didn't and you act horrified."

"I *am* horrified. And besides, you shouldn't be so damned happy and full of yourself," she snapped. Susie's smile wilted.

"Of course I should. You're just tired and irritable. Go to sleep so you don't accidentally give your patient the wrong medicine."

Susie stared her sister down and Faye retreated.

Why not be happy and full of myself? she thought. Why not? She snapped on the radio and unpinned her hair. The uplifting Latin sounds of the Gipsy Kings filled her with excitement and she moved to the rhythms, shaking her shoulders, twisting her hips, repeating the choruses.

Her own laughter echoed around her. Then she heard the sound of an airplane that had just lifted off the runway of the Palm Springs airport and was now circling to pick up its flight path east, carrying people back to Chicago or New York. She went to the window and looked up. There was a whole world out there with endless possibilities. How she wished she could be everywhere at the same time. There were lonely and pathetic people everywhere, people who had just lost loved ones, people who needed her or someone like her.

She looked back toward Faye's bedroom. How could she say that . . . full of myself? She's jealous, that's all. If only . . . if only I had a boyfriend in whom I could confide my secrets, she thought. Most of the time Faye was wonderful and understanding, but it would be nice to have a lover in whose arms she could cuddle, someone with a heart as big as hers and a purpose as big as hers.

But that was not possible, was it? A romance, a relationship, was just not part of her destiny. It was the price she paid for such a meaningful role, for being the Angel of Mercy. For now, she was more than willing to pay it, but that didn't mean she denied her longings, her great desire to have her own beloved, someone to join her when it came her time to depart.

Someone who would want to and wouldn't be afraid. Surely he was out there, waiting.

Corpsy parked in front of the Village Deli and got out of his car cautiously. He couldn't shake the feeling that he was being watched. People might call him paranoid, but during his brief nap in the motel room, he dreamt that his mother had hired someone to follow him and make sure he wasn't making a fool of himself by chasing after some young woman. It wouldn't be the first time she had asked someone to keep an eye on him and report back to her. She often did that when he was in public school and even when he went to college. How did he know? He knew by what she revealed she knew about his activities. That's how he knew. And when he accused her of spying, she always broke down in tears and moaned that she was just trying to look after him properly, just trying to be both a mother and a father. How could he blame her for it?

He couldn't even blame her now, even though it annoyed him to suspect that someone was keeping tabs on him while he pursued the woman he loved. If Susie should suspect they were being watched, she would surely be spooked and want to get away from him. That would enrage him and he would blame his mother for his failure.

He panned the parking lot for a moment, studying the driver in each and every automobile that had entered after him. No one looked especially suspicious. Most were with other people. The only possibility was a young man who parked in front of the video store, but he didn't even gaze Corpsy's way casually when he emerged from his car. It was all right; he wasn't being watched.

He went into the restaurant and ordered a turkey hero sandwich with a side of fries and peas. He had a beer and ate slowly.

He couldn't wait to get back up to their apartment complex and wait for his first opportunity to make contact. Perhaps Faye had an evening shift. If she did, he would follow her to the hospital and make contact there. Maybe he would pretend to have taken a position at this hospital, just to temper her initial shock at seeing him and not frighten her. Once she accepted him, he could tell her the truth. He was glad now he had put his hospital blues in the car trunk.

After dinner, he went out and got them and then went into the bathroom to change. When he emerged, the waiter looked at him with surprise, but he didn't linger long enough for the man to question him. He got into his car quickly and drove back to the Sullivans' apartment. He parked his car in the same dark spot and waited, his eyes on their door, his heart beating a little faster, his tongue moving over his lips.

He saw Faye come hurrying out of the apartment, get into her car, and drive off as if she were heading to an emergency. He started to follow, but then he thought about Susie, alone in the apartment. At least he assumed she was in there. He tempted himself with the idea of going right up to that apartment door and pushing the buzzer. He would just introduce himself to her, go for it head on. It was a tantalizing idea.

He rubbed his fingers up and down the door handle, caressing it, pressing down and then pulling back before the door lock snapped open. He was parked in a dark area of the lot so he wasn't afraid of being discovered, but when he opened the door, the car light would go on and he knew he couldn't start out and then stop and then start again. That would attract attention.

Still, the thought of getting out and walking up to that door excited him. If he only had the courage, he thought. It was just that he was so terrified of making a mistake at the beginning of the courtship, a mistake so big he couldn't correct it and he would lose his Susie. He put his hands in his lap and closed his eyes and tried to get control, but the little animal in his stomach kept clawing away, climbing up to his heart, tickling it, and then scurrying down to his loins and curling up around his penis.

Why couldn't he simply walk up to that door? Other men approached women they admired and introduced themselves, didn't they? He wasn't without charm, without intelligence. He would know what to say. He wouldn't stumble and stutter and look stupid. He certainly wouldn't frighten her.

I can do it, he chanted. I can.

He took a deep breath and then with an impulsive energy, snapped open the car door. The car light had seemed brighter than it was and when he caught his reflection in the glass, he looked ghostly. He swallowed and pushed on, nevertheless. He closed the door softly and then, almost tiptoeing, headed toward the apartments, reciting his words.

"Hello. I'm Arnold Ratner. We haven't met, but I'm a friend of your sister's from back in Phoenix. I just arrived in Palm Springs and decided to pay you guys a visit."

He took the first step.

"Hello, I'm Arnold Ratner . . ."

On the patio, he paused. He was so close now, so close. Susie was just on the other side of that door. His heart was pounding. He thought he could actually feel his blood surging through his veins and arteries. His hand trembled and shook as he raised his finger toward the buzzer. Inches from it, he hesitated and listened. There was music coming from inside. It sounded like soft rock. He liked soft rock, too. He smiled to himself. He had just learned something else about his beloved before he had even met her. But if she was listening to music and relaxing, she might not want to be disturbed, he thought.

It was wrong. It was wrong to just appear like this, unannounced. He pulled his hand back, but he couldn't stop being intrigued. He looked around and saw that there was no one in the parking lot, no one walking on the pathways, no one would see him. Then, he leaned to the right and peeked through the open blinds. The lamp was on in the living room, but Susie wasn't there. He saw what he thought was her shadow on a wall through another doorway that he imagined to be the kitchen. Maybe she was cleaning up after dinner. He perused the living room and spotted what looked like Susie's maid uniform draped over a chair. Over that was a bra.

It was as if he had seen her nude. He pulled back, his heart thumping, the sweat trickling down his temples and over his cheeks. His neck was soaked. He took a deep breath. She might be walking about nude. If he looked through the window again . . .

The sound of a car coming into the complex sent him scrambling down the steps and into the sanctuary of shadows. He walked slowly toward his own vehicle, and fortunately so. It was Faye returning. He crouched down as she pulled into her parking space and quickly came out of her car. She hurried up the pathway and at one point was so close to him, he could see her teeth pressed down on her lower lip. When she entered the apartment, he ran back to his car and got in. He sat there, catching his breath, calming the animal.

Where did she go and come back from so quickly? He didn't notice any bags in her hands. After what seemed like only minutes, the apartment door opened, and this time his beloved appeared. She came down the steps slowly. Mesmerized, he watched her hobble along. His heart went out to her as she headed toward their car. Where was she going? he wondered. Maybe she was going supermarket shopping. That would be great. He'd follow and then he would pretend to just happen to bump into her. It would make it all so much easier.

When she drove out, he followed behind her, but she didn't head toward any malls or supermarkets. She drove away from Palm Springs into Rancho Mirage and pulled off Highway 111 into a side street that led to a row of upscale homes. They climbed up a rise until she stopped in front of a house and turned off her lights. He slowed down and pulled to the side, expecting her to get out. But she didn't. She remained in her car, waiting.

Waiting for what? he wondered. What was she doing? She sat there in the dark for nearly forty-five minutes, and he sat in his car, his eyes fixed on hers, not moving, not doing anything to alert her to his presence. Finally, another car came down the street and turned into the driveway across from Susie. The car entered the garage and the garage door closed. Not more than a minute later, Susie got out of her car and approached the house. Corpsy watched intrigued as she went up to the door and pushed the buzzer. An elderly man opened it. They said a few words to each other and Susie entered the house.

13

Tommy Livingston had just come into the house through the garage when he heard the doorbell. He wasn't in the mood for company. Dinner at his son Todd's had been more than he could take.

"Susie," he said with surprise. "What are you doing here?"

"I was just returning from a movie," she said, "and thought I'd stop by since I was so close."

"You went to a movie in your maid's uniform?"

"Oh," she said smiling. "I wear it so often, I don't even think about it anymore. I did some cleaning for one of our neighbors today. So how was your dinner?" she asked, but before he began to say something, she put up her hand to stop him. "You don't have to tell me. I know what it was like."

"You do?" He started to smile, but he saw she was deadly serious.

"May I come in?" she asked. He started to step back and then hesitated.

"You and your sister really don't have to waste any more time on me," he said. "I'm fine."

"Sure you are," she said, smirking, as she stepped past him and into the house.

He shrugged, smiled to himself and followed her in. She had already switched on the kitchen light. She started for the stove, took the teapot, and began to fill it with water. As she did, she spoke with her back to him, relating her thoughts in a manner that made it sound like she was reciting.

"You didn't eat very much, did you? They tried to get you to eat everything. And everyone talked incessantly. Every moment of silence during a period of mourning seems deadly and uncomfortable, especially to people in the presence of the deceased's most cherished loved one. So they kept trying to get you to eat this and eat that and take more of this, but your stomach was in knots."

"Sounds like you were right there," Tommy said. This time he did smile widely. He stood in the kitchen doorway with his hands on his hips and watched her put the teapot on the stove and turn on the burner.

She turned around and nodded after scrutinizing him.

"You know what you need?" she said. "You need a warm bath. Like Faye always says, make your body relax and your mind will, too. I'll go draw the water. We'll have a cup of tea and a biscuit afterward."

"Why are you still doing all this for me?" he asked in a little more demanding tone than he had intended.

She drew back and took on a look of great disappointment. In fact, she looked like she might burst into tears. He was sorry he had asked.

"I don't mean to interfere or poke myself into places where I don't belong, so if I am . . ."

"No, no. I guess I just can't get it through my head that someone could be as nice as you are, Susie. I'm sorry. I didn't mean to hurt your feelings."

She smiled instantly and then relaxed her upper body as if he had said the funniest thing.

"You can't hurt my feelings, Mr. Livingston. I know you're the one who's suffering and whatever you do or say, you do or say under great strain. I just want to help ease that strain for you a little, that's all. It's not a big-deal thing for me to do. I'm available; I can do it, so I do," she said shrugging.

"Right. So you're prescribing a warm bath, huh?"

"The best thing for you right now. Then we'll have a cup

of tea and something. Faye told me to give you a sedative
and wait until you drift off to a peaceful repose."

He nodded. He had to admit she was right—the prospect
of a warm bath, something warm in his stomach, and quiet
conversation all looked very desirable at this moment.

She turned off the stove.

"Later, while we have our tea, we can talk a bit about Sylvia." Her eyes grew small again. "I know everyone avoids
talking about her when you're around, right?"

"I don't think her name was mentioned twice tonight," he
admitted. She smiled.

"See. I know just how people act at a time like this and
just how to deal with it."

He nodded.

"Yes, I guess you do," he said, and then he became
thoughtful. "Where did you get all this wisdom, Susie?"

"I'm just blessed, I guess," she said, so innocently he had
to smile. "I'm not as intelligent as Faye. She always got the
A's and I always got the C's, but even she admits I have more
patience and understanding when it comes to people who are
suffering.

"Now let me draw your bath," she said, and she left him.

In Tommy Livingston's bathroom, Susie knelt beside the
tub and let the water run through her fingers as if she were
sifting through a stream for gold dust. The feel of the water,
the sound of it pouring out of the faucet, had put her into a
daze for a moment. When she felt it grow warmer and
warmer, she adjusted the hot and cold until she was satisfied
it was tepid enough. Then she stepped back and watched it
rush into the tub. The sound began to mesmerize her again.

Suddenly she saw Daddy sitting in the tub, the water rushing in around him. He had his hands over his face and his
body shook with his sobs. She knelt down beside him and began to stroke his head softly.

"There, there, Daddy. Don't. You're only tearing your
heart apart. Take a deep breath and close your eyes. Lie
back, Daddy. I'll wash your shoulders and your arms. Go on.
Relax, Daddy. That's it. Relax."

"I'm so ashamed," he kept saying, "so ashamed."

"Of what, Daddy? Of being sad?"

He looked at her as if she were a stranger. The tears were streaming down his face. She sucked in her breath and sighed.

"I'll just get you something to help you sleep tonight," she told him.

Right after the bath, she went into Faye's room and got one of her sedatives. She had him drink it with water in which more of the sedative had been dissolved. Into that restful sleep he went, down, down into the dark, his body sinking through the bed, until he saw the light directly ahead of him. She had such vision that she could see it with him. There was Mommy waiting at the gate, her arms out. Susie saw them join hands and embrace and then they turned and waved back to her, both smiling, both happy again.

"Thank you, dear," her mother called. "Thank you, sweetheart."

"Thank you, honey," Daddy cried. "We love you."

"We love you."

"And I love you. Yes," she whispered. "Yes . . ."

Her reverie ended when she heard Tommy Livingston outside the bathroom door. She opened it quickly.

"It's ready, Mr. Livingston," she said. "I threw in some of Sylvia's bath oil. It's a good relaxant."

"Tell you a secret," he said leaning toward her. He was naked under his robe. "I used to use it."

"I knew that," Susie said, smiling. "All you big, strong men like something soft and sweet and if it happens to be feminine, you keep it a secret. My daddy was just like that, too."

She walked out and he closed the door. She stood there for a moment until she heard him groan and then settle in the warm liquid and sigh.

"Are you all right?" she asked, her face up to the door.

"What? Fine," he said. "Just fine. I'll be in and out," he responded.

"Take your time. I'm not in any rush," she told him.

Tommy Livingston was different from her last few bereaved loved ones. He was stronger, more independent, more able to deal with his loss. She hated his conviction that there was nothing to look forward to after death. This resignation and acceptance toughened him in places where he should be soft and vulnerable, and in many ways made her unnecessary and him far less dependent upon her. Disappointed, she felt some anger building and went out to the living room to look at the albums again. She wanted to gaze at Sylvia's photograph and assure her that no matter what Tommy believed, it wouldn't be much longer.

"He's coming, Sylvia," she murmured when she had one in hand. In it, Sylvia looked thoughtful, sad.

Susie believed the dead contacted special people like herself through their photographs. To others, Sylvia might very well be smiling, but to Susie, she was despondent in each and every picture. Afterward, when Tommy joined Sylvia, the smiles would return to all the photographs, just like they had in the other homes, just like her own father's had.

She touched Sylvia's cheek in the picture and closed her eyes.

"He's coming, dear. Don't be despondent. You'll meet at the gate just like my mother and father met, and you'll be together," she promised.

She hobbled out to the kitchen. There, she set out the tea cups on the counter. While Tommy Livingston was getting into something comfortable, she took the gelatin capsules of chloral hydrate from her pocket. She had taken them from Faye's dresser drawer. She snapped a capsule as if she were breaking an egg over a frying pan. The clear liquid rained down into the cup. She broke another and then another until she was satisfied she would give him enough to make him groggy and tired. The teapot began to whistle.

"Good timing," Tommy said.

"Go to the dining room and I'll bring it in to you," she told him.

"Aye, aye, Captain."

She brought in the tea and some biscuits and jelly and

served him. She smeared some jelly on a biscuit and offered it to him.

"I bet you're a little hungry now," she said, winking.

"A little," he admitted, taking the biscuit.

She smeared some jelly on a biscuit for herself and bit into it, closing her eyes and moaning as if it were the most delicious thing she had ever eaten.

"My son Perry's wife invited me to dinner at their house tomorrow night," he told her. "But I think I'll just hang out here. I'm not the best company and won't be for a while."

"They should understand," Susie said.

"Yep. I got to get used to being alone. Puttin' it off ain't gonna do anyone any good. Me, the least."

"I can stop in tomorrow and fix you something light," Susie said. "It's best to eat, but to keep your diet simple. My sister will tell me what to make. She says grief interferes with so many of our bodily functions, digestion being a primary one," she added.

"She's right about that," Tommy said. He sipped his tea and chewed vigorously on the biscuit. He stopped chewing and stared ahead for a moment. "Time, I guess. That's the only cure for what I feel right now. And maybe keeping busy. I might take on this job I've been avoiding."

"You really think you can do that?" Susie asked.

"Got no choice. It's either push on or . . . or cash in my chips," he said and smiled at her. Susie simply stared at him. He finished his tea. "My boys think that's best, too. And I don't want to be a burden to anyone.

"Sylvia and I once swore that no matter what happened to us, we wouldn't be a burden to our children," he explained. He drank some more tea and thought. "I remember how Sylvia's father was, how he was such a heavy responsibility for her. What that woman went through," he said shaking his head. "Maybe that was a big contributor to the heart problem that developed."

"Faye says stress, especially emotional stress, is the biggest cause of heart attacks."

"I think she's right." He yawned. "Jeez. All of a sudden, I feel dead tired. My eyelids feel like they're made of lead."

"It comes from the inside out, this sort of fatigue," Susie said. "Snowballs."

"Yeah. You're right. I guess I should just turn in."

"Yes, you should," she said. "I'll clean up." She started to put the cups back on the tray. "Don't worry about me. I'll let myself out after I'm sure you're okay."

He smiled and shook his head.

"Thank you," he said rising and headed for the bathroom.

The moment she put down the tray in the kitchen, Susie pounded her small fists against her thighs and began to pace. From time to time, she gazed at a kitchen chair as if there was someone sitting there and listening.

"Children," she muttered. "They can be so insensitive to anyone else's needs but their own. The only reason his daughter-in-law invited him to dinner tomorrow night was to make herself feel less guilty. Sons and daughters don't consider their parents' feelings. They just want them to hang around like some artifact; they just want them to be there for when they have time for them.

"They don't think about the fact that their surviving father or surviving mother has to spend most of his or her day alone in some apartment or condo or house with the walls echoing, with pictures of his or her loved one calling, with memories tearing at him or her. Oh no, just as long as they're there when the kids want them."

She paused and looked at the doorway as if Perry or Todd had been standing there the whole time.

"Well, how about your poor mother waiting at the gate? Did you or your brother ever consider her for one moment? Or did the two of you consider your father's real needs? His needs aren't to be found on any dinner plate or some fill-in work. His needs are out there, lingering," she said stabbing the air. "His poor soul is visiting Sylvia's grave, even now as his body sleeps. I'm sure of it."

She looked toward the bedroom. She had to work fast. Poor Sylvia was waiting. She had promised her. She had sat there in the living room and gazed at her photograph and promised her. Well, she couldn't let her down no matter what, she decided, and she dug her hands into her uniform pocket to pull out her sister's plastic surgical gloves. She wasn't going to be careless this time. She put on the gloves and broke more capsules over a glass until she had deposited the contents of at least thirty, and then she took the glass of clear liquid and a glass of water and went to Tommy's bedroom.

He had his arms around the pillow and his body curled as if he were embracing Sylvia. Susie thought he looked so precious, so loving. She hated to wake him, but she had to send him off. She paused at his bedside and then shook his shoulder vigorously. Nothing happened, so she shook again. This time his eyes fluttered open.

"Mr. Livingston," she called.

Groggy and confused, he turned slowly in the bed. She looked out of focus, hazy, moving in and out of his vision.

"Take this," she ordered.

"Wha . . . what?"

"You've been tossing and turning and screaming out. You're having a bad time," she said. "I called my sister and she told me to give you this."

Her words were so confusing. Where was he? What did she say? Bad time?

"This will help you sleep better. Just swallow this. Go on," she insisted. She knelt down and put her arm behind his head, lifting him off the pillow. He felt light, as if he were floating.

"I . . . screamed?"

"Yes. Over and over," she said. "Just take this."

"What is it?"

"Just a sleeping medication. My sister says it will relax you. Here," she said, bringing the lethal dosage of chloral hydrate to his lips. He hesitated, wondering for a moment why he was doing this, and then, out of fatigue and confusion, he opened his lips and took in the clear liquid. She had him chase it down with the glass of cool water and then she pulled her arm out from behind his head and his head fell back to the pillow as if it were made of stone. He closed his eyes.

"Just think about Sylvia now," she told him. "Sylvia . . . poor Sylvia."

"Sylvia," he said.

"Yes, Sylvia," Susie said. She sighed. How she wished she could be there when they were joined together once again. But she was permitted that only with her own parents. After all, the love other people shared was private. They didn't need an audience.

She turned and left the bedroom. Then she went around the house, straightening it up, fluffing pillows in the living room, making sure everything was cleaned and put away in the kitchen. She couldn't help the cleaning neurosis. It was her way of dealing with the tension and the excitement whenever she sent someone to join his deceased loved one.

When she was finished, she returned to the bedroom and took Tommy Livingston's hands, pressing the fingers around the glass of water. She went into the bathroom to the medicine cabinet and found Sylvia's bottle of chloral hydrate. She shook out all but two and wiped the bottle clean. Then she pressed his fingers around that, too. Faye would be proud of her, she thought.

Satisfied she had done everything right, she put his left arm across his diaphragm and drew his right arm over it so the hands rested gently. She watched him for a moment.

"Goodbye, Mr. Livingston," she said. "I know you'll give my love to Sylvia."

She turned and left the bedroom and paused only to go into the living room on her way out, just so she could check the expression on Sylvia's face in some of the photographs. All the smiles had returned. There was thank you written on the lips in every picture, too.

"Don't thank me," she murmured. "It's why I'm here; what I am to do."

She slipped out of the house and into the night softly, but when she had driven away, she accelerated so she could feel

the warm breeze lift her hair and fill her with a sense of excitement and life.

In Faye's black BMW convertible with her hair in the wind
and her white uniform picking up any light she passed or that
passed her, Susie truly looked like Death Itself, fleeing glee-
fully from Its latest triumph.

Corpsy had sat attentively and watched that house, catching every shadowy movement in the windows. He had
thought about sneaking up to it and peeking in. After all, he
had to know what his beloved was doing. He was afraid to get
out and go up to the house because he thought she might
emerge from it at any moment. When some time had passed
and she hadn't, he got out and scurried across the road. He
climbed over the small brick wall and scampered over the
lawn to the side of the house. He gazed into the first lit window and saw an older man sleeping. Moments later, he saw
Susie come in and help the man drink something.

She was only taking care of him, he thought, and he
breathed in relief. This wasn't any kind of love affair. But he
wondered why she was wearing surgical gloves. When she re-
appeared a few moments later, he saw her do a strange thing.
She put the glass and then a pill bottle into his hands. Why?
To get his fingerprints on them, he concluded. He was sure
it was something her sister had told her to do.

He darted back to his own vehicle and waited until she
emerged from the house and drove off. He followed her back
to the apartment complex and pulled into his dark space just
as she started up the steps to her front door. She heard him
drive up, for when she reached the door, she paused and
turned to look.

She was looking his way, but surely she couldn't see him in
these shadows, he thought. Still, his heart pounded because
she was gazing in his direction. She lingered a moment and
then she went into her apartment. He took some deep
breaths and sat there. He reviewed what he had accomplished this first day. He hadn't spoken a word to Susie, but
he had learned where she and Faye lived and he had learned

she liked soft rock. That was a good start. Tomorrow he would find a way to approach her or Faye. Satisfied, he started the engine and drove off.

He had no way of knowing that Susie had not closed her apartment door completely. She had kept it open a crack and stood there peering out in his direction. She waited.

"What is it?" Faye asked from behind.

"Someone's out there, just sitting in a car in the dark."

"Let me see."

Faye pulled her aside and looked out herself just as Corpsy started his vehicle and backed up. For a moment he and his car were under one of the parking lot lamps. Faye squinted.

"There's something familiar about that car and that man," she muttered.

"That's what I thought."

"How could you have thought that? You didn't see it clearly."

"I just thought so, that's all. Who was it?"

"I don't know . . . I'm not sure."

"Yes you are."

"Never mind that. Why did you rush out of here when I was in the bathroom? Where have you been?"

"I went to see Mr. Livingston," Susie said proudly.

"But he was at his son's for dinner."

"I was there when he returned and he was happy to see me. I helped him relax."

"What else did you do, Susie?"

"I made him some tea and had him eat a biscuit."

"Susie?"

"It was time," Susie said.

Faye stared. Then she crossed the living room quickly and went into her bedroom. She pulled open a drawer and sifted through her pill bottles. Susie was standing in the doorway.

"You used chloral hydrate."

"It was his wife's sleeping pills. Just like Mr. Murray used his wife's insulin," Susie said proudly. "And I wiped everything clean. See, I even wore your surgical gloves." She pulled the pair from her uniform pocket.

Faye sat down on the bed.

"The Livingstons are together again and a perfect love affair goes on into eternity, just the way all Mommies and Daddies should go on," Susie said. After a moment she asked, "Why don't you say something, Faye? You're just sitting there staring at the floor."

"Not all Mommies and Daddies should be together forever, Susie."

"Of course they should. Faye, when I left I looked at Sylvia's picture and she was smiling again. Just like Mommy was smiling in all her pictures."

"She wasn't smiling, Susie," Faye said. "She was crying."

"That's a silly thing to say. Why do you say such things? I'm tired," Susie said quickly, afraid to hear the answer. "I always get tired afterward. I'm going to sleep. Good night."

"Good night," Faye said. When she looked up, Susie was gone, which was good, for she wouldn't see the tears streaming down Faye's face.

14

Perry Livingston jumped in his seat when his car phone rang; he was deep in his thoughts. He couldn't help feeling guilty about returning to work so soon after his mother's death, but the contemplation of all that paperwork piling up on his desk overwhelmed his sense of grief and mourning. He decided he would go to the office for just a little while to clear away some of the more important stuff. He could be in and out without most people realizing it and he would take no phone calls. This rationalization was enough to get him into his suit and tie and send him out of the house.

"What are you doing?" Todd demanded after Perry said hello. "I called your house and Grace said you were on your way to work."

"Just going in for a few minutes to get rid of the ASAP business."

"I can stay home from work and you can't? What's my ASAP business, less important?"

"I just thought . . . even Dad says we've got to get on with our lives, Todd."

"He means after a decent period of mourning. Anyway, Dad's why I'm calling."

"Why? What's up?"

"Did you try to call him this morning?"

"Dad? No, I thought it was too early so . . ."

"I've been calling and calling but there's no answer."

Perry lifted his foot from the accelerator.

"No answer? Maybe he got up early and left the house."

"He wouldn't do that. Where would he go? He doesn't have any ASAP business."

Perry pulled to the side of the road.

"You sure you let it ring long enough?"

"Nearly ten times each time I called."

"Maybe he was in the shower."

"I've called every ten minutes for the last hour, Perry," Todd said. "I'm not stupid."

"Okay, I'll turn around and go back that way," Perry said. "I'll meet you there in five minutes."

"Right."

As he turned around, Perry chastised himself for not calling his father first thing in the morning. His father should have been his first thought, not the pile of papers on his desk.

Why wouldn't Dad answer the phone? He sped up, his pulse quickening so that he could actually feel it vibrating in his neck.

Todd had obviously left his house right after he had ended his conversation, Perry thought, for his brother pulled up behind him only a moment or so after he had turned into the driveway.

"He'll probably bawl us out for rushing over here," Perry said. He smiled a tight, nervous smile as Todd joined him, but Todd's gaze fell on his father's newspaper, still lying on the walkway. He bent down and in one motion took a step and scooped up the paper.

Perry's younger brother was much stouter and broader shouldered. He had been the athlete, the high school and college football player, whereas Perry had been the student, the debater, the thespian. If anyone made a comparison in a deprecating manner, Sylvia Livingston would always claim to be happy her boys were so different. "They're individuals," she would brag, "each his own man and each successful in his own way." She was proud that there hadn't been very much sibling rivalry, but there hadn't been very much sibling love, either.

So unalike in temperament and manner, they could never partner up to inherit Tommy Livingston's business, even if they had been inclined to do so. They had different groups of friends and amused themselves in different ways. Their taste in clothing, homes and cars was dramatically dissimilar, too. And the contrasting personalities of their respective wives—Bobbi, who was more casual and colloquial in speech and more like the California girl of the Beach Boys songs; Perry's wife Grace, who was more concerned about style and elegance, a product of an Eastern finishing school—reinforced the dissimilarity of the two brothers.

Perry tried ringing the doorbell, but they heard no sound from within. After a moment he rapped hard on the door.

"Dad!"

They waited.

"Check the garage. See if his car's in there," Todd ordered. Perry cupped his hands around his eyes to peer through the small window in the door.

"It's there. Maybe he left with someone else in their car."

"Dad!" Todd rapped harder.

"Maybe he just went for a walk," Perry added, but not with any confidence. Todd just shook his head.

"I've got a key to the house on my car key chain," Perry remembered. He rushed back to get it.

"What the hell's going on? Why would he leave the house without letting us know and where would he go?" Todd thought aloud as Perry returned and inserted the key.

They opened the door and looked at each other. No lights, no sounds; nothing was what greeted them.

"Dad?"

"Dad?" Perry followed.

The two brothers hurried down the hallway, glanced in the kitchen and then turned to the master bedroom. The moment they set eyes on him, there was no question in either of their minds that their father had passed away. Neither let the reality set in, however, and both rushed to his bedside. Todd seized Tommy's right hand and shook it hard.

"Dad!"

Perry put out his hand slowly and placed his fingers against his father's neck, vainly searching for a throbbing. But Perry Livingston merely had to look at his father's eyes to confirm his worst fears. Tommy's eyes were glassy and still, that spark Shakespeare had called "the Quick" was gone. They were fixed in his head now like two old marbles, their color faded.

"What happened to him?" Todd cried. Perry shook his head and then fixed his gaze on the pill bottle and the glass of water.

"Sleeping pills," he said lifting the pill bottle to read the label. "They were Mom's. He must have taken too many, there are only two left."

"No, he wouldn't do that. Let's call a doctor. Maybe it's not too late. Maybe . . ."

"It's too late," Perry declared, his words hammering the reality home. Nevertheless, Todd went to the phone and dialed 911 to report an emergency. Then he flopped back into the chair at the side of the bed and stared at his father's corpse dumbly while Perry went to the window and gazed out at the yard in which he had spent many happy hours playing. If only it were possible to blink and send yourself back in time. He'd never long to be eighteen or twenty-one; he wouldn't rush the clock; he'd be a little boy forever, for his mother would forever be young and happy and his father would be strong, immortal.

It was too much: losing their mother and then their father in so short a space of time; it was too much.

Perry turned, tears streaming down his cheeks, and shook his head. The sound of an ambulance siren could be heard in the distance, the anthem of hope now an anthem of futility.

"Nolan wants to see you," Billy Gibson, the dispatcher, told Frankie the moment he entered the station. He nodded and looked around. "Where's everyone?"

"Rosina and Derek are on that car wash stakeout. There was a violent marital dispute in that trailer park off South Canyon and a burglary last night at Pizza Hut."

"Pizza Hut? What they take?"

Billy shrugged.

"Dough."

"Very funny."

Frankie crossed to Nolan's office. The door was open and Nolan was on the phone. He waved Frankie in.

"Yeah, I'm going to bring that up with the city fathers tonight," he said into the receiver. "In the meantime, see what you can do for us. We're cutting it too close." He hung up without saying goodbye and sat back. "How's that loose end coming?"

"I found out there was a maid in the Murray apartment the night before he allegedly committed suicide."

Nolan looked surprised.

"Yeah? And?"

"I haven't been able to locate her yet. No cleaning agency employed her."

"You got a name?"

"Just a first name, but enough of a physical description to ID her."

"Try the neighbors."

"That's how I got what I got. I was going back to sniff around some more this morning."

"Good. But before you do that," Nolan said, his lips quivering as if he were fighting an urge to break into laughter, "I got another loose end for you."

"What d'ya mean?"

"There's another apparent suicide . . . man's name is Thomas Livingston. Here's the address. The paramedics are still at the scene."

Frankie took the slip of paper from Nolan.

"You're kidding?"

"Sure you're up to all this work?" Nolan asked him.

"I'll manage."

"When is your pacemaker being installed?"

"I'm supposed to hear from the doctor any day," Frankie said.

"Okay. Let me know what this is all about," Nolan said, starting to punch out a number on his phone.

The ambulance was still in the driveway and the front door of the house was wide open when Frankie pulled up. He found Jack Martin in the hallway.

"Look who's back in the saddle," Martin quipped.

"What do we have, wise-ass?" Frankie asked.

"Well, I'm no detective," Jack said, smiling, "but it looks like he overdosed on his wife's sleeping pills."

"Touch anything?"

"Just the corpse." Jack lowered his voice and leaned toward Frankie. "The victim's sons are in the living room," he said shifting his eyes toward it.

Frankie nodded and entered Tommy Livingston's bedroom first. Jack's assistant was just putting away their gear.

"Couldn't do much. He's been dead awhile," he said. Frankie nodded toward the pill bottle on the night table.

"That what did it?"

"If he took all that was supposedly in there . . . no problem. That's chloral hydrate. The label says there were fifty capsules. His wife's name's on it."

"Anything else?"

"No marks on his body, if that's what you mean," Jack said. "We called the coroner already."

"Thanks. I better go talk to the sons."

He found Perry and Todd sitting on the sofa, both looking pale and stunned, both with bloodshot eyes.

"I'm Detective Samuels," Frankie said, showing his ID.

"I'm Todd Livingston. This is my brother, Perry. We found my father in his bed and called the ambulance."

"Is your mother here or . . ."

"Our mother died two days ago," Perry said. "That's why he did it."

Frankie stared down at them a moment. A second case of suicide with the same motivation within two weeks?

"When did either of you see or speak to him last?"

"He was at my house for dinner last night," Todd said.

"Did he give you any indication he was going to do this?"

"What do you think?" Todd said angrily. "If he had, do you think I'd have let him go home and be alone?"

"I'm just trying to do this as fast as I can so you guys aren't bothered at what has to be a terrible time of grief for you," Frankie explained softly. "Any unattended death has to be investigated."

Perry looked down.

"Neither of us expected it," Todd said. "My father was made of iron. He was devastated by my mother's death, just like we all were, but he was the sort of man who always came back."

Perry straightened up in his seat. "It's the Livingston backbone," he added. "We come from a long line of independent, strong people who go back to the forefathers of this country, men who overcame extraordinary obstacles to make a name and a place for themselves," he said proudly.

"Did either of you know he was taking your mother's pills or give him the pills to take?"

"No," Perry snapped. Then he looked at Todd. "Right?"

"No, we didn't know. He didn't say anything about them when he was at my house for dinner, and when he left . . . I just thought he was going home to go to sleep. He was tired and he didn't have much appetite. Other than that . . . there was no warning."

"Anyone touch that pill bottle?" Frankie asked.

"I'm afraid I did," Todd said.

"I'll need a copy of your prints," Frankie said.

"Why?"

"Just to eliminate any we find and see if there are any we can't ID."

"What about the nurse?" Todd asked Perry.

"Nurse?" Frankie inquired.

"My mother's private-duty nurse. She was here after the funeral," Perry said.

"What's her name?"

"Sullivan. Susie Sullivan."

"No, that's her sister's name," Todd said. "Her name was Faye."

"Sister?"

"She has a sister who came by to help Dad . . . clean, cook."

"A maid?" Frankie asked quickly. "Named Susie?"

"Yeah," Todd said. "But she wasn't here yesterday."

"Are you sure?"

"Pretty sure. Dad didn't mention she was when he was at dinner."

Frankie thought a moment.

"How about after he came home?"

"I don't know," Todd said. He looked at Perry, who shook his head.

"Can you describe this maid?"

"I never saw her. I just spoke to her on the phone," Todd said. Frankie looked at Perry.

"I never saw her, either."

"But you're positive her name is Susie?"

"Yeah. Why is that so important?" Todd asked.

"I just have to have accurate information," Frankie said as he scribbled in his notepad.

"I've got to call my wife," Todd said.

"Me too," Perry said.

Jack Martin poked his head in.

"Coroner's here, Frankie," he said.

"Thanks."

"What happens now?" Perry asked.

"Your father's body will be taken to autopsy. The coroner has to hold an inquest and determine the cause of death."

They all looked toward the door as the attendants rolled the gurney past the living room.

"I can't believe we're going to be making funeral arrangements again," Todd said shaking his head.

Perry buried his face in his hands.

"My family, my children . . . another nightmare."

Todd finally gave in and started to sob. He turned away.

Frankie closed his notepad.

"I'm sorry," he said. Then he went back to the bedroom to bag the empty pill bottle and peruse the room one more time before hurrying out and heading toward the Desert Hospital.

He had gotten to know most of the hospital clerical staff. Some were very cooperative and pleasant, some were bitchy, complaining about being overworked as it was and resenting him for doing the slightest thing to make their workload any bigger. Henrietta Scheinwald was on duty when he arrived, and the fifty-four-year-old woman liked him. But Henrietta was in the middle of training a new employee, Cindy Kizer. The contrast between the flighty twenty-four-year-old strawberry blonde and her tutor was striking. Cindy listened with half an ear on what Henrietta was explaining and with half on what was going on around her in the hallways and outer offices. She had the attention span of a preteen, but she was skilled enough with the word processor and attractive enough for the hospital administrator to hire her. Now Henrietta was left with the burden.

Frankie watched them for a few moments from the doorway before tapping on the jamb. Cindy looked grateful for the interruption.

"Hello, Frankie. How are you feeling?"

"Fine, thanks, Henrietta."

"You're not working, are you?" she asked grimacing.

"Sorta."

"Frankie," she chastised.

"Just passing the time until I gotta have my implant," he said. "Don't be like my wife."

"Men." She looked at Cindy, who smiled with amusement at the way Henrietta chastised this man.

"I need a favor," he said. "I've got to look at someone's file quickly."

"Uh huh." She rolled her eyes and shook her head. "This is Detective Samuels, Cindy. Occasionally, more often than ever these days, unfortunately, he or one of his fellow officers stops by to get information."

"Really?" Cindy said, wide-eyed.

"What is it you need, Frankie?" Henrietta asked.

"I'd like to look at a nurse's file . . . a Faye Sullivan."

"Oh yes. Well, she's primarily a special-duty nurse here. She works for the agency, but, of course, we have her background."

Henrietta went to her computer terminal and tapped out the commands. What Frankie liked the most about Henrietta Scheinwald was her respect for confidentiality. Unlike most of the others, she did not widen her eyes with interest and try to find out why he wanted the information.

"You want a hard copy or do you want to simply read it off the screen?" she asked.

"I'll just read it," he said. He took out his notepad. Henrietta rose and went back to Cindy, and Frankie took her seat in front of the monitor.

"All right, Cindy. Let's get back to what I was showing you. Whenever we have to process a claim through Blue Cross . . ."

Frankie focused on the information before him and copied down what he wanted as quickly as he could. Then he thanked Henrietta and left for the police station, anxious to a wipe that smug, condescending smile off Nolan's ugly face.

15

Faye stood beside Saul Weinstein in the corridor outside his wife's hospital room as Dr. Stanley continued to explain Lilly Weinstein's diagnosis. Dr. Stanley was rapidly becoming one of her favorite physicians. Despite his age she considered him a prime example of the new breed: doctors who practiced what they preached: sensible diet and exercise, no smoking. He certainly didn't look fifty-one. He stood six feet two with dark brown hair and youthful, vibrant hazel-green eyes.

She especially admired the cardiologist for his tolerance of elderly people, whether they were his patients or the close relatives of his patients. He spoke slowly, but never condescendingly, and always struggled to be certain that his patient or the patient's spouse fully understood what was happening, why, and what would be prescribed. He had a talent for simplifying the most complicated problems without diminishing their significance. This was only the third time she had been on special duty for one of his patients, but she sensed a mutual respect. Early this morning he had specifically requested her from the service.

"If you have any further questions about your wife's condition, you can certainly ask Miss Sullivan. Whatever she can't answer for you, she'll relay to me and I'll get back to you," he said. Saul looked at Faye and nodded, but not without a glint of dark worry in his eyes. He turned back to the doctor.

"It wasn't too soon to take her out of CCU?" he asked.

"As I said, she no longer has any pain or discomfort, and it looks like she's had a characteristic bout of angina."

Saul grimaced and shook his head.

"You're sure it was her heart? Not just gas?"

Dr. Stanley nodded, but saw that the elderly man was not fully convinced.

"Listen Saul, angina pectoris, as it is called, is essentially a symptom. We've ruled out hiatus hernia, gastritis, gallbladder disease. . . . What happened was her heart didn't get enough blood."

"I saw her pressing her hand to her chest often, but whenever I asked, she'd say, 'It's just gas.' "

"It's not gas," Dr. Stanley repeated patiently.

"Why is her heart not getting enough blood? She eats well. She's not overweight . . ."

"One of the major coronary arteries is arteriosclerotic . . . It gets hard as we get older and loses its elasticity." Dr. Stanley made a small circle with his left forefinger and thumb and held it up. He pressed the thumb against the forefinger, moving them both in and out to make the opening smaller and larger.

"Imagine this is the artery. It has to move like this to push the blood through, see?" He gazed at Faye, who smiled, her eyes dancing with amusement. Weinstein nodded, his gaze fixed on the doctor's fingers. "But when it gets too hard, it doesn't move the blood to the heart fast enough, and blood carries much-needed oxygen."

"Then she had a heart attack?" Saul concluded fatalistically.

"No, not in the sense you mean. Her heart muscle remains relatively undamaged. What we're going to do is treat this artery. I've prescribed a vasodilator. It's not blocked enough to warrant any surgical procedure. We're just determining the right dosages, watching her carefully. Afterward, she's got to watch her diet, get plenty of rest, avoid emotional strain . . ."

Faye smiled at the doctor who continued to rattle off the therapy and prognosis, but something drew her back to the doorway of Lilly Weinstein's room and she gazed almost absentmindedly at the heart monitor.

The R wave was on the T.

"Stat!" she screamed, and she rushed into the room to begin CPR. Dr. Stanley and Saul Weinstein came in right behind her. Weinstein gazed at the screen of the heart monitor in terror as the doctor and the nurse continued to work on his wife. In moments, the waves returned to a normal pattern and they both stepped back from the patient.

"Nice going," Dr. Stanley said. Faye beamed.

"What happened?" Saul asked, his eyes wide and his face bone-white. The head floor nurse and an aide stood beside him and two other nurses had rushed up the corridor and stood in the doorway.

"She's all right now. Take it easy, Mr. Weinstein."

"But . . ."

"We're going to move her back to CCU," Dr. Stanley said, nodding at the head nurse. She moved immediately to start the process. "Angina can be the first sign of something more serious going on. Fortunately, whatever it is, it happened here, and fortunately Nurse Sullivan was about as sharp and as effective as any nurse I've seen."

Saul looked back at Faye gratefully as she worked on making Lilly Weinstein comfortable. He nodded and let the doctor lead him out to the corridor where he would continue to explain what the possibilities were and what had to be done diagnostically now that this event had occurred.

Faye was flush with excitement. She had literally pulled this woman back from the dead, reached out and seized hold of her as she was drifting down into the dark, sliding, slipping, falling . . .

Now Faye stood beside her and watched her breathe, watched her chest lift and fall, watched her eyes move, watched her fingers twitch. She drank in all of these signs of life as if she had created it instead of saved it. In a sense she had re-created it, hadn't she? It wasn't blasphemous to think like this. God wouldn't have given her the power and the perception, the skill and the talent if He didn't mean for her to have it. She always acknowledged Him and thanked Him. But that didn't mean she couldn't feel ecstatic. She couldn't wait to tell Susie about this.

Lilly Weinstein groaned.

"You're all right, Mrs. Weinstein. You're all right," Faye reassured her. She stroked her face softly.

"My husband . . ."

"He's right outside. I'll send him in as soon as he finishes talking to the doctor. You two will be together shortly. Don't you worry."

Faye assisted in moving Lilly Weinstein back to CCU. Once that was accomplished, her private-duty responsibilities had ended for the time being. Saul Weinstein was waiting outside the CCU when she emerged.

"She's doing fine. They'll watch her very carefully now, Mr. Weinstein, and they'll know exactly what else happened to her and what should be done."

"Thank you," he said. "When she comes out again, you'll be here? You'll take care of her?"

"Of course, I will, Mr. Weinstein. And I'll be checking in with the CCU periodically to see how she's doing. Now you relax so you don't get sick yourself. When she comes home, you're going to have to be strong enough to take care of her."

"She's always taken care of me. Who would think she would be sick like this?" he said shaking his head.

"Don't upset yourself this way, Mr. Weinstein. You'll only get sick yourself. Trust in your doctor. He's one of the best cardiologists I've worked with."

Saul nodded. Anything this wonderful nurse told him to do or believe was fine with him. The doctor couldn't stop raving about her and he had seen himself firsthand how good she was.

"I'll go see her now."

"Just for a little while and then go home and get some sleep." Faye smiled, the warmth returning as quickly as it had disappeared. "Promise?"

"I promise," he said, smiling. "Somehow, I always have pretty women looking after me."

Faye squeezed his arm affectionately and walked off, never feeling more complete, never feeling happier with herself. She took the elevator down and walked through the now relatively quiet and empty first-floor corridor and paused by the doorway of the cafeteria. She felt like treating herself to a reward, perhaps one of those chocolate fudge nut ice cream bars Susie loved so much. As she leaned over to pluck one out of the freezer, she felt someone come up behind her and she turned to look into Corpsy Ratner's smile.

For a moment the sight of someone from another hospital in which she had previously worked, someone dressed in his blues, confused her. It was as if she had been dropped back through time, or as if all that had passed since were merely a dream. She blinked rapidly and took a deep breath.

"Hello, Faye," Corpsy said. "How have you been?"

"You're . . . Arnold?"

"That's right," he said, his smiling widening. "Arnold Ratner. We used to talk all the time in Phoenix."

"But what . . . why are you here?"

He shrugged and looked around.

"I decided to be as close to you and your sister Susie as I could," he replied with such nonchalance that his words didn't register their impact immediately.

"What?"

"I want to see Susie, Faye," he said sharply, his smile evaporating. "There's no reason for us not to meet now."

"You came all the way from Phoenix, followed us?" Faye asked, the realization of what he had done taking form.

"Of course," he said. "I tried to tell you back in Phoenix how much I wanted to meet Susie, how important it was that we meet and get to know each other, but you wouldn't listen."

Faye started to edge herself away, moving along the freezer. She shook her head.

"You're out of your mind," she told him. "You had no right

to follow us here, no right. My sister is not for you. You leave us alone," she said firmly.

"Now listen, Faye . . ."

"Get away from me," Faye snapped, pivoting quickly to hurry out of the cafeteria. She practically jogged down the corridor, her heart racing, and she didn't look back. She burst out of the hospital and quickened her pace even more, but when she reached the parking lot and turned down the row of cars to get to her vehicle, she heard Corpsy walking just behind her.

"If you don't get away from me, I'll call the police," Faye threatened. Corpsy stopped as if she had struck him, but instead of cowering back, he took slower, more determined steps toward her, his eyes dark and small.

"You're not going to call the police, Faye. You're making Susie do things and I know about it. If you call the police, I'll have to tell them."

"You raving idiot. What are you talking about?"

"I told you in Phoenix . . . amyl nitrate. I know it brings on a heart attack, but its presence could be missed. And I saw Susie last night. I followed her to that house and I looked in the window. I saw her give that man something to drink and make sure his fingerprints were on the glass. Is he all right today?" Corpsy inquired with a smile, confident of the answer.

Faye stared, but did not move or speak. Corpsy was encouraged. It was working; his plan was working.

"Why can't we all be friends and then . . . relatives? Why can't we be a family?"

"I don't know what you're saying," Faye muttered. She shook her head. "My sister is a gentle, loving person. She doesn't hurt people."

"Of course she doesn't. I never said she did," Corpsy replied. He looked angry. "And no one better say anything else, either." He relaxed. "She's just following your instructions, I know. What are you doing, mercy killings? It doesn't matter to me," he added quickly. "I'm sure you're doing the right thing, whatever it is."

Faye stared at him for a moment. The man's madness intrigued her, but more important, relieved her. He did like Susie and wouldn't do anything to hurt her. They were safe . . . safe. She relaxed her shoulders and smiled.

"Susie is a very, very shy young woman," Faye said. "I tried to explain that to you in Phoenix."

"I know, and I don't mean to frighten her."

"Then you have to meet her slowly. You can't just burst in on her. She would be terrified."

He nodded, happy now that he hadn't approached her abruptly during any of the recent opportunities.

"I understand."

"Where do you live?"

"I'm just staying in a motel here. I don't really work in this hospital. I thought I'd tell you that so you wouldn't be overwhelmed at the sight of me," he confessed.

Faye nodded and smiled. He was a patient now, a disturbed young man who needed her professional expertise. She had to win his trust and confidence, just as she had to win the trust and confidence of her patients in the hospital.

"That was very clever of you, Arnold. You're a bright young man. I'll be sure to tell Susie that and describe all that you've done to be considerate of her feelings."

He beamed.

"Will you? That's very nice of you."

"Does anyone else know you came here looking for us?" Faye asked with a warm smile.

"Just my mother," he said. "But she won't be upset. Whatever I want to do, she wants to do; whatever I like, she likes." He blushed and shrugged. "I just told her I was going to Palm Springs to find the woman I love."

"The woman you love? How . . . sweet," Faye said. "All right." Faye gazed at her watch. "Why don't you give me time to explain things to Susie first. She gets so nervous whenever she has to meet a man." Corpsy nodded. "We could all have dinner and break the ice later. Would that be all right?"

"Dinner? Sure. You just name the place. I don't care how much it costs," he said, visibly excited.

"I'll find out the name of a good place. What's the name of your motel, and what's your room number?" He told her and she jotted it down. "Just go back there and wait," she said. "Don't get nervous if it takes awhile. Susie is so afraid to meet new people, it's going to take me awhile to build her courage and get her prepared."

"I understand."

"That's good. You are a smart young man, Arnold. Susie needs a smart young man and a sincere young man."

"I'm sincere," he declared firmly.

"I can see that. I'll be in touch." She smiled at him and he watched her get into her car. She looked back after backing out of her space and smiled again. He nodded and stood there as she drove off.

It was working; it was going to happen. In a matter of hours, he would be brought face to face with the woman he loved, and the woman, he was sure, who would love him. Never more satisfied with himself, he headed for his own car to return to the motel and wait.

He wouldn't just sit there and wait, however. He would decide on things: the best clothes to wear, the things he should say, and how he should behave. First impressions are the most significant, Ma always said. His fingers trembled as he inserted the key in the ignition. Was he ever excited about anything as much as he was excited right now?

"Go on," Nolan said. Frankie looked at his notes.

"This er . . . this private-duty nurse, Faye Sullivan, took care of Dorothy Murray, and I'm pretty sure her sister was the maid who was with Sam Murray the day and maybe the night before he was found dead."

"Yeah?"

"This might explain where the Dilantin came from."

"From the maid?"

"Who could have gotten it from her sister because her sister is a nurse."

"Doesn't mean murder. She gets him sleeping pills and later he did himself in, right? I mean, why would she want to kill the old man?"

Frankie held up his hand to indicate Nolan should give him a chance.

"Faye Sullivan took care of Sylvia Livingston, Thomas Livingston's wife, and her sister was looking after Thomas shortly before his death. Thomas was at his son Todd's house for dinner last night and no one there got the impression he was bent on checking himself out. He also used sleeping pills."

Nolan shrugged.

"Violent methods turn people off. Even a depressed, suicidal individual can be afraid of the sight of his or her own blood."

"I know that, but there's more. I went to the hospital and checked the employee records. This Faye Sullivan's been around. A lot," he added. Nolan was still not impressed. Frankie looked at his notes. "Before here she was in Phoenix; before Phoenix, Miami; before Miami, Richmond; before Richmond, St. Louis; before . . ."

"All right, so she doesn't hold a position long or she likes to travel. So?"

"I called the Phoenix Police Department and I got them checking out some of the recent suicides, especially the ones that follow this pattern: husband or wife dies, Faye Sullivan was the special-duty nurse, her sister stepped in to help the bereaved who then off'd him or herself shortly thereafter. That," Frankie punched, "would be considered a suspicious pattern, don't you think?"

Nolan stared. It was his way of eating crow, accepting, being shown to have been too flippant, and admitting Frankie had done good police work . . . most of all, admitting that Frankie did have a detective's instincts, whereas he . . . he had a ways to go.

"What did they tell you?"

"I'm waiting for them to get back to me."

"Did you question the sister who's a maid?"

"I was going to do that right after I heard from Phoenix."

Nolan nodded, his face finally reflecting his admission of the probabilities.

"What the hell could possibly be the motive?" he wondered aloud.

"I got a feeling we won't find that out until we lock up a case, make an arrest, and bring them in for questioning and maybe psychoanalysis," Frankie replied.

"Rosina's close to breaking that car parts thievery ring over at the car wash," Nolan said in as apologetic a tone as he was capable of. "Otherwise, I'd pull her off and . . ."

"I can handle this myself," Frankie said. "After all, it's just a nurse and her handicapped sister."

Nolan didn't say anything. Frankie smiled to himself, got up, and went to his desk to wait for his phone call from Phoenix, but a call came from Jennie first.

"Dr. Pauling's office just phoned. He's scheduling you for tomorrow."

"What? I thought it would be more like a week to ten days."

"He had a cancellation and can fit you in, Frankie. I thought you'd be happy to get it over with."

"I'm happy. It's just . . . a surprise," he said. "Are you sure?"

"Call them yourself."

"I'll check it out," he told her, and then phoned the doctor. His receptionist confirmed Jennie's message.

"We'd like you to check in early and . . ."

"I got a problem," Frankie said.

"Oh. Let me see if I can patch through to Dr. Pauling."

Frankie waited, his heart pounding. Jennie would be absolutely furious.

"Mr. Samuels?"

"Hi, Doc," Frankie began. He explained that he was at the tail end of an important investigation.

"You're on the job?"

"I not doing anything strenuous, just detailed investigative stuff, but we're sort of short-handed right now and I'm the one who's brought this thing to something of a climax."

"It can't wait?"

"Someone else might die," Frankie said, not meaning to be dramatic.

"Let's hope that someone else isn't you, Mr. Samuels," the doctor replied. It brought the blood rushing into Frankie's face.

"You told me it wasn't a life-or-death situation, Doc."

"As long as you don't get into vigorous physical activity. But I'm just your doctor, Mr. Samuels. I'm not the one who determines your destiny."

This guy doesn't like to be contradicted, Frankie thought.

"Look," Frankie began.

"All right, Mr. Samuels. I'll put you back to where you were on my schedule and move someone else forward. But I'm documenting our conversation. With the malpractice frenzy going on in this country . . ."

"I understand."

"Watch yourself, Mr. Samuels," he warned, and their conversation ended.

All the little white lies accumulated over all the years he and Jennie had been married wouldn't amount to diddly compared to the one he was about to tell her when he called her back.

16

"Why are you home so early?" Susie asked the moment Faye stepped into the apartment. Faye didn't respond. She closed the door and then leaned back against it. Her face was white with rage, the corners of her mouth the color of bone. Susie hobbled into the living room. "What's wrong? Did you lose your patient?"

"No, you little fool. Did I ever come home this upset after a patient expired?"

"Then what is it? What's wrong?" Susie asked, letting Faye's nastiness roll over her.

"He's here. He followed us all the way from Phoenix because of you."

"Who?"

"That . . . man I told you they call Corpsy. Arnold Ratner. He works in the pathology department. I thought it was him the other night when I looked out. He's been spying on us, spying on you!"

"What do you mean?" Susie rested her left hand on the back of the sofa and brought her right hand to the base of her throat. "When was he spying on me?"

"He followed you to Tommy Livingston's house and looked through the window. He saw you give him the sleeping medication. He knows all about you."

"What does he want?" Susie asked, aghast.

"He's in love with you, you fool. I told you when we were in Phoenix. He thinks you'll marry him and we'll all live happily ever after. A family," she said smirking.

"Where is he?"

"At a motel. I told him we would all go out to dinner later and that satisfied him."

"What are we going to do, Faye?"

"Pack and leave. What do you think?"

"But he might follow us again."

Faye thought a moment.

"Right?" Susie pursued.

"Yes, he might. First, we'll pack and then we'll deal with him," Faye said. "I knew you would get us into terrible trouble some day. I just knew it. I should have left you behind."

"That's not fair, Faye. It's not fair to blame it all on me. You know it's not fair."

"Never mind. We don't have time to argue now." She marched through the living room and went to the closet to pull out their suitcases. Then she opened the dresser drawer and began to pack.

"Where will we go, Faye?" Susie asked from the doorway.

"North. Maybe Portland. Start getting your things together," she ordered. Just as Susie turned, they heard the door buzzer and then a pounding.

"He followed me home!" Faye exclaimed. "He's here!"

"What should I do?"

"Nothing. Just let me talk to him. Go into your bedroom and wait," Faye said. She started toward the door. The buzzer went off again, and again there was pounding. "The man's a raving lunatic," Faye muttered, but when she opened the door, she found Tillie Kaufman. Both she and Tillie breathed sighs of relief.

"Oh, thank God you're home," Tillie cried.

"What's wrong?"

"Faye, please! It's Morris!"

"Morris? Oh yes," she muttered. "I almost forgot."

She turned as she stepped out and looked back to see Susie standing in the hallway, smiling.

Twenty minutes later, the paramedics pulled up to their apartment complex. Faye, still dressed in her nurse's uniform, waited in the Kaufman's doorway.

"Stroke," she announced as the paramedics hurried up the walkway.

The two emergency attendants moved quickly into the apartment, barely noticing Tillie Kaufman seated in the living room near her stricken husband, her eyes red with tears, a handkerchief clutched in her hands and pressed to her mouth to stifle her fear and sorrow. Faye had placed a pillow under Morris Kaufman's head and a blanket over him. The paramedics examined him, and in moment they had Morris Kaufman strapped on a stretcher, his vitals analyzed.

"Looks like a cerebral hemorrhage," one of the paramedics whispered to Faye as they went by with Morris, who remained unconscious.

"I know," she said. Tillie stood up and began to gasp at the sight of her husband being carried off. His skin had already taken on the pasty pallor of a corpse and his body jiggled like so much dead protoplasm on a slab as the paramedics twisted and turned to get him out of the apartment.

"He just collapsed," Tillie cried. "He screamed, grabbed his head like this," she said pressing her palms against her temples, "and then he fell to the floor. I couldn't lift him, and there was blood coming out of his nose."

"You did what you could, and you got to me. The paramedics got here fast, too, didn't they?"

"I've got to go to the hospital," Tillie said as if she were just realizing it. "I've got to be with him."

"Of course you do. I'll take you to the hospital. Wash your face and get hold of yourself."

"Thank you, Faye. Thank you. You're better than a daughter to us. We're so lucky to have you and your sister next door. So lucky," she said. She hurried to the bathroom. Faye stepped onto the patio and looked at her doorway. Susie had opened the door far enough to peer out.

"What are you doing?" Susie asked.

"I'm going with her to the hospital."

"My pocketbook," Tillie realized aloud after she came out of the bathroom. "They always want those damn insurance cards. How do they expect you to think at a time like this?"

"I said I would help you. Stop making yourself so sick," Faye called back. Then she looked at Susie. "Don't answer the door and don't answer the phone, you hear me?"

"I hear you," Susie said. She backed into the apartment. A moment later, Faye and Tillie were going down the steps.

They arrived at the hospital minutes after the paramedics had brought Morris into the emergency room. Tillie waited with Faye on the cool red vinyl sofa in the emergency room lounge, twisting her handkerchief in her hands as if she expected to squeeze some precious juice out of it. Every time they heard footsteps in the corridor, her eyes spun up in anticipation.

Finally, the doctor emerged from the examination room and came looking for them in the lounge. Faye stood up. It was that young intern, Dr. Hoffman. He had emergency room duty. He smiled at her and then turned to Tillie, the smile quickly evaporating.

"You're Mrs. Kaufman?" he asked. She nodded. He looked at Faye.

"She's my neighbor," Faye said. "It happened just after I had gotten home from the hospital."

"Oh." He gave her a conspiratorial look, telegraphing the seriousness of the diagnosis.

"Your husband's had a cerebral hemorrhage."

"Brought on by his high blood pressure problem, I'm sure," Faye inserted.

"Most likely," Dr. Hoffman said. "At this point we don't know the full extent of the damage. We've got to run more tests, and then he'll go to ICU. It will be a while before we know enough to make a complete diagnosis, Mrs. Kaufman. You might be better off going home."

Then he pulled Faye aside.

"Looks like middle cerebral artery," he said softly. "He won't come out of the coma," he predicted with deadly certainty. She nodded and turned to Tillie.

"We'll go home and return later, Tillie. There's nothing more to be done right now, and you need some rest."

"Who can rest?" the elderly lady said. She was no longer crying. A deep resignation had set in. "I always hated it whenever he was in the hospital and I was home alone. It's a small apartment, but it always seemed so big when I was by myself."

"I'll give you something to help you sleep, Tillie. You need some rest."

"And you'll stay with Morris? Be his nurse in the hospital?"

"Absolutely."

"We have a little money and there's some insurance . . ."

"Don't worry about the money. I'm not doing this for the money."

Faye drove her home and helped her into the apartment and took her directly to the bedroom.

"See how I always lay out his pajamas," Tillie said, nodding toward the garments draped over a chair. "I've taken care of him so long, I won't know what to do with myself."

"Don't think about that now. Just get some rest."

"I should straighten up a little," Tillie said.

"I'll send Susie in later."

"You're such dolls, you two. Such dolls. Your mother must have been very proud of both of you."

For a moment Faye didn't respond. Then she snapped back the blanket on the bed. "Yes, she was."

She helped Tillie undress, and then she got her some water and handed her some pills.

"This will help you get some needed rest," she said. Tillie eyed them suspiciously.

"I've got my own sleeping pills. Little blue ones."

"These are better, believe me."

Tillie studied them a moment longer, shrugged, and put them into her mouth and followed them with gulps of water. Then she fell back against the pillow, her thin gray hair framing her tired, old face. Faye fixed her blanket and tucked her in.

"He won't die today, will he?" she asked. "I don't want him to die while I'm away from him."

"He won't die today," Faye promised. "And when he does die, you'll be right beside him."

She said it with such certainty and confidence, Tillie Kaufman relaxed. She closed her eyes and let herself sink into the mattress.

"I am tired. So tired. Thank you. Thank you," she muttered.

Faye watched her sleeping for a moment and then quietly left the apartment.

Susie was waiting in the living room.

"Well?" she said the moment Faye stepped in.

"He's got a massive cerebral hemorrhage."

Susie nodded.

"Now we know we have to leave Palm Springs," Faye said.

"Whatever you think is best, Faye," Susie said.

"That's what I think is best. Were there any phone calls?"

"It rang, but I didn't answer it, like you said."

"Good. It must have been that horrible man. He'd surely have called by now."

"What are we going to do?"

Faye dug into her purse and came up with Corpsy's motel number. She went to the phone and asked for his room. He picked the phone up so quickly she was sure he had been hovering over it, anticipating.

"I'm sorry I didn't get back to you sooner," she said. "But our next-door neighbor had a stroke, and I had to get him an ambulance and take his wife to the hospital."

"Oh. Can we still go to dinner?" he asked quickly.

"Yes. We're going to go someplace close to your motel. We'll come by early so we can go someplace and talk?"

"You'll come here?"

"It's all right. Susie is excited about it."

"She is?"

"Yes. Just wait for us in your room," Faye instructed.

"It's a crummy room."

"You don't think Susie cares about that, do you? She's not overwhelmed by a person's material possessions. She's a sincere person."

"I know," Corpsy said. "I guess it's all right. We won't stay here long, anyway."

"No, we won't. Expect us," Faye said. After she hung up, she turned to Susie and smiled.

"Will we be all right, Faye?"

"We will if you do what I tell you to do," she said.

"What?"

"You've got to go see this man and keep him from following us."

"Me? Why me?"

"Because he loves you, so he'll trust you," Faye replied sharply.

"But this is different."

"It isn't different. Do you want to continue doing your good work, or do you want him to stop you?"

"I'm afraid," Susie said softly.

"You don't have to be afraid. I'll tell you exactly what to do," Faye whispered. She smiled. "I'll be with you each and every moment."

Susie took a deep breath.

"Okay?"

"Okay," Susie said, and Faye began to describe her plan.

Frankie jumped on the ringing phone.

"Sorry it took me so long," the detective from Phoenix said. "I had to go out to Scottsdale for you."

"Why?"

"Well, I was able to locate two recent suicides, the spouses of whom died shortly before, and in both cases, your nurse was the private-duty nurse, but I couldn't find anything about any sister who was a maid, so I paid the daughter of one of the suicide victims a visit."

"And?"

"There was a sister, who, as you described, wore a brace

on her leg. She took care of this woman's father after her
mother died. Woman's name was Ruth Kaplow. But I gotta
tell you, she had only laudatory things to say about the maid.
Who, by the way, is this nurse's twin sister. Did you know
that?"

"No, I didn't." Todd and Perry hadn't seen her, so they
hadn't mentioned it. "Twin, huh?"

"Yeah. Ruth Kaplow told me the maid was very considerate and very compassionate. She claims she treated her as if
she were her sister and the old man were her father, too."

"How'd her father do it?"

"He was drinking booze and took Seconals. Ruth Kaplow
says the maid, Susie, tried to stop him from drinking. She ri-
fled through his room until she located every hidden bottle,
but the old guy got some more."

"What about the pills?"

"Her mother's prescription."

"Part of the pattern," Frankie muttered.

"I thought so from what you said. I spent about an hour
with this Kaplow woman. She couldn't stop talking about this
maid and her sister. But she did say something I thought you
might want to follow up."

"What?"

"Apparently their father committed suicide after their
mother died."

"She told her that?"

"Yeah."

"Thanks. I will look into it. What about the other suicide?"

"Couldn't find anyone to tell me whether the maid Susie
tended to him or not. He was a loner."

"How did he go?"

"Something called physostigmine. Cause of death was pul-
monary edema. Sounds very unpleasant."

"And physostigmine or whatever, that was the wife's medication?"

"Yep. She had some kind of heart irregularity. I didn't dig
too deeply into the medical wells here, so that's all I've got at
the moment."

"That's fine. You did great."

"Gotta tell you, this nurse gets rave reviews. One doctor claims she saved one of his patients with her quick thinking."

"So displeasure with her work, or lack of it, wasn't any motive for the move to Palm Springs?" Frankie asked.

"Hell, no. She could get work here tonight, if she returned."

"Thanks," Frankie said. He thought a moment and then called Jimmy McDermott, an old friend of his in the LAPD.

"Jimmy, Frankie. I need you to tap into your famous computer again for me, buddy," Frankie said.

"Frankie? I was just talkin' about you with Jack Sussman. He said he heard from his brother-in-law in Palm Springs that you were retired."

"Minutes away. I'll tell you about it all when I come into L.A. next. In the meantime, I need to know about a suicide that occurred in Pacific Palisades. Name's Sullivan." He looked at his notepad and the information he had copied from the hospital records on Faye. "Edward R."

"When?"

"Well . . ." He checked his dates to determine when Faye and her sister had left the L.A. area and started on their various trips and jobs. "Looks like about six and a half, maybe seven years ago."

"Give me twenty minutes, or will you be retired by then?" Jimmy kidded.

"It's close," Frankie said, and Jimmy laughed.

Frankie sat at his desk organizing his information. He lost track of time, so when the phone rang, it seemed like only a few minutes had gone by since he had spoken with Jimmy.

"Got it for you. Edward R. Sullivan. Overdosed on sleeping pills. I'll fax you the whole story if you like."

"Yeah, thanks, Jimmy."

"Don't forget to invite me to your retirement party."

"You'll be the first."

After Frankie hung up, he brought the information in to Nolan who slowly digested everything.

"Looks like you have your patterns, all right," he concluded. "I'll call the coroner and tell him about our suspicions and ask him to take another look at Livingston. In the meantime, I guess you better call the Sullivan sisters in for questioning."

"Let me visit them first and speak to them in their own surroundings. I have better luck that way. This isn't your typical deranged serial killer, if what we suspect is true. This is a sophisticated and intelligent psychotic. I mean, are they both guilty or is it just the nurse or just the maid? Is one aware of what the other does? I'd like to have something more, that old smoking gun, before I read them their rights and clamp the handcuffs on one or the other or both."

Nolan thought a moment and then nodded.

"Okay. Play it the way you think best," he said. His acquiescence made Frankie feel proud of himself, but he recognized that the man wasn't motivated by his respect for Frankie's abilities as much as by his fear of being held accountable for missing something very dramatic and very big.

Frankie was on his way out when the dispatcher signaled to him.

"It's your wife. She doesn't sound too happy," he whispered loudly.

"Tell her I just left," Frankie said.

He hurried away feeling very guilty but also full of that special excitement that came whenever he was on the verge of breaking a case or making a major crime discovery. Surely the gods would permit him just one more, and Jennie would forgive him.

17

The door buzzer took Faye by surprise. Her first thoughts went to Tillie, but she also feared that it might be Corpsy Ratner. He had sounded so anxious on the telephone. People as mentally unstable as he was were capable of doing anything impulsively, she thought. Susie, who had been preparing herself for visiting Corpsy, popped her head out of her doorway.

"Faye? Was that the door buzzer?"

"Yes. Just stay in there. It's probably Tillie, but it might be that idiot. If it's him, I'll tell him you're not here. Don't make any noise."

"All right." Susie left the door open a crack.

"Close it," Faye insisted. After Susie did so, Faye went to the front door.

"Faye Sullivan?" Frankie asked. Faye sensed immediately that he was a policeman. It was revealed to her in the way he carried himself and the way he scrutinized her quickly, his eyes sweeping over her and then moving off to look behind her.

"Yes?"

He produced his identification.

"My name is Frank Samuels. I'm with the Palm Springs police. May I come in?"

She didn't accede to his request instantly, as most people

would, even most guilty people who were anxious to put up
a facade of innocence immediately. She hesitated, her shoulders stiffening. After all, she was someone who usually carried authority, someone who bore responsibilities and had
self-confidence. She wasn't easily intimidated.

"Why? What is it you want?" she demanded.

Frankie started to smile but stopped and became firm himself instead.

"I'm investigating an alleged suicide," he replied. "You
were one of the last to see this person alive."

"Who is it, or was it, I should say," she asked, still unflinching.

"Thomas Livingston."

Her eyes softened, the tiny lines around them deepening
as her lips curled inward. If she were pretending this shock
and sadness, Frankie thought, she was real good at it. She
looked like she was on the verge of tears. But she sucked in
some air and pulled herself out of it.

"I'm really sorry to hear that. He was a very nice man."

"There are just a few questions remaining," Frankie said.
"I don't mean to take up much of your time."

"I do have to go some place soon . . . to meet my sister,"
she said.

"Oh, she's not here?" he asked with disappointment.

"Not at the moment. Why?"

"From what I understand, she was with Mr. Livingston the
day before he died. I'd like to talk to her. When do you expect her to return?"

"I don't. I mean, not right away. We're meeting an old
friend for dinner. She's already gone to be with him."

"I see. Well, maybe I'll be able to talk to her tomorrow. In
the meantime . . ."

"Yes," Faye said finally stepping back to permit him to enter. "Come in."

He gazed around quickly. The apartment, from what he
could see of it, had that transient feel to him. Nothing very
personal was in view, no family heirlooms, no pictures, except
for what looked like an album on the coffee table. All the liv-

ing room furniture looked like the inexpensive rental package that included lamps. It reminded him of motel rooms.

"Please, sit down," she said and moved forward quickly to take a copy of *People* magazine off the small sofa.

"Thanks."

"Can I get you anything? A cool drink?"

"No thanks. From what I understand," he said, wanting to get right to business, "after the funeral, you remained behind at Mr. Livingston's house to be with him after all the mourners, including his family, had left." He read from the notes he had gotten from a telephone call to Todd Livingston.

"That's correct. He was obviously overwrought, but he was the sort of man who hated to be a burden to anyone, especially his family."

"Yet he was willing to rely on you?" Frankie asked quickly.

"I'm a nurse, Detective Samuels. It's my work, helping sick people. Mr. Livingston was sick with grief."

"What did you do for him?"

"I got him to relax and then to sleep."

"Did you give him any pills?"

"He didn't have anything, but I found his wife's prescription. It was fine."

"You gave him the pills yourself? Brought them to him?"

"Yes," she said and smiled. "It wasn't the first time I've given someone pills."

"What I meant was, you went into the medicine cabinet, found the pill bottle, opened it and took out . . . what, two?"

"That's correct. Two was enough."

"Do you remember how many pills remained?"

"I didn't count them, no."

"Were there a great many left?"

"Most of the prescription, I'd say," she replied and finally sat down across from him.

"So you handled the bottle?"

"Yes." Now she knew what he was driving toward. "I left it out on the night table by his bed in case he needed some the next night," she added quickly.

Frankie nodded, looked at his notepad and then without

looking up, asked, "When did your sister come to work for him?"

"Susie relieved me that evening. I had promised the family I would look after him, but I had to go and I had already discussed his hiring my sister to do some work in his house. She does that sort of thing on a part-time basis."

"She's your twin?"

"That's right."

"How long did she stay with him that evening?"

"She remained through the evening, made him breakfast the next day, cleaned up, and came home," Faye said. Her lips trembled. "She's not going to take this well. Susie gets so involved with people. She's very shy, but when she gets to know someone, she . . . devotes herself to him or to her."

"Really?" Frankie said.

She looked up at him.

"Yes, really. It's painful to just get to know someone, to commiserate with him, and think you're making progress, you're doing something good: you're helping him deal with his great sorrow and then, what amounts to only hours later, to discover you were no influence at all."

"Well, people with a great deal more training and experience than your sister do no better. I take it then he was talking about suicide, either with you or your sister?"

"Yes, but from what I've seen working with other lonely people, especially elderly people, that's not unusual. What's usual is it's just talk. They feel sorry for themselves and they say things like that so we'll feel sorry for them, too."

"Susie didn't mention his taking any more pills that night?"

"No. He slept through the night, and he ate well when he got up."

"How much longer did your sister remain?"

"Just to clean up the bedroom and the kitchen. She was tired herself. She didn't sleep well, worrying about not hearing him call or something. She's like that."

"I see."

"Is there anything else, because I do have to go," Faye said.

"I have just a few questions about another suicide that oc-curred in Palm Springs recently, Sam Murray."

"Oh yes," she said.

"Your sister worked for him too?"

"That's correct."

"Did you give her a pill called Dilantin to give him to help him sleep?" he asked quickly. She stared a moment and then smiled, but so coldly it made his spine feel like it had turned into an icicle.

"Hardly, Detective. If anyone should know not to give someone Dilantin without his doctor's knowledge, you'd think it would be me, wouldn't you?" she asked disdainfully. "There can be some serious side effects. You should know the patient's medical history and condition."

"Dilantin was found in his body, and there wasn't any in the apartment, nor was any prescribed for him or his wife," Frankie said. "It's a prescription drug."

"My experience with older people is that they often lend each other their medications. Some of them have been deal-ing with the medical community for so long, they see them-selves as doctors and nurses. Have you asked any of his neighbors?"

"Some. What did you think about his injecting himself with insulin?"

"I wasn't surprised. He used to administer it to his wife, so he was comfortable with the hypodermic," she said.

"And how long did your sister stay with him?"

"Not long. She left the night before he died."

"And she thought he was all right, too?"

"She was worried about him. He had no immediate family nearby. I was going to check on him in the morning, but by the time I got around to it, I found out it was too late."

Frankie studied her a moment. She looked so confident or else . . . she really didn't know what her sister was up to. He couldn't decide.

"Why all these questions, Detective?"

"Why? Well, sometimes we take note of patterns. Believe it or not, most everything fits into a normal average . . . your normal average homicides, burglaries, car thefts—based upon the population, of course."

She nodded.

"When something breaks out of the average and forms an unusual pattern, we look twice. Most of the time, it's nothing," he added forcing a smile. "But sometimes the pattern is our first clue."

"It's the same in medicine. If a man of your age and weight started to behave differently from other men of your age and weight, we'd think it justified an investigation. Only we call that a physical."

Frankie laughed.

"You don't know how close to the truth you are," he said.

"Oh? You have a physical problem?"

"Hypertrophic . . ."

"Cardiomyopathy?" she said.

"Yeah, that's it," he said. He couldn't help but be impressed. She was really a very good nurse.

"Sometimes it can be treated with medication, but most often a pacemaker is recommended," she recited. "Did you have a pacemaker implanted?"

"I'm about to."

"It's not a big deal," she said. "But if you need a private-duty nurse . . ."

"Thanks," he said, nearly laughing. Wouldn't that be a twist? "Anyway, getting back to what I said about patterns. I noted from your work history that you were working in Phoenix recently."

Faye finally shifted nervously in her seat. He noted that she also gazed quickly toward the rear of the apartment.

"Yes, that's true."

"A bit of checking revealed that there were a couple of similar situations there."

"Similar?"

"Suicides with the same MO."

"I'm sorry, I don't keep up with the jargon. MO?"

"Modus operandi. How the crime or the act was committed," he explained.

"I see. And these suicides all have the same MO?"

"Well, these people all turned to some form of medicine to use as a poison. And when you see something like that, naturally, you get curious about it."

She didn't respond, but she fixed her eyes on him intently.

"And there are some other coincidences, shall we say."

"Namely?"

"Well, I checked the records, and you were the private-duty nurse for the spouses on each occasion."

Faye sat back, her shoulders straight.

"If you please one patient and his or her family, they often recommend you to friends in need."

"Yeah, well, I suppose that's true, but . . ."

"It's more than true, Detective Samuels; it's very common. The rule instead of the exception, as they say."

"I've had the opportunity to look at only a few with more attention, but in every case so far, your sister was employed to care for and clean the home of the surviving spouse."

"Oh, I see. That coincidence troubles you. Well," she said leaning forward, "my sister was born with one leg shorter than the other, which caused a problem that can only be alleviated by wearing a brace. Consequently, she grew up very shy, introverted. I'm the one who goes out and gets her the employment. She thinks everyone's looking at her limp. She's very self-conscious about wearing the brace. I've always had to look after her. If I didn't find her the work, she'd remain in this apartment cleaning and recleaning it, watching those inane soap operas all day, reading those gossip magazines," she added, nodding toward one on the table, "and eating junk food."

"I see. Well, there are other interesting details. Like the time factor. Every one of the men who committed suicide did it soon after his wife passed away."

"Losing a loved one, one you've been with for years and years, is devastating." She paused and stared at him, her expression becoming hard, cold. "What are you suggesting, Detective Samuels?"

"Remember what I said about the unusual pattern? If I

research your work in Florida, will I come up with similar circumstances? You the nurse, your sister their maid?"

"I'm not sure I like where this conversation is headed," Faye said. "Maybe we shouldn't be having this conversation. I know of too many instances of wrongful malpractice cases that ruined good nurses and doctors."

"I wasn't thinking in terms of a malpractice case, Miss Sullivan. I was thinking in terms of someone helping a depressed individual take his own life. Do you believe people are sometimes better off dead? Did you or your sister ever advise anyone to do himself in? Maybe show him how?"

Faye glared at him.

"I'm a nurse, someone dedicated to alleviating pain and suffering, someone dedicated to helping people get well. I don't advise people to die. I advise them on how to get well. And Susie, Susie couldn't hurt a fly. That's literally true. She won't kill an insect when she cleans. She'll spend hours trapping it and then throw it out of the house."

"Nevertheless, I'm afraid I'm going to have to have a talk with her. I'd like you to bring her into the police station tomorrow," he said standing. "What's a convenient time for you?"

"I'm on call tomorrow," she said, "but I should know by nine if I'm getting an assignment. Can I let you know then?"

"Sure. If there's a problem, I'll come here," he said.

"Fine," she said, "but I must warn you, Susie is very shy and can become very nervous, burst out in tears . . . It's best that I'm with her when you speak to her."

"Well, we'll do the best we can," Frankie said. Faye didn't like his tenacity. She followed him to the door. "If your sister has such serious problems," he said, "you wouldn't be helping her by ignoring them." His implication was clear.

"I think I know best how to take care of Susie," Faye replied.

"Okay. Thanks," he said. She watched him leave and then closed the door. Susie was already standing in the living room when Faye turned.

"Did you listen to that conversation?" Faye asked. Susie

nodded, her face nearly in tears. "Now do you understand why we have to do what we have to do, and do it quickly?"

"Yes, Faye." Susie stepped back. "How do I look?"

Faye inspected her.

"Open another button on the uniform," she instructed. "I want him to see more cleavage."

Susie complied.

"My perfume?" Faye asked.

"I put it on. How do you like my hair?"

"It's fine."

"I feel funny not wearing a bra. You can see my nipples."

Faye smirked.

"Only Corpsy will see you, and that won't matter very much, will it?"

"I guess not."

"You had better not mess this up, Susie," Faye warned.

"I won't," Susie promised. "But I can't help being afraid. I wish I was more like you."

Faye finally smiled.

"I told you: I'll be with you every moment. Whenever you get frightened or nervous, just listen for my voice and the things I've said. Okay?"

Susie nodded.

Faye went to the window and looked out to be sure Frankie was gone.

"Give me a few minutes," she said. "And then we'll go, and you'll do what has to be done."

Susie nodded, but her heart was beating so hard, she felt sure Corpsy Ratner would hear it and know what she had come to do to him.

18

Susie sat in the car and looked anxiously at the door of unit 31. Beside her on the passenger's seat was her purse, inside of which was only one thing: the hypodermic filled with Tubarine, a neuromuscular blocking agent Faye had prepared in a lethal dosage. She had assured Susie that the effect would be immediate.

All the way up to the motel, Faye had recited the plan move by move, as if she were writing a screenplay for a feature film: how Susie should enter the room, how she should speak and behave once she was inside, even how she should flutter her eyelashes. She was still whispering behind Susie's ear, sitting in the back in the shadows and whispering, chanting at her like some cheerleader of the damned, encouraging her, building her confidence to commit murder.

Of course, they didn't view it as murder. It was killing only in the sense that a doctor kills a germ or a surgeon cuts out a cancer. "We kill bad things so that good things can live," Faye told her. "Death is just another tool in the arsenal against the evil that lurks in and around our precious bodies. If we're not healthy in mind and in body, and we don't live in a protected environment, we can't do good deeds, can't we?"

Susie didn't need to be convinced of their motives; she just needed to be bolstered and sustained. She had to know her strong, intelligent sister was with her, behind her, ready to come to her aid if need be.

"You'll do fine," Faye whispered. "You won't have any problems with him. He idolizes you. Look at what he has done . . . come all this way just to see you. You're all he thinks about, talks about. He lives and breathes you. He will not be suspicious. We do not suspect those we love and who we think love us," she added, but with some bitterness. "This won't be the first time someone who had such faith in another person was betrayed.

"But you mustn't think of it that way," she added quickly. "Think only of us and what we must do to go on together. You want us to be together, don't you, Susie?"

"Yes."

"Then there is no choice. You have what you need, and you know what to do. If you get nervous or afraid, just think about me and what I would do and how I would act, okay?"

"Yes, Faye."

"It's time, Susie. There's no one around here right now. Get out and go to the door before someone pulls into the lot and sees you entering his unit. Go ahead, honey," she said, and she kissed Susie on the cheek.

Susie took a deep breath, grasped her purse carefully, and stepped out of the car. She looked back once, but Faye wasn't visible in the window. Without further hesitation, she hobbled over the gravel to Corpsy's door and knocked.

Corpsy had just finished shaving. He wiped his face dry and dabbed on his favorite lotion, maybe putting on a little more than most men would because of his paranoia about that formaldehyde thing. He was in his briefs, no shirt, no socks, when he heard the rapping at his door.

It couldn't be them, he thought quickly. It's too early, even for drinks before dinner, isn't it? But who else could it be?

He wrapped a towel around himself and went to the door.

"Who is it?" he asked. For a moment there was no response. Maybe it was a couple of kids pulling a prank, he thought. He was about to turn away when he heard, "It's me. Susie."

If he had stepped on an exposed electric wire, he couldn't have had a more sudden shock pass through his body. He was numb. The charge that shot through him left the back of his neck ice cold. He started to stammer and then closed his mouth and seized control of his tongue.

"Susie?" he said, and he opened the door to see her standing there, not more than a foot away from him. "But you're so early. I didn't . . . expect you and . . ." He looked beyond her. "Where's Faye?"

"She'll be here later," Susie said. "May I come in?"

"Oh, but . . . sure," he said stepping back quickly. "It's not much of a room, as you can see."

She paused inside the door and gazed around at the worn carpet, the stained wallpaper, the unmade bed, and the dull brown night table and dresser. There was one chair by a small table to the left.

"I was just finishing dressing," he said, permitting himself to look directly at her. Of course, he had never been this close to her before, but he wasn't disappointed. If anything, he thought she was prettier than Faye, especially because of the way her hair framed her face. Faye's short hair made her face look chubbier.

He was surprised to see that Susie wore her maid's uniform. Maybe she really didn't have any wardrobe. But why couldn't she have borrowed something from Faye? However, the uniform looked different. With the buttons undone and the collar pulled apart, it was a far sexier garment. Enough cleavage was revealed for him to see that there was a tiny birthmark on the inside of her left breast. He longed to touch it with the tip of his finger.

When he looked up and into those cerulean blue eyes, his heartbeat not only quickened, it skipped. His own partial nudity added to this unexpected but delightful excitement. The erection that was building nudged against his briefs. He felt his skin warm. She smiled softly, her lips wet, the tip of her tongue just visible between them.

"It's okay," she finally said. "A room is a room. What makes it nice is the people who are in it, don't you think?"

"Oh sure. Yeah. Sure. Um . . . I don't have anything to offer you. Just water."

"I don't need anything. She turned her shoulders in just a little, but the move pushed her breasts up, giving them even more exposure. "Faye thought it would be nice for us to have a chance alone first," she said.

The revelation of this motive put Corpsy into a frenzy for a moment. They were actually alone, weren't they? He looked about, trying to decide what move to make next, what to offer.

"That's very nice of her. I guess I should finish getting dressed, though, huh?"

"No," Susie said quickly. "Let's just relax. When people are relaxed, they are more honest with each other, right?"

"I suppose. Yeah," he said. There wasn't anything she could say or do that he would disagree with right now, he thought.

She surprised him by sitting on his bed.

"Oh, I'm sorry I didn't make that. I don't usually leave things messy. I took a nap this afternoon and . . ."

"I don't mind." She ran the palm of her hand over the exposed sheet. "It still feels warm. You must have a warm body. Faye says some people's normal temperature can be a full degree or two above what's considered normal." Suddenly, she sat forward and put that palm against his chest. He started to pull back, but Susie touching him and him feeling her so soon was too wonderful and unexpected a pleasure to deny. "Yes," she said, "you are a warm man." She smiled and laughed. "Well?" she asked.

"What?" He didn't know what to say or where to put his nervous hands.

"Aren't you curious about me?"

"Curious about . . . you mean, whether you're warm or not?"

"Yes, silly." She reached down and seized his left wrist, bringing his hand up to her exposed chest. She pressed his fingers on her bosom and looked into his shocked face. "So?"

"You're warm, too," he said, pulling his hand back.

"I know. Sit down beside me," she said, patting the bed. "You must tell me about yourself. I don't remember seeing you in Phoenix."

Gingerly, he sat down and held his towel closed.

"Well, I was nervous and shy about meeting you then," he said. He blushed. "I used to watch you from a distance."

"You used to spy on me?"

"Yeah, I suppose you could say that. But the moment I set eyes on you . . ."

"What?" she asked in a breathy, excited way.

"I thought you were beautiful and someone I had to know and maybe could love," he confessed.

"That's so nice. No one has ever said anything like that to me before. Probably because of this," she said, lifting the skirt of her uniform so her brace was fully visible.

"Oh, that's nothing," he said. "Why should your handicap make any difference. It doesn't make you less of a person or less beautiful. In fact . . . it kind of makes you more beautiful to me."

She stared at him with her warm smile, her eyes brightening.

"My sister said that any man who would come so far to meet me must be sincere," she said.

"I am. I don't even like the idea of your being in here alone with me. I never intended . . ."

"Oh, I don't mind. I know you're not that sort, but we should be alone and we should see if we do care for each other, shouldn't we?"

"I guess so," he said.

"We already know we like touching each other," she said, laughing.

"Oh, I love touching you. There's nothing I want more."

"As long as you're always gentle with me and understand that I'm . . . I'm not very sophisticated," she admitted.

"That means nothing to me. I'm far from what you would call sophisticated."

"Oh, I bet you've had a lot of girlfriends."

"Me? No, ma'am. No."

"You mean we're both . . . virgins?"

"I guess so," he said.

"That's good, because we'll make discoveries together and Faye says when two people do that, they find it easier to love each other."

"I bet she's right."

"Oh, I'm sure she's right. She's usually right about most things."

"She's a very good nurse. I know," he said nodding.

"Will you kiss me?" Susie asked.

"What?"

"Will you just lean over and kiss me?" She closed her eyes and pursed her lips.

Corpsy took a deep breath and looked around the room as if he wanted to be sure this wasn't all a dream. Then he swallowed and leaned forward to press his lips to hers. It was a quick kiss, and to illustrate that she didn't think it was enough, she kept her eyes closed and her lips pursed. He swallowed again and leaned forward to kiss her harder and longer. The moment he did so, she put her hand on his shoulder. She kept it there when he lifted his lips from hers.

"That was very nice," she said.

"Thanks."

"You know that I'm shy."

"Well . . . I thought you might be, but . . ."

"I am shy. I'm just very excited right now and very happy. Aren't you?"

"Yes, I am," he said, nodding.

"Kiss me again," she said. "Go on."

Corpsy did as she asked. He thought he was on fire. She moaned and leaned against him, kissing his neck and his shoulders. Her caresses both excited and frightened him. It wasn't supposed to be like this, was it? He was sorry now that he had had such limited experience with women. What was he supposed to do? Was she testing him? If he turned her away, would she resent him and be angry? Or would she be angrier if he returned the kisses and the caresses?

"Your sister might be coming soon," he said to test the waters.

"No. She won't be here for a while. Besides, she'll call first. Girls know what to do," Susie said, winking. She kissed him on the tip of his nose before pressing her lips to his again and pushing herself on him so that he fell back on the bed. He kept his hands at his sides as she kissed her way down his chest and then fingered the towel around his waist.

"Don't you like me?" she asked when he didn't respond.

"Oh yes, I just thought you'd be angry if I . . ."

"I won't be angry, but you've got to hold me and kiss me and do love the way I want to do love the first few times, because I'm shy. I told you. I've never been with a man like this."

"Of course," he said, and he kissed her quickly. She laughed and stood up to unbutton her uniform. But she paused before taking it off.

"Turn over," she said. "I don't want you to look at me right away."

"Okay." He turned over.

"I'll help you, though, if you don't mind," she said, and he felt her fingers under the elastic of his briefs. He lifted his body as she pulled them down. Then he felt the palm of her hand on his buttocks. "You're as smooth as a baby," she said. He laughed, too.

"I've got to go into the bathroom first and do something girls do," she said. "Faye would be very angry if I didn't."

"Of course," he said. He started to turn.

"No," she said sharply. "Don't move and don't look back at me, okay?"

"Okay."

He lay there while she picked up her purse and went into the bathroom. His erection was so full and firm, it nearly lifted his lower body off the bed. A few moments later, he heard her approach the bed and then he felt her naked body over his, her breasts on his back, her pubic hair against his leg as she clamped her legs around his. Her brace was cold against his hot skin. She moaned, and he closed his eyes and moaned softly, too.

"Susie," he murmured, "my Susie."

Was this really happening? He was in the greatest ecstasy of his life.

"Don't look," she said when he started to turn his head. He pressed his forehead to the sheet and obeyed. Then he felt her body lift from his. A moment later, there was a pin-prick pain in his neck that grew and grew. He started to lift himself up, but she pressed her knees against the small of his back and the pain continued for a moment more. It was as if a giant bee had gotten stuck in him.

Finally he screamed and flailed out, pushing her off him. Then he turned and sat up. She was on the floor, naked, but in her right hand there was a hypodermic needle, its contents emptied.

The effect was immediate. He started to speak but experienced a tightness in his throat. His eyelids felt like they had turned to stone and his breathing shortened until he was gasping for air. He struggled to stand. Susie got to her feet and scooped up her uniform as he fell to the floor and then grasped the bed to pull himself up again. She put on the uniform quickly, gathered her purse, dropped the hypodermic into it, and rushed to the door as he collapsed to the floor again, his guttural noises ugly. When she looked back, he was clutching his rib cage. His face was turning blue.

She looked around the parking lot as Faye had instructed, waited to be sure it was clear, and then closed the door quietly and moved as quickly as she could with her limp to the car.

"Well?" Faye asked as soon as she got into the car.

"It went just as you said it would, Faye," Susie said, gasping slightly. She was so excited she couldn't find the key, and Faye had to tell her it was still in the ignition.

"Go on, get us out of here quickly," Faye said, sitting back.

Susie started the car and drove out. In moments they were down the street.

"I'm proud of you, Susie," Faye said. "So proud."

Back in the room, Corpsy had managed to drag himself toward the door. He put all his strength and determination into reaching for that doorknob. When his fingers found it, he closed them as best he could and pulled and pulled, but it seemed like his arm was pulling away from his body. He wasn't rising and he wasn't getting any air into his lungs. He did manage to turn the knob so that the door clicked open. He fell back to the floor, his nose close to the opening.

And there he died of respiratory failure, looking like a fish out of water, his eyes bulging, his lips swollen, his tongue a pale pink, his ecstasy cut short forever.

19

Jennie was sitting in the living room with the lights low.
Frankie closed the front door softly and almost tiptoed into
the house. At the moment, he would rather charge into a den
of terrorists, guns blasting. He paused in the living room
doorway. The weak illumination cast a long, dark shadow
over Jennie's face, making it look as gaunt as death.

"Why are you sitting in the dark?" he asked.

"Isn't it funny," she said, "how even when things can
be simple, we make them complicated. We are our worst
enemies."

"Jen . . ."

"I called Dr. Pauling. Something told me your story was a
fabrication. That's a nice way of saying you lied to me,
Frankie. Now I don't know who's more furious, me or the
doctor."

"Oh, those specialists," Frankie said, stepping into the living room. "If they don't get things exactly their way . . .
They're prima donnas, that's what they are, the prima donnas
of the medical world."

"It's not Dr. Pauling who has to be worried."

"It's no big deal. It's just a matter of schedules," Frankie
claimed. "If I were in the middle of a life-and-death
situation . . ."

"You could be," Jennie snapped.

"Jennie, I haven't so much as walked fast since I was in the hospital. I haven't lifted anything that weighs more than . . . than a pencil."

"Why did you do it, Frankie? Why did you postpone getting this over with?"

"Jen," he said sitting on the sofa, "I stumbled on something . . . you wouldn't believe. You see," he said becoming visibly excited, "I had this warning bell go off in my head when Rosina told me about this suicide the other day. I never liked loose ends. If something is cut-and-dried, it shouldn't have loose ends. Anyway, there was this medication . . ."

"I heard about this already, Frankie."

"Yeah, but you didn't hear the follow-up. Turns out there was a maid looking after the victim the night before. No one knew her and only this old gent saw her. His description was worthless until he mentioned this leg brace she wears, see.

"Anyway, turns out the maid's the twin sister of this private-duty nurse who took care of the victim's wife. That situation in and of itself isn't a bell ringer, but . . ."

"Frankie."

"No, wait, listen," he said, hoping to infect her with his enthusiasm. "The two of them are involved in the same way with the next suicide victim, Tommy Livingston, who again is killed with an overdose of medicine. I check out the nurse's background and find she worked in Phoenix . . ."

"Frankie, for God's sake, you're actively involved in a potential murder case, and a suspected serial killing to boot!"

"It's not a big deal physically. I'm not wrestling with anyone. I'm doing some hard-nose, nitty-gritty police work: phone calls, a little research, some interviewing . . ."

"Couldn't this be done by someone else, Frankie? You're not the only cop in Palm Springs."

"Well, the department's been a little busy and . . . Nolan . . . that smartass bastard . . . ridiculed my suspicions from the start."

Jennie leaned forward into the light and nodded.

"So it's not so much a matter of cracking a case as it is keeping your ego intact, is that it, Frankie?" she asked.

"No. I mean, I don't mind shoving it to Nolan, but there are people in grave danger out there if I'm right, and I'm about ninety-five percent convinced I am. I just don't know to what extent both sisters are involved, if both are."

"So you have a ways to go?"

"Not much. That's why I wanted to put off going in tomorrow, see? Once I do . . ."

"You're retired."

"Exactly, and this case might fall through the cracks. They'll leave Palm Springs and prey on other people, Jen."

She stared at him a moment.

"What does Nolan think now?" she asked softly.

"He's come around to my way of thinking and he feels like the horse's ass he is," Frankie said happily.

"So then he won't let the investigation die if you go into the hospital."

"It's not that simple, Jen. This is my baby now. A good detective develops a passion for his cases, and another detective coming on might very well not have the same passion. These women, they're . . . very intelligent, and the MOs are sophisticated. I mean, they've gotten by coroners from here to the East Coast."

"But they won't get by Frankie Samuels. No sir," Jennie said bitterly.

"Jen." He sighed and sat back. "Most of my adult life," he began, "I've been a cop. I've eaten, worked, slept cop. It's been who and what I am. Now, practically overnight, I'm told I've got to become a different person. I've got to bury the identity I've had. All right, I've come to terms with that, but let me say goodbye my own way," he pleaded. "Let me give the old flatfoot one last moment of glory."

"Oh Frankie, I'm just scared," Jennie said. "I don't want that old flatfoot to take you with him."

Frankie nodded.

"He won't, Jen. I promise. If I don't wrap it up before I'm supposed to go in now, that's it; it's over."

He saw the tears streaming down her face and went to her, kneeling beside her and wiping the tears off gently. Then he kissed her and embraced her, lowering his head to her lap. She put her hand on his head and stroked his hair.

"I love you, babe, and I'm sorry I lied to you and I'm sorry you've suffered at all." He looked up at her.

"I've been afraid, Frankie. I've always been afraid. I know you go to war every day. Most of the time, I filled my life with things just so I'd keep busy and not think about it. But every time you came home to me, I felt this great relief and this great surge of love. I know I became complacent at times, overconfident, maybe; and I just came to believe I've been lucky. I'm sorry you had this heart problem, but I didn't look at it as tragically as you did. I saw it was a way out. Maybe I'm selfish for wanting you all to myself, but I want you, and that flatfoot Frankie Samuels is just going to have to give you up."

"He will, Jen. I swear."

She put her hands under his chin and he rose to bring his lips to hers.

"Hey, I'm home in time for dinner for a change," he said, and she laughed. "What?"

"I was so angry at you, I didn't make any dinner."

"What?"

"You'll have to take me out."

"Fine thing. A man comes home from a hard day's work and . . ."

"And takes his wife to dinner. Get used to it," she said. "I'm close to retirement age myself."

They both rose just as the phone rang. He stared at it.

"It might be Beth or Stevie," she said with confession in her eyes.

"You ratted on me?"

"I had to vent my feelings on someone. Isn't that what your grown children are for?"

He laughed and lifted the receiver. It was Beth.

"What are you doing, Dad?"

"Just living up to my idealistic beliefs," he kidded. "How do you like it?"

"It's not the same thing."

"Why, because it's me?"

"Oh, Dad."

"Look, you and your brother don't have to worry," he said. "I've got it all figured and . . ."

"I want you around, Dad. I want you there to see my children."

"Children? You've got children?"

"Eventually."

"Sure you want them around Dirty Harry?"

"I'm sure, Dad. You'll be careful, won't you?"

"No sense in stopping now," he said. "How was your date?"

"How did you know about that?"

"Little bird flew in from L.A.," he said winking at Jennie. "So?"

"He's very nice."

"Nice?"

"We seem to share a lot of the same beliefs, ideals . . ."

"Did he wear sneakers?"

"What?"

"Just an in-joke. Look, I've got to take your mother to din-ner. It's some sort of punishment."

"I'll call tomorrow."

"Okay. Call the counselor right now and get him off my case, will you?"

"You want me to do that?"

"Why not? You're good when it comes to talking to peo-ple," he said. He could almost feel her pride and happi-ness.

"Okay, Dad. Have a good dinner," she said. He hung up.

"What?" he asked when he saw Jennie staring at him with that smile on her lips.

"You really are a pussycat, Frankie Samuels."

"Meow," he said and she laughed.

"What will it be: Chinese, Italian, Mexican . . . ?"

"Let's go to that cozy little Italian place on North Palm Canyon and make believe we've just met," Jennie said.

"Well, you do have to get to know the new me," he said.

"In that case I'd better put on something sexier and fix my face. There's a new me just waiting to burst out, too, you know."

He watched her go off and felt himself lose years. That's what being in love meant, he thought, staying young at heart for the woman you worshiped. It made the prospect of a new identity and a new life that much less difficult to accept. He decided to change his clothes and freshen up himself. After all, he had to make a good impression on his date.

Susie went to bed almost as soon as she and Faye returned to their apartment. She had no appetite, and Faye did not push her to eat. It was better she went to sleep; she was emotionally exhausted.

Faye, however, had a hearty appetite. The tension and the excitement had burned up calories. She was absolutely ravenous, going at every leftover like a pack rat, mixing foods, eating things without warming them, and drinking one glass of wine after the other as if it were water. She had all the dishes on the table and was picking from one after the other when the phone rang.

At first she wasn't going to answer it, thinking it might be that policeman checking to see if she and Susie were home. Then she thought she could easily say Susie was still out on her date. After the fifth ring, she relented and picked up the receiver.

"Where the hell you been, Sullivan? I've been trying to reach you for hours," Sue Cohen said. Her agency supervisor sounded peaked.

"Visiting dear friends," she replied.

"I told you a dozen times if I told you once, check in with

me when you're between assignments. I want to know if you're around and available."

"I'm sorry," Faye said.

"Yeah, well, apparently you've made a very good impression on Dr. Stanley because of the way you handled that crisis with Mrs. Weinstein. He had this new family specifically ask for you when they called me."

"Really?" She couldn't help feeling great pride in herself and a little sad that she had only Susie with whom to share it.

"Yes. We have a man about sixty-six coming out at about midafternoon. He had a heart attack a little under a year ago, retired with his wife, and moved to Palm Springs. A little less than a week ago, he had a severe angina attack. They kept him in CCU under observation. He's done well, so they want to move him out, but the family would like some private duty, and as I said, Stanley had them ask specifically for you."

Faye blushed with pride. "You have the morning shift tomorrow. Any problems with that?" she demanded quickly.

Faye thought a moment. She really wanted to get herself and Susie away.

"I'm afraid there is."

"What now?"

"I meant to tell you yesterday, but I got too involved in things. We're leaving Palm Springs. Going north."

"Leaving? Well, I'm sorry to hear that," her supervisor said softening. "Good private-duty nurses are harder and harder to find."

"Thank you," Faye said. "If I need a recommendation . . ."

"No problem. Keep in touch, and if you should return to Palm Springs . . ."

"I'll call you immediately," Faye said.

She cradled the phone but stood there thinking for a moment. Mrs. Cohen had sounded jealous over Dr. Stanley's enthusiastic recommendation. She knew why her supervisor was jealous. She took a deep breath and turned slowly. Her bedroom door was open and she heard someone taking off his clothes. He had been waiting there patient all this time. How like him, she thought.

She began to unbutton her blouse as she walked toward the bedroom. She paused in the doorway. He was standing there naked, his back to her, gazing out the window. But he knew she was there.

"Get undressed," he said, "and lie down. I'll be right with you."

She unzipped her skirt and stepped out of it and then lowered her panties to her ankles. He kept his back to her, but it was such a strong, muscular back and those shoulders . . . She could see the turn in his waist and the firm lift in his buttocks. When she was naked, she placed herself on her back on the bed and gazed up at the ceiling.

"Ready, Doctor," she said. After a moment he was at the side of the bed gazing down at her. She watched him slip on his surgical gloves and then tie his mask around his face.

"The heart," he began, moving his fingers over her breast, "is a remarkable organ. It's slightly bigger than your fist and beats about forty million times a year, every year of your life."

"Yes, Doctor," she said.

"It reacts to your thoughts and feelings. Right now, your heart is starting to pound, isn't it, Miss Sullivan?"

"Very much so, Doctor."

"Take a deep breath and close your eyes," he ordered, and she did so. "Try to control your breathing, try to control your body, try to control your heart," he said, but he continued to move his fingers over her breasts, the tips of those fingers just touching her nipples. They became erect so quickly they stung.

Then his hands traced the lines of her body and moved down to her stomach.

"Breathe in, breathe out. Gently now." His fingers turned into a spider, crawling over her pubic hair and settling against her pelvis. His palm began to rotate over it, and her entire body moved with it. Then his assistant and his nurse, who had been waiting in the shadows, quickly moved to his side.

"Heartbeat?" he asked.

"Eighty-five," his nurse reported.

"Blood pressure?"

"One-thirty over eighty but rising."

"Temperature?"

"Normal."

"Heartbeat?"

"One hundred."

"Blood pressure?"

"One-thirty over eighty-five, Doctor."

"Thank you. Lift those legs, please," he told his assistant. "Good. Now spread them, please. Okay, Miss Sullivan, breathe in, breathe out. Here we go," he said, slipping his hard phallus into her. At first it was as cold as a surgical instrument, but it quickly became warmer and warmer. She gasped. His hand was over her heart. "Easy, Miss Sullivan. Easy. Relax. That's it. Now we're doing well."

Her skin felt as though it were on fire. Despite her efforts to control it, her heart broke free of any restriction and pounded madly. Her breathing quickened and quickened as the doctor moved himself deeper into her, touching her so profoundly within, she thought he had nudged her very soul.

She cried out as he continued to build her toward one explosion after another. She reached around to take hold of his buttocks, the wonderful, muscular buttocks, but the assisting nurse quickly seized her wrists and pulled her hands down to her sides.

It went on and on until she could barely breathe and then suddenly it stopped and she felt herself sink into the bed. She kept her eyes closed.

"Sew her up, please," Doctor Stanley told his assistant. She felt his hand over her forehead. "You did very well, Miss Sullivan. Very well, indeed. I'll see you in recovery," he said, and he left her.

She lay there, enjoying the aftermath, waiting for her blood to cool, but that was interrupted by screaming and a pounding on her front door. She threw on her bathrobe and rushed out. The noise had woken Susie, but she remained behind in her own doorway, waiting.

It was Tillie.

"They're on the phone. I don't understand what they're saying. . . . Please come talk to them."

Faye followed her into her apartment and picked up the receiver.

"This is Faye Sullivan, Mrs. Kaufman's next door neighbor. What's going on?"

"Hello, Faye. Dr. Pauling. I'm afraid Mr. Kaufman had a cardiac arrest a little while ago. He just passed away. We did all we could."

"Oh, I'm so sorry," Faye said.

Tillie began to cry.

"If there is anything I can do for Mrs. Kaufman . . ."

"I'm here with her, Doctor. She'll be fine."

"We'd like to do an autopsy, of course, but we'll need her permission."

"I'll speak to her, Doctor, and we'll get back to you."

"Thank you, Faye. Sorry."

She hung up and went to comfort Tillie, who had collapsed on the sofa.

"Now, now, Tillie. We knew this was going to happen."

"I know, I know. To know is one thing, but to have it happen . . . Oh, poor Morris, poor, poor Morris," she wailed. "What am I going to do? What will I do?" she asked, rocking herself.

"I'll be here for you, Tillie. We'll do what has to be done. You'll tell me who you want to contact."

"Who do I want to contact? I have one living sister, and she's sick and alone herself. She can't travel to a funeral. None of our nephews and nieces have had much to do with us, and all of Morris's brothers and sisters are gone. I'm alone, all alone."

"No you're not," Faye insisted, hugging her.

"Oh, Faye, oh, dear, dear Faye. You and your sister inherited the troubles of two old people when you moved in here."

"We've been through it before, Tillie. Many, many times."

"Oh God, oh God," Tillie moaned, rocking again.

"Tillie," Faye said, sitting back. "You don't especially like autopsies. I mean, your people, your religion . . ."

Tillie paused.

"No," she said firmly.

"I don't see why you should agree to it, anyway. We all know the cause of Morris's death. Why cut up his body just to satisfy some doctors who seize every opportunity to experiment and toy with dead people's organs?"

"Oh, how horrible. No, no autopsy."

"I'll let them know your feelings, and then you and I will sit down and quietly plan out what has to be done. I'll do all the phone calls for you."

"You're a godsend," Tillie said, her tearful eyes full of love and awe. "You're a true nurse, Faye. Such a Florence Nightingale. I know you did all you could to help Morris."

"All I could," Faye said smiling. "Just as I will for you," she added.

After she made the phone calls, she returned to her apartment and found her sister pacing in the living room. She stopped the moment Faye entered. Her eyes were wide and tearful.

"She's suffering, isn't she?"

"What did you expect?"

"It had to be done. You said so yourself."

"I never said so."

"You did. I don't have to hear you say it, Faye, to know it's in your mind."

"Let's not argue about it now."

"No. No," Susie said, looking toward the Kaufman's residence. "We've got to think about her."

"What do you mean?"

"We can't leave Palm Springs and just let her linger here, suffering, being lonely, can we? Morris needs her, and she needs him."

"She doesn't need him. He was a drain, a dead weight."

"He was her husband, and they spent most of their adult lives together. It's for better or worse, remember? Before we leave Palm Springs, we've got to help her leave, too. Okay? Okay?" Susie pursued.

"I don't want to talk about it right now. I've got too much to do," Faye said. She left Susie mumbling to herself about what had to be done.

20

Frankie and Jennie did have a wonderful dinner. They both drank too much wine and were giggling like teenagers when they returned home. Frankie thought that if it was possible to fall in love again and again with the same woman, he would do so. Impulsively, groping each other with an abandon that revived their memories of earlier days, when it seemed impossible to keep their hands off each other whenever they were alone, he and Jennie embraced in the entryway and kissed so passionately, neither cared that they were standing in a window in full view of anyone in the street.

Frankie started to unbutton Jennie's blouse. She kept her eyes closed, her head against the wall as he planted kiss after kiss on her neck. She continued to giggle, but once he had her blouse undone and he kissed her breasts and then her stomach, her giggling stopped and she moaned softly. He undid her skirt.

"Frankie, wait . . ."

"What for?"

"Let's go into the bedroom," she pleaded.

"Anyone can make love in his bedroom." He started to lower her to the floor.

"Frankie, stop. Wait."

"Don't move," he said. "We've never made love in this entryway, and I've always wanted to."

"What?" She laughed, but he rushed into the living room, got some cushions off the sofa, and hurried back. "Frankie, you're not serious?"

"Hell, I'm not," he said. Moments later, they were both naked, embracing and making love as fervently as ever they had. Midway through, Jennie paused. He saw the concern in her eyes.

"The doctor didn't say anything about strenuous lovemaking," he told her. His heart was pounding, but he wasn't going to stop now. "Besides, what better way to go?"

She closed her eyes again, her facial expression a mixture of pleasure and prayer. Even so, they continued the best lovemaking they had experienced in a long time. Afterward, they lay there on the entryway floor, neither wanting to end the moment too soon. Finally, Jennie burst out in laughter.

"I can't believe where I am and what I've done here," she said.

"What if the Mortons came to the door with a senior citizen discount?"

"Stop," she said giggling uncontrollably.

"Don't all married couples make love in their entryways occasionally?"

"No. Most normal people don't." She started to gather her clothes. He followed her into the bedroom. A little while later they were snuggled together.

"Now this makes more sense," she said.

"Ready for an encore?"

"Frankie!"

"Just testing," he said. "I had a great time tonight."

"See? It's not so hard to live like everyone else. You don't have to be afraid of retirement."

"Are you kidding? This is more strenuous than police work," he said.

They kissed and held each other until they both grew too tired to keep their eyes open. Sleep came quickly and deeply, so deeply, in fact, that Frankie didn't hear the phone ring early the next morning until it had rung for the third time; and it was on his side of the bed, too.

"I really debated whether or not to call you this early, Frankie," Rosina said. "Nolan insisted I do. Now that I know I woke you, I wish I hadn't. It could have waited until you came in, but you know our relentless chief of detectives. He always gets his man or . . . woman."

"It's all right," he said in a loud whisper. Jennie, remarkably, had not woken. "What's up?"

"Nolan filled me in on your investigation earlier. He was quite excited and even said some nice things about you."

"He's getting religion."

"Anyway, we've got a homicide. Been working on it most of the night. There are some aspects of this that might interest you, considering your case, that is."

"Hold on a minute," Frankie said. "I'm going to another phone." He slipped out of bed as quietly as he could. Jennie moaned, but she didn't turn over or open her eyes. He tiptoed out and into the kitchen where he picked up the receiver.

"Okay, what do you have?"

"Last night the receptionist at the Sunny Dunes Motel noticed the door of one of the occupied rooms was open and, on closer inspection, saw a hand sticking out. She went over, gazed in, and found one Arnold Ratner, naked and dead on the floor. Derek and I attended the scene. No signs of any struggle, no bruises, except I noticed a small trauma on the back of his neck."

"Yeah?"

"Just got a report from pathology and thought immediately of you."

"Come again?"

She laughed.

"I don't mean you personally. Seems someone stuck a hypodermic into Mr. Ratner and injected him with . . . something called Tubarine. It's a nueromuscular blocking agent, normally used to promote muscle relaxation during surgical anesthesia and occasionally used to control convulsions. Highly lethal in an overdose, with rapid results when injected. That's word for word on the report," she said.

"Another medical murder," Frankie muttered. "Who was this guy? Any recently deceased relatives?"

"No, he doesn't fit that part of your MO, Frankie, but who he was and where he came from will be of great interest to you."

"You've got my full attention, even at this early hour," Frankie said, noticing it was not quite six-fifteen.

"He was from Phoenix, a hospital technician in the pathology department at the hospital in which your suspect, Faye Sullivan, did some private-duty nursing."

"That is very interesting. How old was this guy?"

"Thirty-two. Lived with his mother. Don't know much more about him at this point, but we've been in touch with Phoenix and they're digging up what they can. I'm expecting a phone call from them at any time."

"I'll get dressed and come down now. Didn't Nolan have you on some car wash, car parts scam all day yesterday?"

"That he did. We had just made the arrests and finished all that paperwork when this call came in. Derek and I are both beat."

"You're working too hard, Flores."

"Just getting used to filling your shoes," she replied. He thought a moment.

"Yeah, well maybe that ain't such a big deal. Look at where hard work got me."

"Retired on a pension," she said. "Quit complaining. How are things at home? Or shouldn't I ask?"

"Actually, we're experiencing a delightful period of calm."

"Eye of the hurricane, Frankie."

"Thanks. See you at oh seven hundred or so," he said. She laughed.

After he hung up, he stood there thinking. He was afraid that he wouldn't be able to wrap this thing up neatly before he had to go in for his pacemaker, even after he had interviewed the twin who was a maid. But if she or her sister or both of them were involved in this new murder, it might wrap it all up very quickly.

Christ, he thought, shaking his head, what a way to go

about killing people . . . using medicines that were designed to ease pain, cure illnesses, and defeat death. How could he ever look at a nurse or a doctor again and not think about this? We place such trust in the medical world, let them poke and prod, cut and snip our bodies with relative impunity. We trust them more than we trust our own mothers. We take their word for it that the medicine that's supposed to be in that hypodermic or in that IV bag is the right medicine in the correct and safe amounts.

What a betrayal, he thought. What a cruel, sick betrayal, especially of older people who are far more dependent?

I'm going to end it all today, he vowed, and then he returned to the bedroom and moved as quietly as he could in the bathroom. Jennie didn't wake up until he had most of his clothes on and was just pulling on his socks.

"How did you get out of this bed and dressed so quietly?" she asked.

He shrugged.

"I wasn't especially quiet. You were just dead to the world. Face it, you can't take the fast life."

"Never mind. What time is it?" She gazed at the clock. "Why are you leaving so early? Did you have any breakfast?"

"I'll get something on the way."

"No you won't," she said, sitting up. "What's going on, Frankie?" She ground the sleep out of her eyes quickly.

"I have a chance to finish this thing off today," he replied. "There was a homicide yesterday that looks like a tie-in." He checked his watch. "I've got to report to the command bunker."

"Frankie, you're not going to do anything alone, anything . . . dangerous, are you?"

"I once told you, statistically it's more dangerous to smoke a cigarette."

"Neither of us smokes, Frankie. Answer my question," she insisted.

"These people don't kill in your usual violent manner with guns and knives. They poison their victims with medicine. I ain't about to accept a Coke from my suspect," he replied.

"Anyway, Nolan's putting a few of us on this now. I'll probably just be riding shotgun. You know Nolan—he'll want to claim full credit for breaking the case."

"Let him. You don't have to prove anything to anyone."

"But myself," he corrected.

"I want you to call me if you're not meeting me for lunch," she said.

"Yes, dear." He stood up and then leaned over to kiss her. "I'll call you." He started out.

"Frankie!" She got out of bed and rushed to him as he turned. She kissed him again. "Be careful. You're almost home."

"Okay," he said softly, and he walked out. Before he got to the front door, the phone rang again. He picked it up in the living room.

"Samuels."

"Frankie, Rosina. We just got the call from Phoenix. They interviewed the mother and she told them her son was going to Palm Springs to find the woman he loved."

"Woman he loved?"

"Yes. He told her the woman's name . . . Susie Sullivan."

"Son of a bitch."

"Forensics has lifted loads of prints from the motel room, so if she touched anything, we should be able to tie her to the scene."

"Right."

"Looks like you hit the jackpot with your urban cynicism and good old policeman's instinct, Frankie. I never saw Nolan this impressed."

"Leave out that old part," he said.

"Nolan wants you to come down to talk strategy. He's pacing back and forth in his office like a tank commander."

"I was almost out the door when you called, but what strategy? The thing to do now is simply pick up the sisters."

"Nolan says . . ."

"I can swing by their place on the way. You want me to do it by myself or you gonna meet me there?"

"Frankie ..."

"Most probably they killed that man last night, Rosina. They might already be gone."

"I'll tell Nolan I didn't reach you. You had already left," she said. "I'll meet you there in twenty minutes. Wait for me and Derek."

"Gotcha," he said and cradled the phone. Then he hurried out of the house and into his car. When he pulled away, he gazed up at his rearview mirror and saw Jennie. She had come to the front door to watch him drive off.

The image of her standing there lingered in his eyes. He wasn't sure if it was a good or bad omen, but he knew he had better not dote on it. Those who were too careful usually made fatal errors, he thought as he drove on.

Tillie sat at the kitchen table like someone who had been lobotomized. She chewed mechanically and swallowed with great effort. Susie sat across from her, observing, her heart aching with sympathy. Faye was still sleeping and didn't know she had left the apartment to visit Tillie. But she had to move quickly, didn't she? Faye was determined to move on and might very well pack their things in the car today and just leave. She had done that before.

"How about some tea, Tillie?" Susie asked. "Those Danish Mrs. Solomon brought you last night look good."

"I don't taste anything," Tillie said, but she eyed the Danish with some interest. "Maybe a little tea would help."

Susie nodded and got up to prepare the cup. She cracked in four tablets of Dilantin.

"Just lemon, right, Tillie?"

"Please."

She brought her the cup and cut a piece of Danish, placing it on a small plate and setting it beside the tea. Tillie fed herself with a teaspoon for a few moments and then nibbled on the Danish.

"How long were you two married, Tillie?" Susie asked. Questions about Morris and her were the only questions that rekindled the light in Tillie Kaufman's eyes.

"Forty-five years this November sixth. We got married twice, though."

"Twice? Why twice?"

"First," Tillie said smiling, "we ran off and got married in Atlantic City. We spent a week together as man and wife before we told our parents. Then they insisted on a big Jewish wedding. My father spent what was a fortune in those days. Morris was so handsome in his tuxedo. You saw the picture?"

Of course Susie had. The picture was at the center of a dozen or so photographs arranged neatly on a sofa table. Tillie laughed.

"We returned to Atlantic City for our second honeymoon."

"When did you come to California?"

"About ten years after our marriage. Morris's uncle Leo had started a plumbing supply business in Ventura and needed a good manager. Morris did the books, too. It was a good business, but Leo was a terrible businessman, always investing in some crazy real estate deal. A dreamer. Eventually, he lost it all, but Morris was conservative with our money and we had enough to retire on when the time came."

"You still have the house in Ventura?"

"No, we sold it when we moved back East."

"And then you started to spend your winters here in Palm Springs and decided this was where you wanted to retire?"

Tillie nodded. She drank some more tea and bit more eagerly into the Danish.

"Most people back East go to Florida when they retire," Susie said.

"Morris said he didn't want to winter in Florida with all the other senior citizens. He said he agreed with Buddy Hackett, Florida was God's waiting room." She started to laugh but then looked around the empty apartment. "So this turned out to be God's waiting room instead."

Tears emerged. She took a deep breath and sat back in a daze. Susie stared at her a moment and then smiled.

"You mustn't think of him as too far away. Think of him as

standing in the distance by a doorway, waiting for you," she said.

Tillie nodded. She finished her tea.

"He waits, he waits," she said, placing the empty cup neatly on the saucer. "Morris was good at waiting. A more patient man you couldn't find."

"But he doesn't want to be alone either, does he?"

"I always said it would be better for me to die first. Morris was stronger. Now look."

"He can't be that strong," Susie insisted. "He's lonely without you."

Tillie shifted her eyes toward Susie curiously.

"What lonely? He's probably with his gin rummy buddies who were all dead before him. When he and they were all alive, the world could blow up and they'd still be playing cards."

Susie rose and began to clear the dishes off the table.

"I should help," Tillie said. She started to rise.

"I don't need you to help. It's nothing."

"I always take a bath in the morning," Tillie said. "But this morning I barely put water on my face."

"So take your bath now. I'll draw you a bath. I know you like to soak in the tub."

"Such a good girl. I'll miss you," Tillie said.

"Miss me?" Susie smiled. Did Tillie understand? Did she know she was soon to join Morris in Paradise?

"I'm going back East. I called my sister Sophie and she wants me to come stay with her."

"When?" Susie demanded.

"A couple of weeks, maybe."

"But Morris . . ."

"What about Morris?" Tillie asked. Susie stared at her. How could two people be married so long and not think about being together forever? She's just confused now, Susie concluded. She doesn't know what to do. She smiled.

"Morris would want you to be happy. He doesn't want you to be lonely," she said.

Tillie shrugged.

"I'll live. Why, I don't know, but I'll live."

"I'll run your bath," Susie said. "A good soak will make you feel better."

The Dilantin had begun to take effect. Tillie moved in a daze and let Susie lead her to the bathroom.

"Maybe I should just rest on the sofa," she said gazing down at the water rushing into the tub.

"After a quick bath. You need to relax your body. You said yourself, you didn't get much sleep."

"My body feels asleep already," she said. It made Susie laugh, but she pushed on, helping Tillie off with her clothes and then guiding her carefully into the tub.

"I'll wash your back for you."

Tillie nodded.

"Everyone's jealous who comes here and sees how much you and Faye have helped me."

"They have no reason to be. We'd help them, too, if we had to," Susie said. Tillie nodded and leaned forward as Susie scrubbed her back in small circles.

"That feels good."

"I'm glad. What was Morris's and your favorite song?" Susie asked.

"Song?"

"Didn't they play a song at your wedding?"

"Oh yes. You wouldn't remember it."

"I know a lot of old songs. Try me."

"It was 'I Can't Help but Say I Love You.' "

" 'Won't you say you love me, too?' " Susie continued.

"You know it?" Tillie asked, surprised. But of course Susie knew it. She had heard Tillie singing it before, and Morris had told her it was their wedding song. Susie started to hum the melody. Tillie's body shuddered with her small sobs. Then she sighed deeply.

"He was so handsome," she said. "So handsome."

"Close your eyes, Tillie. Lean back and relax for a while. Just soak," Susie said. She guided the elderly woman back in her tub until she was comfortable, and then she put the washcloth over her forehead and stood up. Tillie's eyes fluttered. She took a deep breath and relaxed. Her eyes closed slowly, opened, and then closed and remained closed.

Susie continued to hum Morris and Tillie Kaufman's song as she returned to the kitchen and went to her pocketbook. She plucked out her surgical gloves and put them on, still humming away. Faye had said the detective was interested in her because she had used the same . . . What was it? MO? Well, she would change the MO this time. She had thought it out carefully, however, and had decided something of Morris's should be used. It would join Tillie with Morris in the afterlife more quickly.

Back in the bathroom, Tillie Kaufman's breathing had become slow and regular. The sleeping pills had kicked in. Susie smiled and then looked up at the ceiling.

"Are you listening in, Morris? Do you have your ear to the ceiling just the way you used to have it against my sister's wall? She's coming. Be patient.

" 'I'm singing my love for you . . .' "

She went to the medicine cabinet and located Morris Kaufman's straight razor. It was something of an antique and had originally belonged to his father. It had a white pearl handle and a blade of the finest tempered steel. It was made when craftsmen took pride in their work, when they made something to last. If Morris had had a son, he would surely have passed it on.

She opened the blade and brought the razor to the tub. Tillie's body was limp, the wrinkled skin around her shoulders and breasts slightly crimson from the heat of the water. Susie put the blade into Tillie's right hand, taking great pains to keep her fingers over Tillie's, and then brought it to Tillie's left wrist. With the precision of a surgeon, she made a neat, deep incision through the artery. The blood rushed to the opening as if it longed to escape the confines of Tillie's body. It streamed out and spiraled in the water, creating the prettiest red tint. Susie released the blade from Tillie's hand and let it fall to the bathroom floor. Then she dropped Tillie's wrist into the water and watched for a moment as the bath began to take on a ruby glaze. She sighed deeply.

"Together again, forever and ever. Goodbye, Tillie." She looked up at the ceiling. "You don't deserve her, Morris, but she misses you terribly."

Susie returned to the kitchen, took off her gloves and continued to clean up. Content with how the apartment looked, she returned to the bathroom and felt for a pulse in Tillie's throat and checked her eyes. She was gone. She and Morris were together again. She and Faye could leave Palm Springs and not feel that they had left some good work undone.

21

Frankie pulled into the apartment complex parking lot, found a space and shut off his engine. This was one of those complexes populated by more permanent Palm Springs residents, so there was a lot of activity with people going off to work. He checked the cars under the carport and spotted what he knew to be Faye Sullivan's automobile. She and her sister hadn't left town. He suspected that whenever things got too warm for them, they just upped and left. That was why they had moved from one place to another so often during the last few years. They were here; the question was, should he go any further by himself? A week ago, he wouldn't have hesitated to apprehend two women not considered armed, but that image of Jennie standing in the doorway, the worried wife, lingered, and he had made promises.

He decided to wait for Rosina and Derek, and he had every intention of doing so; but suddenly he saw the door of the apartment adjacent to the Sullivans' open and a woman emerge dressed in a maid's uniform. She paused, looked up at the sky and smiled strangely. It was Faye Sullivan's twin sister, all right. She looked just like her sister, Faye.

She didn't close the door of the apartment. She looked back, and then she limped her way across the patio. But what caught his interest even more was what looked like a bloodstain on the skirt of her otherwise clean white uniform.

He thought a moment, gazed at his watch, drummed the dashboard impatiently, and then got out of his car. Why did she leave that apartment door open? Why hadn't anyone come to close it? He approached slowly, looking from the Sullivans' door to the open apartment door. He stepped up to the patio, quickly reviewing the possibilities.

Maybe no one was home. He checked the name on the door and read Kaufman. Perhaps Susie Sullivan had been hired to clean their place while they were away, he thought, and he gazed through the doorway into the living room. What struck him were the sheet over the television set and the sheet over the mirror in the entryway. He knew enough about Jewish religion to know this was a house of mourning. Someone had recently died. The new possibilities sent him reeling for a moment. Surely they wouldn't do anything right next door to their own home, he told himself, but then he thought, it wouldn't matter to them if they were psychotic.

"Hello," he called after poking his head in. "Anyone home?"

Silence drew him farther into the apartment. It was immaculate, nothing in the kitchen sink or left on the counters. The floors looked vacuumed and scrubbed; everything was in its place. The maid had most certainly been working in here, he thought.

But if it was a house of mourning, why wasn't anyone here? Had the individual just died? Was everyone at the funeral? Not this early in the morning, he reasoned. No, he sensed something was wrong. His heart started pounding and he felt his breath grow alarmingly short, as his doctor warned him it might; but nevertheless, he continued into the apartment, gazing into the bedroom, where he saw the bed made. Just like everywhere else in the apartment, everything was neat and organized, perhaps too neat and organized.

Even so, he was about to retreat when he heard it: the drip, drip, drip of water, encouraging him to go on. He entered the bedroom, listened, and then turned to the bathroom. The door was slightly open, the light on.

"Mrs. Kaufman? Mr. Kaufman?"

He waited. Just that drip, drip, drip.

He went to the bathroom door and gently pushed on it. It swung open and revealed the dead old woman sitting in a pool of her own blood and water, her mouth dropped open, her eyes shut tight. Her skin had taken on the pallor of a corpse. He noted the straight-edged razor on the tile. Another murder made to look like a suicide, he thought.

Dead people weren't an unfamiliar sight to Frankie Samuels, but confronting his darkest suspicion was a jolt. He didn't expect the physical reaction. For a moment, his head spun. He took hold of the door jamb and waited for his equilibrium to return. The raw stench of human death filled Frankie's nostrils, so he turned away and walked toward the front of the apartment. Then he went to the phone and called the station.

"Where's Rosina, Billy?" he asked.

"She just left, Frankie. Nolan held her up awhile. She said she couldn't raise you on your car phone, but said if you called, to tell you she'll be there in a few minutes."

He described what he had found and told Billy to patch the information to Rosina.

"Tell her I'll be next door," he said

Next door Faye Sullivan had slipped into her skirt and then buttoned her pearl silk blouse. She stepped out of her bedroom and looked toward the open bathroom door. She heard Susie in her bedroom, but she peered into the bathroom first and saw her uniform hanging over the shower rack. On closer inspection, she spotted the bloodstain and Susie's poor attempt to get it out of the garment. Her eyes widened with realization and she gazed toward the Kaufman apartment.

"Susie!" she screamed. She pounded the floor as she hurried out of the bathroom to Susie's bedroom. Susie was standing there in her bra and panties, brushing her hair. She looked like a twelve-year-old girl again, innocent, sweet, and very dependent on Faye.

"Good morning, Faye. I knew you were tired, so I tried not to wake you. Oh, I didn't put up the coffee yet."

"Where were you? Why is there a bloodstain on your uniform?"

Susie's smile faded and she took on the expression of a child who knew she had done something wrong.

"I'm afraid I was a little careless."

"Careless with what?"

"Tillie," she said. And then she smiled again. "But it's all right. She's gone. By now, she and Morris are together again."

"You did something this morning? Already?"

"I thought I would do it as soon as I could so we wouldn't have anything holding us back. I know you want to leave as soon as possible."

"But I told you . . . what did you do? Why is there blood on your uniform?"

"Oh, that was the best idea, Faye," Susie said with excitement. She put down the hairbrush and turned to explain. "I knew how worried you were about the . . . MO, so I thought and I thought and I came up with a wonderful alternative— Morris's razor. Tillie didn't get a wink of sleep all night. I gave her some tea, and some Dilantin, of course, and then we decided she should take a warm bath and rest for a while. Almost as soon as she went into the bathtub, she fell asleep . . . because of the Dilantin . . . and then, I helped her leave. I didn't watch what I was doing after I cut her wrist and some blood dripped off the razor, I think. But all the rest of it went into the tub with Tillie. Wasn't that smart? Using Morris's razor? It was practically an antique."

"No."

Susie looked disappointed.

"Why not? Daddy was thinking of doing that, wasn't he? One night he had his razor out and on the edge of the tub when he was bathing and you thought that was just what he was going to do. Then he asked you to shave him. You told me that. You did, so don't deny it."

"Daddy didn't have the courage to look at his own blood," Faye said.

"But he was desperate. You said he was desperate, Faye."

"He was. Even if he wasn't, he should have been," she replied.

"Why, Faye? Why do you always say things like that? You never heard me say anything like that about Daddy."

"He never . . ."

"Never what, Faye? What?" Susie demanded firmly, her hands on her hips.

"Never . . . put his hands on you," she said.

"I don't understand, Faye. What do you mean, put his hands on you? Hit you? Hit me?"

"No, no," she said and pressed her hands to her ears. There was a horrible buzzing in her head, but Susie didn't seem to notice or care. She stepped toward Faye, pursuing.

"Where did he put his hands, Faye? Where did Daddy put his hands on you?"

"Shut up."

"You said it. I want to know. Tell me. Show me."

"I said shut up. Get dressed. We're leaving. Right now. Right now, do you hear?"

Faye turned and went back to her bedroom, where she had one of her suitcases packed and closed. She seized the handle and lifted it quickly, practically lunging at the front door.

When he heard the front door of the Sullivan apartment open and close, Frankie stepped out quickly and confronted Faye.

"Where are you going?" he demanded. Her gaze went to the Kaufman's open doorway and then back to Frankie.

"Who are you?"

"What? You know who I am, Miss Sullivan. I'm Detective Samuels," he said. "I spoke to you only yesterday."

Her eyes blinked rapidly. She did look like she had no idea who he was.

"You don't remember me?"

"Yes, I'm sorry. I forgot for the moment."

"So where are you going?" he asked.

"I have to make a trip."

"Because of the things your sister has done?"

"My sister?"

"Next door, for starters," he said.

"What are you talking about?"

"Didn't she tell you what she did to Mrs. Kaufman?" Frankie asked. Faye didn't reply. "Care to see?" he stepped aside and held his hand toward the open door.

"This is ridiculous," she said. "My sister told me nothing. I have to go someplace."

She started for the stairway. He reached out and hooked her at the elbow.

"You are not going anywhere, Miss Sullivan. Let's go talk to your sister."

"She's not here. Let me go," Faye said, pulling her arm free. She started away. He hurried down the steps after her and seized her arm again, much more firmly this time.

"Let me go," she cried. "You have no right . . ."

"We can do this hard or do this easy, Miss Sullivan. Now let's go back to your apartment and talk to your sister."

"I told you . . . she's not in there."

"She's there. I saw her go into the apartment not ten minutes ago. Now either you open your door or I'll break it open," he threatened.

"What dramatics," she said, her eyes flaring. "I'm telling you, she's not in there. You're going to feel like the fool you are," she said.

"Right. I know she's not in there," he said dryly. "But open the door."

Faye glared at him. Then she walked back reluctantly, but made no effort to open the door. She simply stood sulking. He shrugged and started toward the door, his posture suggesting he would break it down.

"All right," she relented. She dug into her purse and came up with the key. He stepped back as she opened the door. "See for yourself if you must. But hurry, I have someplace important to go.

"You not going anywhere, Miss Sullivan. Not anywhere you want to go, that is. Just relax," he said.

He entered slowly. She was right behind him, hovering as

he paused in the living room and then at the doorway to the kitchen. When he didn't find Susie, he went to the first bedroom on the left, Faye's bedroom, and peered in. There were two other suitcases on the bed, both open, a nurse's uniform visible.

"Doing a lot of packing," he said. "Looks like this isn't such a short trip, is it?"

She didn't reply. He entered the bedroom, checked the bathroom, and then looked in the closet.

"Really, Officer, do you expect to find my sister hiding in the closet?"

He came out and paused at the doorway of the second bathroom. Susie's uniform was still hanging over the shower rack. He looked back at Faye. She had put her suitcase down and was standing with her arms folded under her bosom.

"That's your sister's uniform, isn't it? I saw her wearing it a short while ago."

"It's her uniform, but it's not her. I told you she wasn't here," Faye said. He looked at the second bedroom. The door was closed. He started toward it.

"She's not in there," Faye assured him. Frankie looked at her and then opened the door on an empty bedroom. "Are you going to check the closets in there, too?" she asked.

It was her calmness that unnerved him. He thought he would rather be facing a street criminal. At least he would know what to anticipate, but this cool and bizarre woman made him feel anxious and somehow at a disadvantage. It was as if he had stepped into dangers he couldn't imagine.

He studied the room for a moment and then went to the closets. They were empty. Naked hangers dangled on the rack. He checked the dresser drawers and found them empty, too.

"Isn't this . . . your sister's room?" he asked, confused. "Are all her things in that suitcase?" She didn't reply. He looked around the room and then fixed his gaze on the bed. How childish, he thought. He looked back at Faye and smirked, but she didn't change expression. "Come out, come

out wherever you are," he sang, and then he started for the
bed.

"What are you doing? Don't touch that bed. My sister is
very particular about other people touching her intimate
things. Don't!" she shouted, but he reached out and pulled
back the comforter, exposing the leg brace lying just where it
would had it been on the leg of someone in that bed.

Then his eyes fell on the pillow that had been under the
blanket, too. Just a few strands of hair were visible. He lifted
the pillow and pinched the wig in his fingers, holding it as if
it were something contaminated.

"What the hell . . . ?" Leg brace, wig . . . The realization
sent a shock through him. The excitement was tantamount to
his having run five miles. His heart thumped and his head
felt heavy.

"Stop!" Faye screamed. "Put that down!" She lunged forward. Frankie turned to sidestep but took the brunt of her
charge. She struck him in the chest with both closed fists and
for a moment, it was as if he had been shot. The surprise, the
power of the blow, the excitement, and the beating of his
heart collaborated to bring on an attack. He reached out to
push her away, but his arms felt like they were made of
marshmallow. The room spun, his eyes went back, and his
legs folded, dropping his torso with a heavy thud at the feet
of Faye Sullivan.

She stepped back and gazed down at him. His face was as
white as mashed potatoes and his lips had begun to take on
that familiar blue tint. She heard his gasps and shook her
head. Her eyes blinked rapidly as she tried to sort out the
confusion. The wig was on the floor, but it looked unfamiliar.
Where was she? A gurgle echoed in Frankie's throat, and she
went to her knees beside him.

Quickly, she turned Frankie on his back and then, placing
one of her hands over the other and interlocking the fingers,
she pressed down on his chest with the heel of her hands on
his breastbone. She leaned forward and began a rhythmic
movement, alternating it with mouth-to-mouth respiration.

"What are you doing?"

She paused and looked up at Susie.

"He's having a heart attack," she replied.

"But he's a policeman. He's come for me."

Faye gazed down at Frankie as if seeing him for the first time.

"I can't let him die," she said, shaking her head.

"You can't let him live," Susie retorted. "Get away from him. Come on. Let's get everything else in the car and go. Come on, Faye."

"He'll die," Faye said. She looked at Susie. Her face was twisted in a grimace of fear. Never did her sister look more pathetic.

"But he knows about us, about me. And now he knows about Tillie. Get up. Quickly. Don't you know what you're doing?"

"Of course I know what I'm doing. I'm a nurse," Faye said proudly. She turned back to Frankie just as Rosina Flores came rushing into the Sullivan apartment. With her service revolver drawn, she hurried through until she spotted Faye Sullivan on her knees beside Frankie Samuels.

"What's going on?" she demanded, her gun pointing at Faye. "Get away from him."

"He's having a heart attack," Faye said calmly. "I'm giving CPR." She started again. Rosina stepped closer. "I'm losing him," Faye said. She got up and started out. Rosina didn't move. "Get out of my way! Quickly!"

Rosina stepped aside and Faye ran into her bedroom where she began to rifle through her dresser drawers.

"There's a dead old woman in the bathtub next door," Derek said coming in behind Rosina. "What the hell's going on?" he asked, seeing Frankie on the floor. Rosina nodded toward Faye, who pulled out hypodermic needles from the drawer and shoved something out of the way to find the medicine she wanted. She ripped off the protective cover of a needle and began to draw the medicine from the bottle.

"She says Frankie's having a heart attack. Call the paramedics."

"Right," Derek said. He rushed to the nearest phone.

"What is that?" Rosina demanded when Faye returned to Frankie's side.

"Digitoxin. It's a cardiovascular drug used for congestive heart failure, to regulate the heart rhythm."

She went to her knees and quickly prepared to inject Frankie.

"Wait," Rosina cried. Faye turned.

"If we wait any longer, he's sure to die," Faye said. "Look at his lips and his pupils!"

Rosina's mind reeled. Where was the other sister? What had caused Frankie's seizure? Is this woman a murderess or a nurse? she wondered. She, a policewoman, could be standing by and willingly watching someone kill another person; in effect, giving her permission to do so. On the other hand, Faye Sullivan might actually be saving Frankie Samuels' life.

"Well?" Faye waited, poised with the needle. "I'm losing him!" she screamed.

"Do it." Rosina lowered her pistol to her side, closed her eyes, and prayed.

EPILOGUE

With Stevie, Beth and Laurel at her side, Jennie held Frankie's hand and watched the medicine in the IV bottle drip through the tube and into his arm. There was subdued noise and chatter around her in the CCU, but Jennie heard only the beep, beep, beep of Frankie's heart monitor. His eyelids fluttered and slowly lifted. When he focused on Jennie's face, he smiled. Then his gaze went to his son and his daughter and daughter-in-law.

"Did I miss something?" he asked.

The tears rolled down Jennie's cheeks, but she didn't make any effort to wipe them away.

"You missed something," she said with a tone of chastisement.

He stared at her a moment.

"I had the craziest dream," he said, "that I had come out of the hospital, recuperated, gone to my retirement dinner, and then moved to Palm Springs."

"Very funny, Frankie."

"How are you doing, Dad?" Stevie asked moving closer to the bed to take Frankie's other hand into his.

"I'm all right as long as you guys leave me in here and don't let her take me home, where she's sure to beat me to death," he replied.

Beth laughed and then just started to cry. She turned away quickly.

"Hey," Frankie said. "I've got a new cause for you to picket and protest: the treatment of retired policemen, especially retired detectives." Beth's shoulders stopped shaking. She wiped her face and turned back to him.

"Maybe I will," she said. He took her hand and held it. Then she leaned over and kissed him on the cheek.

"Guess I don't look much like Dirty Harry anymore, huh?"

"No," she said sadly.

"Don't tell me you're sorry, that you'll miss him."

"I won't," she said, smiling.

He laughed and looked at Laurel. "You mad at me too?"

"I'm with Jennie, if that's what you're trying to find out," she said.

"Figures you women would stick together," he said, and then he took a deep breath and turned back to Jennie.

"Let's hear it," he said.

"What's there to hear? You knew what you were doing and you went and did it anyway." She softened. "Rosina says you're being awarded some sort of citation for outstanding police work as soon as you're able to leave the hospital and receive it."

"Check this, Dad," Stevie said, and he held up the *Desert Sun*. The front page had Frankie's picture on it and a story about his cracking the case they labeled "The Medical Murders."

"Well isn't that nice," Frankie said.

"Yeah, it's nice. I could have put it in a nice frame and looked at it whenever I returned from the cemetery," Jennie quipped.

"That's a woman for you," Frankie said to Stevie. "Always looking at the dark side."

"Rosina's here." Jennie smirked. "I'm sure you're anxious to hear the details, even in this condition. There's only a few minutes left to this visit. We'll go out and let her come in. I'll be back on the hour."

She leaned over to kiss him.

"I'm sorry, Jen. I really didn't think this sort of thing would happen."

"Of course you didn't. You're Charles Bronson," she said. The children kissed him, too, and they all left. A few moments later, Rosina was at the side of the bed, shaking her head.

"You know what I feel like now, don't you—an accomplice to a capital crime."

"Come on, Flores."

"I shouldn't have told you anything about the Ratner murder I should have just closed all this myself."

"What, and get all the glory?" She laughed. "So, tell me all about it. What did I do? I'm still not sure what the hell I found in that apartment."

"You found someone with what the doctors call a multiple personality syndrome."

"Then there wasn't a twin named Susie?" he asked.

"Yes, there was, but she died when she was twelve. She was born with the handicap, just the way Faye played it. Apparently, from what I could gather up to now, her twin was a very disturbed young lady with many psychological problems exacerbated by the fact that she was handicapped and not as bright as her sister. Whenever comparisons were made, she always came out on the short end, and there was even evidence their father favored Faye and neglected Susie."

"What did she do?"

"She took too many of her mother's sleeping pills," Rosina said. "To escape the turmoil and disappointment. And she was only twelve. Can you imagine?"

"But that's where the idea to do people with pills originated?"

"It probably got planted there and developed when Faye became a nurse. Anyway, after Susie died, Faye's mother went off the deep end and became obsessed with cleaning, organizing, regimenting her life to the point that there was no real living. She and her husband became estranged, whatever, and . . . here's the other ugly part . . . he began to sexually abuse Faye."

"When?"

"Not long after her sister's death. It went on for some time, until Mrs. Sullivan had heart trouble and died. He began to suffer some guilt himself, went into a depression and eventually was thought to have committed suicide."

"Thought?"

"The psychiatrist tells me he now believes—I should say, he's now convinced—Faye, who was a nurse by this time, helped him off to the hereafter, and thus the so-called Medical Murders began."

"Is that when this multiple personality business began?"

"The doctor believes so."

"Why did that happen?" Frankie asked. "Does he know?"

"The psychiatrist feels Faye reinvented her twin sister to compensate. She had trouble living with the guilt, of course, but she had more trouble living with herself, living with whom she had become. Susie became her alter ego, encompassing all the qualities and beliefs she wished she had, such as believing in the magic of love and marriage, that relationships between men and women could be perfect and go on forever and ever, even after death.

"Most importantly, Susie was that part of her that denied what had gone on between her and her father. Susie was the innocent."

"Innocent? She murdered people as Susie, didn't she?" Frankie said.

"Yes, but the doctor says those killings validated Faye's killing of her father."

"Huh?"

"Believing she was helping these loved ones reunite in a better world continually justified Faye's killing of her father, sending him off to join their mother in a more perfect life. Death, killing, wasn't so terrible then. In fact, it was in Susie's and I suppose Faye's mind, nothing more than the ticket, the means of transportation. When the doctor talks to the Susie part of her, Susie says she was just helping them leave, providing them with the means."

"The Susie side," Frankie said shaking his head.

"There are definite, clear personalities in her mind, Frankie, and you're alive because those two personalities are so sharply delineated. That's what the doctors say."

"Come again?"

"Don't you know? No one told you?"

"What?"

"Faye Sullivan saved your life. She was a perfect nurse, giving you the right emergency treatment. As Faye, she couldn't be a murderess. She had to become Susie to do anyone in."

"The killer saves the life of the policeman who's coming to arrest her?"

"You've got to understand . . . she wasn't the killer. Not in the sense you mean."

"But what about this Ratner guy?"

"We're not sure if he came to blackmail them or what."

"Them?"

Rosina laughed.

"I can't help it. Does that make me nuts, too? Anyway, Susie says she had to kill him in order for them to continue their good work. She reverted to a medical analogy, comparing him to a cancer. They merely had to cut him out and go on helping loved ones reunite."

"Lovely young women. I mean . . ."

"Even the doctors have trouble thinking of Faye as only one person. They talk about Susie and Faye the way you would talk about two different people. It's as if her brain split in two distinct parts and those two parts communicate with each other," Rosina said.

"Anyway, they're calling you the instinctive detective. You should see Nolan talking to the press with his chest out, describing how unhappy he his that he is losing his best man, a man of age and wisdom who can smell out a crime. I feel like puking at his feet," she said.

"You're just jealous."

"You know what he asked me this morning?" Frankie shook his head.

"Can't imagine."

"He wondered if your doctor would permit you to be something of a consultant for the department."

"No shit? Nolan said that?"

She shrugged and leaned over.

"Who knows, maybe he's a multiple personality, too."

Frankie laughed and the nurse came over.

"I'm sorry," she said. "But time is up."

Frankie smiled.

"You'd better listen to her, Rosina." He lowered his voice to sound ominous. "She's a nurse."

"All right," Rosina said. "Get better."

"Get a life, Flores. Don't end up like me. Say yes to that accountant from Palm Desert and raise a herd of *niños* and *niñas*," Frankie advised.

"I might. We've got a date tonight," she said, and she flashed an impish smile at him before turning to go.

Frankie lay back and closed his eyes. He was alive; he had survived. He would live to become a different sort of man. Maybe, in a sense, we're all multiple personalities, he thought. There's someone else living within us, just waiting for his or her time to emerge. There's no sense fighting it, he thought. I'm too tired to resist. Come on, Frankie Samuels the Second, whoever you are. Come get me.

He drifted off and dreamt about Jennie and him walking toward the famed Palm Springs Indian Canyons, just down from their house. In his dream there was a nearly cloudless sky with a turquoise tint. The sun had created pockets of shadow and strips of darkness along the brown San Jacinto Mountains. Here and there along the range, he could see a clump or two of bushes and palm trees, suggesting a mountain spring.

As he walked with Jennie, the vista seemed to come alive. The shadows shifted, presenting the illusion of the mountains moving and turning. It was magical. The farther into the valley they walked, the younger Jennie and he became, until he turned to look at her and saw her as she was when they first met. It filled his heart with joy and made him feel they would be together . . . forever.

Faye yawned. It seemed to her she had been sitting in this office for hours and hours, explaining it repeatedly to Dr. Clark, chief of the psychiatric staff. He sat there taking notes and nodding stupidly, occasionally asking what she considered the most obvious questions:

"How did your sister know these people were waiting for their loved ones? How did she know the people she helped off wanted to go off? Tell me again why you thought she saw this as her private duty."

It amazed her, truly amazed her, how incompetent some doctors were, especially psychiatrists. When would the malpractice lawyers turn their money-hungry eyes to this segment of health care and haunt and pursue them with as much vigilance and tenacity as they did medical doctors?

"You've been a great help, Faye," the doctor said. "I'd like to talk to Susie now. Can you get her for me? Please."

Faye stared at him, shook her head and then rose from the chair. She walked down the corridor and turned to go down another corridor, stopping at Susie's room. She knocked on the door and waited until she heard her say, "Come in."

"He wants to see you," she said. Susie was sitting on the bed, her hands in her lap, twirling her fingers nervously. She looked up at Faye.

"They're all angry at me, aren't they?"

"They're not angry. They're just confused. You have to explain, make them understand. I tried, but it needs to come from you."

"You're not going to leave me here, are you?"

"I told you I wouldn't, didn't I?"

"Because it wouldn't be fair."

"I said I wouldn't. Now, are you going to go to the doctor on your own or do I have to drag you down the corridor?"

"I'm going," Susie said and stood up. She smoothed down her dress. "How do I look?"

"What possible difference does that make?"

"I care about my appearance, even though you don't care about yours."

"Will you stop that? Will you finally, once and for all, stop that?"

"Stop what?"

"Making comparisons. You're who you are and I'm who I am. We just happen to look a lot alike."

"Of course we do. We're twins."

"But we're two different people, and when you finally accept that . . ."

"What?"

"I'll be free, that's what," Faye said, a little harder than she had intended. Susie's eyes revealed her pain, but she didn't cry.

"Okay," she said in a tired voice. "I'll try. I'll try to be a separate person."

Faye stepped back to let her hobble by.

Down the corridor she limped. Now that she had her back to Faye, she could permit a tear or two to escape and flow over her cheeks.

It seemed to her that she sat with the doctor for hours and hours before he looked up from his notepad to ask his final questions of the day.

"So how do you feel about this now?" he finally asked. "Considering what's happening to you, where you are . . ."

"I feel terrible. I'm locked up here, unable to help the countless others out there who are depending on me."

"If you were released, you would go back to Palm Springs and continue your work?" he asked.

"No, not Palm Springs. Faye and I are ready to move on," she said.

"I see. Well now, next time I'd like to talk about your parents more. Is that all right with you?"

"Of course," she said.

"You look fidgety today."

"I happen to be hungry. It's after twelve," she said nodding toward the clock. Dr. Clark smiled.

"So it is. All right. Why don't you go to the cafeteria. We've had a good session today."

"Good for whom? It's wasting precious time," Susie said. "There are people in pain."

"I understand," he said.

She smirked and got up.

"Let me ask you a question, Doctor."

"Sure."

"Are your parents alive?"

"No. My mother died two years ago and my father died last year."

"See," she said. "He couldn't live on much longer without her."

She spun on her heels before he could reply and left the office. She got her food quickly and sat at the same table she had been sitting at since she had first arrived. The gentleman across from her, Mr. Keach, stared ahead blankly and chewed mechanically. He had yet to say his first word to her. She looked behind her at the attendants chatting by the door and then turned to Mr. Keach, just as she had every single time before.

"You miss your wife, don't you? That's why you won't say anything to anyone. I know. I'm probably the only one here who knows."

He continued to chew and to stare.

"I'm going to help you," she said. "I figured it out last night. That's why I've been sent here. That's why all this has happened."

He turned slowly toward her. She was heartened. Her words were finally getting through. He was beginning to understand. She widened her smile.

And then she looked across the cafeteria and brightened even more. All of her couples, including her parents, were seated at the various tables looking her way, holding hands and smiling gloriously.

She had been given the gift of bringing them all together. What more could she ask for?